AN INVESTIGATION
OF MARS

CJ DEARLOVE

LADY EDITH PUBLISHING

LADY EDITH PUBLISHING

CJ DEARLOVE

Ontario, Canada

Printed Worldwide
First Printing 2023
First Edition 2023

ISBN 978-1-7389734-2-2 (Hardcover)
ISBN 978-1-7389734-1-5 (Paperback)
ISBN 978-1-7389734-0-8 (eBook)
ISBN 978-1-7389734-3-9 (Audiobook)

10 9 8 7 6 5 4 3 2 1

Cover Art by Daniel Eyenegho

Content Warning: this book portrays the use of substances and should be read by a mature audience.

Statement on use of Artificial Intelligence: Not a word of this book was created by AI. An actual human being, with access to the universal consciousness, wrote this book.

AN INVESTIGATION
OF MARS

DEDICATION

For my daughter, and her generation:
I'm so sorry for what we've done to your beautiful world.

May you forgive us for our neglect,
may your generation reconcile with nature,
may you create new systems based on oneness and unity,
and may you lead us on a new and courageous path.

AUTHOR'S NOTE

All characters and events in this book are fictional, even those that bear resemblance to real individuals. This book weaves varied ideas and theories into the story, partly in hopes others will pick up these breadcrumbs and add to a new understanding of the universe. Similarities to real people may exist, since this book was written with tremendous appreciation and admiration of all the intrepid researchers, experiencers, philosophers, and spiritual leaders whose gifts informed this work.

I know I did not write this book alone; though when tapping into the universal consciousness, has a human ever had a truly original idea?

Prologue

"One morning I had a report from the CIA that a small twin-engine plane had gone down somewhere in Zaire, and that it contained some important secret documents. We were searching for the crash site using satellite photography and some other surreptitious high-altitude overflights, but with no success. With some hesitancy, a CIA agent in California recommended the services of a clairvoyant, who was then consulted. She wrote down a latitude and longitude, which proved to be accurate, and several days later I was shown a photograph of the plane, totally destroyed and in a remote area. Without notifying Zaire's President Mobutu, we sent in a small team that recovered the documents and the bodies of the plane's occupants."

Jimmy Carter, from A Full Life

During the Cold War, any information that could bring one side an advantage was coveted, and both the Americans and Soviets conducted espionage that spanned the world, trying to solidify that advantage.

In the 1970s, the CIA and DIA had intelligence that the Soviet Union was making advancements in psychical research, and were using it to spy on the United States.

Not to be outdone, the Americans launched what would come to be called Stargate Project. Launched by the DIA with SRI

International, a California contractor, Stargate Project also included a secret U.S. Army unit that would research psychic phenomena, with a focus on Remote Viewing.

Remote viewing (RV) is the practice of seeking impressions about a distant location in one's mind.

One example of an experiment in remote viewing is having an individual, the target, travel to a location that is unknown to the subject. The subject is given a set of coordinates in an envelope, which they typically don't open. The subject, or RVer, settles their mind and waits for images to begin to appear. They then start to draw what they see. If the elements of the drawing match the location of the target, the RVer has a match.

When the CIA closed the program in 1995, they did so stating that remote viewers consistently failed to produce any actionable intelligence information. Proponents of remote viewing challenge this assessment, and point out that the program operated and was funded for twenty years, a lot of time and money for an unsuccessful program. And while the CIA downplayed the effectiveness of the program, the participants in the program disagreed, feeling that the intelligence they produced was not taken seriously by the Intelligence Community.

Afterall, what serious person would listen to psychic spies?

Despite what was stated publicly at the time, documents from the program were eventually declassified, revealing a program that explored fascinating and unexpected areas. The documents showed that not only was it believed that RVers could visit distant locations, but they could also obtain information contained within, such as viewing a document in a locked filing cabinet.

Even more incredible than the attempts to visit distant locations, were the attempts to visit distant locations *in the past.*

Time, like distance, is not a barrier to a remote viewer.

This program, funded for twenty years by the American government, was staffed by serious people who believed they could psychically travel not only the world, but across cosmic distances, and completely bypass our linear experience of time.

Psychic-spying time-travellers.

Through the release of classified documents relating to Stargate Project, one particularly fantastical - yet real - transcript was released.

In 1984, a remote viewer was given the following location and time to access:

The planet Mars.

Time of interest approximately 1 million years B.C.

In this episode in American military-intelligence history, the U.S. government sent a psychic spy, paid for by the taxpayer, on a remote viewing mission to Mars, because they wanted to know what was happening there one million years ago.

Of all the times and places, of all the information that might be valuable in the heat of the cold war, someone wanted to know what was happening on a "dead" planet a million years ago.

Why?

This book is a work of fiction, though fiction is where some of our deepest truths are found.

~ 4 ~

Chapter 1

"Unfortunately, however, the theory that flying saucers are material objects from outer space manned by a race originating on some other planet is not a complete answer. However strong the current belief in saucers from space, it cannot be stronger than the Celtic faith in the elves and the fairies, or the medieval belief in lutins, or the fear throughout the Christian lands, in the first centuries of our era, of demons and satyrs and fauns. Certainly, it cannot be stronger than the faith that inspired the writers of the Bible - a faith rooted in daily experiences with angelic visitation."

Jacques F. Vallée

Within seconds of hearing the doorbell, Tomi was out of bed and in front of the mirror, frantically pulling her hair back into a ponytail, trying to hide the fact that she was still in bed at - *what time was it?* - 1:30 in the afternoon, at least.

She was pulling on the pants she'd stepped out of the night before, getting her foot caught in a twisted pantleg and almost losing her balance, when she heard John call upstairs to her from the front door. "Uhh, Tomi? It's for you."

She'd known. She thought she'd known before the doorbell rang, just a feeling that she would be brought in today. *And this is how they do it,* she thought. Now that she's being brought in for operational work, she's at their beck and call. Usually it's Barry at the door, one of the researchers at PSI, sometimes accompanied by an intelligence or military client. Tomi assumed they – the clients - usually want to supervise everything, to make sure that the staff of PSI haven't influenced the subjects or slipped them information in any way. *Most of the agents are highly dubious of our work,* she thought, *and probably want to have eyes on every step, right from my front door.*

Tomi scratched a crusty food stain from her pantleg, and almost left the bathroom without applying deodorant. *Maybe that's why they show up unannounced,* she thought, *to test us. If I'm really psychic, I should be showered and ready for them.*

With one last turn in the mirror, she felt like she'd done enough to pass herself off as ready. Her wavy black hair was pulled into a bun, light deep blue eyes in contrast to her dark skin. Tomi headed down the stairs of her home, and to the entryway, where she saw John standing beside a closed front door. *Odd,* she thought. Usually he would invite Barry and whoever was with him in and have a friendly chat, or offer coffee if she was taking some time.

"Is it Barry? You didn't invite him in?"

"Yes, Barry *and* Dr. Johansen. And a couple others. I invited them in, but one of them let me know that would not be necessary," John said, with a bit of a furrow that she knew well, meaning whoever was on the doorstep was probably a dick. John was usually too nice and polite to ever give it back.

His "this fucking guy" furrowed brow was his way of showing her that he wasn't thrilled about this unannounced visit.

"Dr. Johansen? Huh. That's different. Ib's never picked me up before. I'd better go. I have no idea how long I'll be, but I'll text when I ca-," she stopped, realizing she'd paused even before he actually interrupted. She knew it was coming. He hadn't said much, but she could tell he was uncomfortable with her work at PSI. Which she thought was especially unfair since he had initiated it, in a way.

"I know. You don't know how late you'll be, but you'll let me know, which usually isn't until you're already on your way home," he said.

Tomi nodded, trying to speed this up, fully aware there were several people outside the door waiting on her. She knew now wasn't the time to get into it, but felt John's attitude was unfair, considering the unpredictable and long hours he'd always put in.

"Sorry, just," he paused to find his phrasing. "Just be careful you don't get too deep into this. And them." John tilted his head to indicate the people outside.

Tomi nodded, said goodbye, and sped through the door, closing it behind her. She was met with Barry and Dr. Johansen, along with two other men, one in a dark suit, the other in uniform - *Air Force*, she thought. She never paid much attention to this world of military and intelligence, and couldn't recognize branch or rank, but gathered from the medals on his uniform, along with his presence, that he was a figure of some power. He had deep lines on his face, making his stern, impatient expression even more potent.

She said a tentative hello, feeling immediately out of place with this group.

"Hi Tomi, sorry for the crowd here," Dr. Johansen said, his near-perfect American TV accent betraying his Danish roots. He was an older man who had long ago decided his intellectual pursuits were of greater priority than being clean-shaven or ensuring his shirt was tucked in all the way around. "We were hoping you would come in today for a session."

Before she could give a response, the man in uniform extended his arm towards the black SUV running in her driveway, giving her a nod that said he wasn't often made to wait.

In the three-row SUV, Tomi sat alone in the back row, all passengers silent as the vehicle drove down the Durham Freeway, bypassing downtown and heading towards Duke.

These streets still don't feel like home, Tomi thought. They had moved here a year ago for John to pursue a private sector job after a dozen years in intelligence, but they both secretly hoped that new scenery would somehow give their marriage some new life. Instead, Tomi just felt more isolated and disconnected; at least she had before she joined PSI, and found an almost forgotten feeling of having a community.

This drive, though, was different; the air in the vehicle was thick with tension. And these men oozed seriousness. She realized she didn't know their names, which was odd, as in the past she would get an introduction to *Agent* or *Lieutenant So and So*. Usually only last names, but there was at least an introduction. She wondered if she would ever get one.

The vehicle made a left onto Morreen Road, and pulled into the parking lot of a long two-story building, a typical suburban office building housing various businesses and organizations. In this case, the red brick and yellow siding building was mostly rented as overflow office space for the university, as well as a few private labs and research groups. Their destination was at the end of the parking lot and the back of the building. The typical business-park entrance, just a frosted glass and steel door, had simple, black, two-inch letters spelling out *Perceptual Studies Institute (PSI)* at eye level.

The first time Tomi saw it, she laughed at the ridiculously generic and boring exterior and entrance for a parapsychology research centre. John, who had been beside her as they approached the building that first time back in April, smiled as he heard her laugh, realizing that it had been a rare sound for some time.

She didn't laugh this time as they silently exited the vehicle and walked single file up the sidewalk, and into PSI. No, *this time is different*, she thought, as she rolled her shoulders, already physically feeling the tension and stern energy of their guests. No, this was certainly not what John had had in mind when he brought her here that first time for a "laugh."

"I thought, you know, because of your grandmother, and her history, that you would get a kick out of this. I mean I didn't say anything about her to anyone."

No, John wouldn't say anything, she thought. He knew his clearances and what shouldn't be disclosed. He knew he wasn't supposed to know about her grandmother's background.

Sure, he could know most things about her. Tomi talked often about her grandmother, who was like a gust of fresh air into a sealed-up and stagnant room. She was creative and laughed loud and often. She was warm and loving, and knew what Tomi was feeling before she could even articulate it, so buried were Tomi's emotions, so unlike her grandmother. Her grandmother somehow had these huge emotions but could bask in them and let them flow with grace, and share love with those around her, whereas Tomi had learned early to hold in and contain her emotions.

Her grandmother always seemed to know more than she should. She was a psychic, an intuitive. She didn't have a fortune telling business or anything of the like, but the more time you spent with her, the more you knew that she *knew*.

Tomi remembered being a child and looking at a painting in her grandmother's house that scared her. It felt dark and creepy. On it was scrawled in messy paintbrush lettering: "We are the daughters of the witches you didn't burn."

As a child, Tomi didn't understand. One day she asked her grandmother about it.

"Why do you have that, Nan?"

Her grandmother considered the piece, breaking into a smile. "Because I'm a witch!" she said, and let out a cackling laugh.

Tomi got chilled. "Isn't it bad to be a witch?"

Her grandmother's face turned serious faster than Tomi could even process.

"Who told you that witches are bad?" her grandmother asked.

Tomi thought about it. Every story she'd heard that involved witches had taught her that witches were bad.

"Stories, I guess," Tomi had replied.

"Well, you've heard the wrong stories then."

Over time her grandmother told her lots of stories about strong women and what the world does to them. And about how nature provides so much of what we need to heal and be healthy, about how the universe resides within every cell of our body, and about how you could see places and times in your mind, when your body isn't even there.

That's what Tomi had told John that she shouldn't have. But Tomi *had* told him. Not everything she knew, but that her grandmother had been in *the program*. That her grandmother had been recruited into, and worked with the CIA - or DIA? Tomi was fuzzy on the details - doing psychic spying.

Tomi had told him so many years ago, back when they were falling in love. *I didn't think he'd remembered*, she thought. It was one of those family stories that young lovers tell to stoke that feeling of intimacy, when you empty out secrets as a means to say 'I trust you'.

"I trusted you with that," she said, aiming to sound cold but not icy. John, reminding Tomi that he *knows* her, pulling a thread from the start of their quilt, just reminded her how far they'd veered from those days of naked intimacy and trust.

"I didn't tell anyone. We're assessing this program, and they need volunteers, so some of the guys thought we would bring our spouses along and have a laugh. It was meant to be a fun thing. You don't really know anyone here. It was meant to be thoughtful," he said, sounding deflated.

She loosened. *He's a good man*, she thought. *He's making an effort.* Which she surely hadn't done in some time.

If she were stronger, she might have left him long ago. *He's a good man*, she thought again, *but didn't she need more than that?* She ached for something – or somewhere - she couldn't describe. Like an itch that keeps coming back, preventing you from ever getting comfortable.

But with bouts of depression, struggling to find her way professionally, and just not seeing any better options, she always stayed.

And John would never leave. It wasn't in his nature. *What was in his nature is arranging a trip, or tickets to the theatre, or signing us up for a remote viewing study, apparently - these were the things he did instead of talking*, Tomi thought. *This is him trying.*

"Okay, sure. Let's do it. It'll be fun." She forced a smile to show she was done talking about it.

The subject wasn't brought up again until Saturday came along, when over toast and coffee, John stopped reading his paper long enough to say, "The thing starts at one, so we should leave here by twelve-thirty or so. Maybe dress a bit nice, we were talking about going out for dinner after."

The "thing" of course, was this remote viewing experiment that had disrupted her sleep the past few days. Not knowing why, she didn't want John to know that this had affected her, so she tried to be light and breezy, and go along with it all. She didn't have the heart to burst the bubble of this kind, dedicated man.

"Is Jeff bringing Kirsten along?" Tomi asked.

Jeff was one of John's colleagues and, since moving to Durham and knowing few people, one of John's closest friends in town.

"Think so," John responded, without looking up from the paper.

"That's good," said Tomi. "I like her."

This time John did look up, giving her a *'really?'* look. Jeff had recently separated from his wife of 18 years when they had moved to Durham, and Jeff had recently started dating Kirsten. Tomi didn't know what the age difference was, but it was significant enough for everyone to share a smirk when Kirsten was brought up. Perhaps worse than the age difference, Kirsten was a free spirit who had no idea about, and seemingly no interest in learning about, Jeff's work and life in the intelligence community.

Within the IC, people like this weren't tolerated well, but for Tomi, Kirsten was a breath of fresh air. Kirsten had no idea of the secrecy, the stresses, the politics. She had her own life that included pole dancing classes, yoga, horseback riding, and vegetable gardening. She was even a vegetarian, yet another oddity in a place famous for its shrimp and grits. Kirsten had a life force that was just hers, and it called to Tomi. She felt both familiar and safe.

Perhaps a little, if she was really honest, she appreciated that Kirsten was even more on the outside than herself. It's a sad fact of humans that we often gain a sense of belonging in a group by denying access to another.

"Yeah, she's very nice," John finally replied politely. "Summit is bringing Meena also. Should be fun."

Tomi rested her forehead on the windowpane as she watched Durham fly by their vehicle. It still didn't feel like home. It looked about the same as any other place she'd lived, though she had struggled to call any of them home.

The car sped along silently. One of John's quirks was that he didn't listen to music. Not on the radio, CD, not in the car, not in the shower. He didn't mind music. If it was on, he didn't complain. He just never chose music. He'd hop in the car for a six-hour drive, and ride along content in silence.

Tomi eventually lifted her head off the passenger-side windowpane and broke that silence.

"I thought they cancelled the program," she said.

"Huh?" John had obviously been deep in thought, not making the connection between her question and their destination.

"The remote viewing program," she said. "The secret one. I thought they closed it in the 90s."

"Stargate Project. They did," John said.

"So what's this, then?"

"Well sometimes a program may be closed," John said. "A program under a certain name or department is closed. But the activities sometimes carry on. Maybe under a new name."

Tomi considered this for a moment. "Why would they close a program, but really continue it?"

"Lots of reasons," said John. "Maybe the focus of the program is shifting. Or maybe it's moving to a whole other branch of government. Or maybe, it's not secret enough anymore, and by saying it's closed, people interested in it stop looking for new information about it. Or if it has a new name, they don't know what to ask for through Freedom of Information."

"Right," said Tomi. "So what, remote viewing is real then?"

John smiled and breathed in a laugh. "Well, it doesn't mean that."

"Why would they keep it going if it wasn't?" Tomi asked.

"Again, lots of reasons," said John, though he didn't offer any.

A short silence fell until Tomi spoke again. "It doesn't sound like you take this very seriously."

John gave a quick flash of his eyes before darting them back to the road. "Well, it's not serious. I told you, we were asked to look into the program, and we just thought it would be fun. A laugh"

John's mouth stayed smiling while Tomi considered this. She wasn't sure how she felt about it, but hearing her husband say that it wasn't serious felt dismissive of her grandmother's experiences.

But she knew John didn't believe in psychics. Or ESP. Or ghosts or anything paranormal. If it wasn't physical, something he could touch, it couldn't possibly exist in John's eyes.

And I'm just not sure, thought Tomi. She knew her grandmother had some psychic abilities. So much so that she was involved in this *Stargate Project*. But while she accepted this of her grandmother, it was still too much to square with the world she saw in front of her.

They pulled into the lot of a long two-story office building, a mix of red brick, for the look, and yellow siding for the affordability. John drove the car slowly, scanning the entrances and signs. Remarking that he saw both Jeff and Summit's vehicles, John accelerated towards the back of the building, parking beside Summit's SUV.

"Guess we're the last to arrive," John said as he opened his door and slid out of the vehicle. Tomi opened her door, stepped out, and turned to see a glass entrance door with black film over the glass, and a small sign: "Perceptual Studies Institute (PSI) Unit 108."

Her left leg began to move towards the building, but she stopped suddenly, like the air in front of her had formed a wall. A feeling she couldn't quite identify came over her. It was similar to déjà vu, but not quite. With déjà vu, you feel like you've done something or been somewhere before. Instead, it felt like she'd had a flash forward, a momentary vision of her entering this building many times.

"Coming?"

She realized John was standing a few feet from the door, waiting for her to come out of her sudden trance. As soon as his voice washed over her, the feeling was gone and the wall of air in front of her disappeared. She started in his direction and stepped inside.

There was no reception area. Instead, the door opened into an open space, set up like a large living room, where several uniform blue couches formed a circle. In the centre was a small coffee table, with a projector on top, pointed towards a white pop-up screen.

On one couch were Jeff and Kirsten, Jeff with a tucked-in golf shirt and his shiny, shaved-bald head, and Kirsten in a green flowing summer dress with an elephant pattern. Tomi felt more at ease whenever she saw Kirsten.

Summit and Meena were settled on another couch, Summit with shirt and jacket - but no tie, as it was Saturday - and Meena in a blouse and long skirt. Tomi, in stretchy black pants and a long shirt/skirt, was as usual underdressed by comparison.

On a couch facing the couples were three men: one older man in a brown cardigan, his thin grey hair looking like someone had just tussled it. The one in the middle looked to be in his forties, with a tucked-in golf shirt that highlighted his belly, and the man on the right looked to be in his 50s, in faded blue jeans and a John Prine t-shirt. *At least I'm not the most underdressed*, thought Tomi, who smiled as her eyes landed on the t-shirt man.

"Ah, welcome, come in, come in and have a seat on that couch over there." The man on the left, in the brown sweater, pointed towards the empty couch and gave them a smile. He had just a slight accent, which Tomi couldn't place. She heard kindness in his voice.

The man looked at his clipboard, and said: "Mr. John Haywood, and Ms. Thomasina Newton?" John and Tomi smiled and nodded as they took their seats.

"Please, get comfortable, we are just about to get started. These are my colleagues who will be assisting us today, Chris Law," he said, as the man in the golf shirt nodded without a smile. "This is Barry Class," he said, pointing to the John Prine fan. "And I am Dr. Ib Johansen, and we are researchers here at the Perceptual Studies Institute, which we usually just shorten to *PSI*."

Ib nodded his head and looked around the room, as though he expected a question. None arose.

"Well okay then, Chris will go over the Participation Agreements, which we mentioned in the invitation, and then we'll get started."

"I'll just start by introducing myself, PSI, and the work we do here." Ib paused to sip his coffee. Tomi noticed his face react to the coffee, his lips curling up slightly as though his face said 'mmm.' He had a casual way about him, *like he wasn't in a hurry*, she thought. It was such a little thing, but when everyone around you is always in a hurry, a small act like enjoying the taste of coffee is noticeable.

"As I mentioned, my name is Ib, and I am a Doctor of Psychology. You might have noticed my accent, and that's because I come from, and did my studies in Denmark."

"You speak English so well!" Tomi blurted out, surprising herself. "Just, you have almost no accent," she said, as everyone shifted their gaze back to Dr. Johansen.

"Ah, thank you, the credit for that goes to Danish television, because they didn't dub American shows. So, you could say I owe my accent to reruns of Degrassi High and Major Dad," he said with a laugh.

"Chris and Barry are two of my research assistants here at PSI," continued Ib. "We are connected with, but not formally affiliated with the University. Here at PSI we do research into perceptual studies, or you might just say psychic phenomenon."

John and Jeff shared a quick grin and a glance, which Ib noticed, as though he expected it.

"That's okay if don't believe in such things," Ib said, his voice still sounding kind. "You don't need to believe in it to participate."

John apologized.

"Oh no need to apologize," said Ib. "We aren't here to convince anyone, though you might be surprised that a quarter of the world's population believes in psychic phenomenon. You see, I'm a man of science, trying to find evidence on the phenomenon one way or another. Let me ask you, how do you know that psychic abilities, or say any paranormal phenomenon, doesn't exist?"

John thought for a moment. Jeff jumped in, "There's no evidence. No scientific evidence."

Ib nodded and considered this. "Well, I wouldn't say *no* scientific evidence, but I would agree there isn't enough. So, if you're right, and it doesn't exist, shouldn't we prove that it doesn't exist once and for all, so we can all move on?"

John and Jeff agreed. "Totally," said John. "Sorry for the interruption, please keep going, we're excited for today."

"So am I," said Ib kindly. "Today you will be engaging in a study on Remote Viewing. Do any of you know what that is?"

The group looked at each other to see who would be the first to speak, and Meena awkwardly put her hand halfway into the air. Ib nodded to her in encouragement.

"It's sort of shifting your consciousness to another place. Like seeing pictures in your mind, and those pictures are of a place you're trying to get information about."

"I couldn't have said it better myself," Ib said, giving his head a small shake in appreciation.

"We do many experiments using remote viewing here at PSI, and usually with people with purported psychic abilities, or people who have experience in the field. Today, you are subjects in an experiment where we will examine the effectiveness of remote viewing among people with no experience or expertise in the subject. It's really quite a classic remote viewing experiment we will do today. Barry here," Ib said, pointing towards the John Prine fan, "will travel to a location of his choosing. In fact, he's the only one who knows where he will go. Well, he and his envelopes. He's written the geographic coordinates of the location he is going to on a card, and sealed it in these envelopes."

Ib held up the blank white envelopes, then continued. "Barry will go and wait at that location. While he's there he will launch a little drone to take an aerial picture of his location. Meanwhile, you will each take turns being remote viewing subjects. Chris and I will give you the envelope, though you won't open it. We'll ask you to move your thoughts to the location in the envelope. You will try to let pictures form in your mind, without thought or judgement. You'll draw the pictures that come into your mind."

He held up a clipboard with blank white paper in one hand, and fine-tip markers and pencils in another.

"And that's it," he said, with an innocent enthusiasm, "that's all you have to do. Then Barry will return and show us the aerial picture of his location. We will compare his actual location to what you drew in your sessions, and assess the degree of accuracy in your pictures. Make sense?"

The three couples looked around at each other, nodding or shrugging their shoulders as a way of collectively saying yes, it makes sense.

Just when Ib was about to move on, Kirsten broke the silence. "Why the coordinates?"

"I'm sorry?" asked Ib, not understanding the question.

"Why the coordinates?" Kirsten repeated. "In the envelope. If we don't look at the coordinates, what's the point?"

Ib smiled and nodded. "What a great question! It is to show consistency in the experiment, that the location was set, and by sealing the envelopes, it shows the other researchers didn't have knowledge of the location that they could impart to the subjects."

"Right," said Kirsten, "that makes sense, but why hand the envelope to us if we aren't going to open it?"

Ib was taking a moment to consider his answer when Barry spoke. "It's conscious intention. I create the intention when I write down the location. That conscious intention is shifted to you, or accessed by you, when you concentrate on the envelope. One consciousness to another."

Ib smiled uncomfortably. "That's one of our theories of how it works, but not one we really understand just yet."

He scanned the room and waited for someone to take issue with Barry's theory, or ask follow-up questions, but when one wasn't immediately visible, he nodded and said, "Okay then, let's get started. Barry, safe journey, please give us a call when you get into position."

While Barry travelled to his secret location, Ib and Chris left the group to prepare the interview rooms. The couples mingled, with the men shifting seats and getting into a chat about their golf club. Meena moved to the corner of the room to take a call, and Kirsten moved over to sit beside Tomi.

"Hey," said Kirsten, giving an obvious look at Jeff, "I don't think our guys buy any of this stuff! What about you?"

"Oh, I guess I'm open-minded. How about you? Have you ever done anything like this?" Tomi asked.

"Oh, like I've been to psychics before, and I had a roommate who would read my tarot, that kind of thing," said Kirsten, "but I've never imagined someone at some coordinates or whatever this is! Have you?"

Tomi tended to be a private person. She was very warm and friendly, but few people ever knew her deeply. Which is why she was surprised by a sudden urge to tell Kirsten about her grandmother, not just about the way she would know things, but she even wanted to tell Kirsten about her top-secret work. She felt warmth and openness in Kirsten. And Tomi realized it had been a long time since she'd had a good friend.

Before she answered, Ib and Chris came back into the room.

"Okay," said Ib enthusiastically, "Mr. Barry Class has called in to say that he is in place, so we are ready to begin. We will go in two at a time. Who's first?"

"We'll go first!"

Before Tomi registered who Kirsten had volunteered, she was being pulled off the couch by the hand, as she and Kirsten headed towards the interview rooms.

"Good luck, go do some psychic shit," Kirsten said with a laugh, as they parted into their individual rooms.

The rooms were small and plain, with dull white walls. There were two couches facing each other, and a reclining chair off to the side.

"We have clipboards, so you can write and draw sitting on the couch, or you can use the chair, dealer's choice," Chris told Tomi as she entered the room. She silently picked up a clipboard with several pieces of white paper already clipped in. Beside it was a mug with pens, pencils, and fine-tipped markers. She picked a blue Bic pen.

Tomi sat on the couch across from Chris and nodded that she was ready. Chris clicked on a small recording device.

"The date is April 21, 2023, this is Chris Law as Monitor, subject is Thomasina Newton. In this envelope," he said, as he nodded towards the envelope on the small coffee table between he and Tomi, "are coordinates to a location unknown to both the Monitor and the Subject. Researcher Barry Class is currently present at that location. Now Thomasina, I…"

"Tomi. Sorry, you can call me Tomi." She felt immediately awkward for interrupting him, remembering he was recording.

"Tomi, sure. Tomi, I will take you through some breathing and relaxation exercises to help focus your mind."

After focusing on her breathing, Chris led her through visualizing images.

"Now, Tomi," his voice had softened by this point, and she found it soothing and trustworthy. "I want you to focus your mind on the location written on the card and sealed in that envelope. Focus your mind on the place where Barry Class, who you met earlier, is located right now. With your eyes closed, through the darkness, you'll start to see lines or shapes or colours start to appear. Don't judge them, don't try to interpret them. Just let them form, and describe what you see. It may help to move your pen on the paper, whether drawing or just moving the pen. Just be patient, and let the images come forward."

Chris became quiet. Tomi didn't see anything. She waited. Her mind started to wander. He'd said 'dealer's choice', which her grandmother used to say. She suddenly could see, in vibrant colour, her grandmother's living room. She was laying on her grandmother's couch, and her grandmother was in her armchair. She could almost make out the autumn-coloured pattern, could almost feel the soft velour of the couch. Her grandmother was telling Tomi to breathe in and out, to focus on her breathing.

Had she tried to teach me this? she wondered.

"If your mind wanders, just clear your mind, go to black, and focus again on the target," Chris said. "Focus and be patient." While his voice was soothing, it made the image of her grandmother dissolve back into darkness. *Clear your mind and focus,* she reminded herself.

Through the darkness of closed eyes, she thought she could see vertical lines forming. They became clearer, solid.

"Four vertical white lines. Coming up into a point," she said softly. "And horizontal lines. They're supports. And it's not a point. It's like a big cylinder, a container. It's…it's tall. Then two long rectangles. Buildings, I think. They are kind of angled and this tall thing is in the middle, in between the buildings. Taller than them."

"Okay, that's great," said Chris. "What else do you see?"

Tomi was quiet, trying to make sense of the picture as it came together piece by piece, like a puzzle.

"Something else taller than the buildings. Like a tall rectangle. Like a big chimney. And water. Why water?" Tomi questioned herself. Water seemed out of place here. What she saw felt urban, and the water seemed natural.

"You don't need to question or interpret what you see. Just let the images guide you," reminded Chris.

"There's…like, water in the middle. In between these buildings…like a little river," she said. "It just seems weird but that's what I see."

The image in her mind focused more and more on the water. It felt like she was zooming in. Getting closer to it.

"I'm getting closer…like I can touch…" A hand came into view. Her hand. She watched it slowly dip its fingers into the water. She thought she felt the cold water on her fingertips.

She gasped and opened her eyes.

"Tomi, are you okay?" asked Chris, surprised by her abrupt wake up.

Was she okay?

"Sorry," she said, not wanting to share what she had just experienced. "I sort of lost the image there."

As Chris told her it was no problem, she looked down at her hand, then shook her head. Her hand was dry, of course.

Her eyes shifted focus from her hands to the clipboard and pen in them. She'd been sketching what she saw. She realized she was vaguely aware she was doing this, but thought she was mostly just scribbling. Instead, there was a drawing of what she saw, albeit a bit rough.

"So, once you're ready, you'll place your sketch in this manila envelope here with your name on it. Once everyone has done their sessions, and Barry returns, we'll take a look at them." He paused and looked at her. "You okay?"

Tomi realized she wasn't making eye contact, and was looking instead at her drawing with a slight look of confusion. She was surprised how much she felt like she was actually there, at this place, wherever it was. It almost felt like she was beside the water. Like she could dip her toes in.

"Yeah, guess I just got pretty relaxed there. I'm fine," she said, and forced a smile.

She put her drawing into the envelope, handed it to Chris, gave an awkward thanks, and left the room.

When Tomi exited the room, she headed directly to the bathroom to get a few moments alone and collect herself. She looked in the mirror, and told herself she had fallen asleep, just at the end. *Sometimes dreams can feel so real*, she thought.

She splashed some water on her face, dried up, and went back into the main room. Meena and Summit were now in the interview rooms, and John and Jeff were on a couch chatting.

"Where's Kirsten?" Tomi asked John as she approached them.

"Oh, hey hun. How did it go in there?"

"It was fine." *It was fine,* she repeated in her mind. "Where's Kirsten?"

"We sent her for food! She was done before you," Jeff said to Tomi, then turned to say to John, "Dude, you should see her hungry. It's scary, seriously."

Tomi was happy to see them continue chatting, and curled herself up on the furthest couch and closed her eyes. She didn't feel tired as much as mentally drained.

After a time, Kirsten returned with an extra-large tray of sushi rolls for the group. She came over and sat on the edge of the couch beside Tomi. "Hey Tomi, I brought us sushi. How was your session? You okay?"

"Hey, oh thanks, I'm good," said Tomi. "Just have a bit of a headache so I'm just resting my eyes a bit."

"Oh, I've got this peppermint oil in my purse, you rub it into your temples, it really works!" Kirsten said as she started to rustle into her bag.

"I've taken some Advil, but thanks, I appreciate it," Tomi said and closed her eyes again. She could hear them eating and chatting. Shortly after, Meena and Summit exited, and John and Jeff took their turns. After they finished, Chris came out to say they were just scanning the results, and that they would all go over them once Barry returned, which he did shortly after. Dr. Johansen's team came into the main room, and while Chris set up his laptop and switched on the projector, Ib addressed the group.

"Thank you so much for your patience, and again thank you for your time today. Now, my friend Barry here, as you know, went to a location of his choosing. Chris, would you put up the picture Barry took with his drone? Barry, would you tell us where you went?"

"I wanted to go to a place that had some distinctive features, as that makes it easier to identify matches with your drawings and interviews. So today I went to the American Tobacco Campus here in Durham, and parked myself just under the Lucky Strike tower."

A few in the group let out an *ohhh* sound, though Tomi wasn't familiar with it. Chris finally got the projector turned on, and an aerial image popped onto the screen. There was a tall water tower in between two long buildings. Behind the water tower was a tall, rounded smokestack. Barry could be made out standing just under the water tower, holding the controls for the drone. And in between the two buildings, and flowing around the water tower, was a small concrete river of water.

Tomi's stomach twisted. Her lip started to tremble. She had nailed it, and she wished she hadn't.

"Now, Chris scanned each of your drawings," said Ib. "Chris, can you put the first one up? Ah yes, this one is Mr. Haywood's."

Beside the aerial photograph was a rough pencil sketch. It had two rectangles. In between was a taller rectangle. Elsewhere on the page were some scribbles and squiggles, and in one spot was written the word '*tall.*'

"So, this is interesting," said Ib. "I mean it's not exactly a carbon copy, but you can see some similarities. Are these meant to be buildings?"

John looked a little proud that his sketch was deemed interesting. "Yeah, I sort of imagined two buildings, with a taller building there in the middle."

"Right, and that's why you wrote 'tall' here," said Ib. "Interesting, well we assess these based on the number of corresponding items, so though it's not detailed, you have three shapes that do match up."

"John, I didn't know you were a psychic," Jeff teased. "I mean psychotic, we knew that, but not psychic!" John laughed, perhaps more because Jeff was his senior at work, but he appeared to be uncomfortable.

Tomi was numb. She sat silently, staring at the screen, dreading her drawing being projected for everyone to see. She looked at the exit. *Leaving would cause a scene. It's already done*, she thought.

They shuffled through sketches from Meena, Jeff, and Summit. None had any real similarities, and the group had a laugh at Summit's stick figure drawing of Barry.

"Barry, you've lost a lot of weight," Ib joked, and got halfway through a laugh when the projector flashed Tomi's drawing on the screen. "This is, uh…oh my…"

Ib stopped his thought and stared at the screen. Tomi's drawing was a bit crude, but there were clearly two long buildings. In between was a water tower, complete with four tall metal legs, with horizontal support bars going up the tower. Behind it was another tall figure - the smokestack. And there with wavey lines to indicate flowing water, was a small stream between the buildings. The perspective was even similar to where the drone had taken the photo.

"This…is remarkable," Ib finally said to a silent room.

"Holy shit Tomi, you're legit psychic!" Kirsten said with excitement and a laugh. The group got suddenly light, as everyone expressed amazement at the drawing. In between the compliments and jests, a deep voice caught everyone's attention.

"What the hell is that?"

Everyone turned to look at Barry, who was focused on the projection of Tomi's sketch, mouth hanging open.

"What is that, in the corner?" Barry asked, pointing to the screen.

On the bottom right corner of her drawing, a bit apart from the main sketch, was a lightly drawn circle. In the circle was a crude sketch of Mickey Mouse, with both arms pointing upwards, one up and to the right, the other up and to the left.

"Well, it's Mickey Mouse," Ib said with a laugh. "Mickey wasn't with you, was he Barry?"

Barry didn't lighten. He pulled out his phone and turned the screen to Ib.

"Look at the time. I called Chris at 1:54 to say that I was in position. I looked at my watch when I called, so I could say the time that we would begin," Barry said, sounding incredulous. He then held up his left arm, showing Ib his watch.

"It's a Mickey Mouse watch," Ib said quietly, more to himself than anyone else. He turned to look back at the sketch projected on the screen. One of Mickey's arms was pointing to where one or two might be on a clock face, with the other arm pointing to where eleven would approximately be.

Then he turned to look at Tomi, who was crawling out of her skin.

"I must ask," said Ib, looking slightly awestruck. "Have you ever exhibited psychic abilities? Or a family member?"

Tomi opened her mouth as if to speak, but nothing emerged as she looked around the room at the eyes fixed on her. Bringing up her grandmother, who the other kids called the witch lady, would not lower the tension in the room.

"So she saw the watch before he left," Jeff said, proposing a rational explanation.

"And she would know the time he called because we would have started a few minutes later," added Summit. "And everyone knows the Lucky Strike water tower. Did someone tip you off?"

"I don't think my wife would cheat," John said flatly.

"No, not cheat," said Jeff, with Summit agreeing. "I mean like subconsciously, maybe she saw it on him, and it was in her head."

"I wasn't wearing it." Everyone turned back to Barry, who looked not only confused but solemn. "I wasn't wearing it earlier. When I was driving, I put my hand in the cupholder and the watch was in there, and I put it on. I think. I don't think I was wearing it earlier."

"Oh, but you don't know for sure, well-"

"My head hurts. John, would you take me home?" Tomi said softly to John, interrupting Jeff's rationalizing.

Although the group had plans for drinks and dinner after, they didn't put up an argument about the party being over. The researchers thanked the group, and the pairs headed to their cars and waved as they drove off.

When they got in the car, John looked at Tomi and asked if she was alright. She nodded, he squeezed her knee, and then proceeded to drive silently.

Tomi felt uncomfortable. She felt exposed, as though she had done something wrong, something she wasn't supposed to do. In front of so many people. John's colleagues.

It was a feeling she'd had before, and feeling it now brought it to mind clearly. It was a memory that had always been there, but fuzzy, unwanted, and one she chose not to visit.

When Tomi was a kid, she was quiet. She wasn't afraid to speak. Mostly she didn't have others to speak to, as she was a bit of a loner.

Not really a social outcast, and not really bullied. Just not really thought of, not considered, and not one to insert herself.

Even though she was a loner, she was fascinated by the other kids. How they could just get along, feeling their place in the world, as though daily life was the most normal and natural thing. For Tomi, life always felt a little more confusing, and getting along in life always felt a little harder.

At night, resisting sleep, Tomi would imagine she could float into the sky, right through her ceiling, and see the whole town, rooftops, streetlights, and trees from above. She would fly to the homes of her classmates, drift through the walls of their houses, and imagine she could snoop around. Sometimes she imagined people were still awake, parents or an older sibling watching late night TV. One time a kid's parents were fighting, screaming at each other. She imagined floating along, into the rooms of her classmates. Usually she imagined them sleeping, once or twice they were reading. Once, the kid was crying into their pillow.

She didn't know why she imagined these things, but usually, it would end with her returning to her bed and drifting off to sleep. It was a harmless fascination, until she opened her mouth and exposed herself to her peers.

One day at school, Stacy Marland, who was a nice kid but who seemed younger and more childish than the rest of the kids, brought her stuffy to school and held it in class. One kid asked the teacher why she was allowed to have it in class since there was a rule not to bring toys from home. The teacher explained Stacy's mom thought it would be good for her, so she would allow it. Some of the kids snickered and shook their heads.

Later that day, the girls were in the change rooms switching to their uniforms for PE, when a few of the girls approached Stacy and asked to see her stuffy. She said no, but one of them grabbed it. They passed it around and teased Stacy, calling her a baby.

Before she could stop the words leaving her mouth, Tomi spoke up: "Stop it! Adeny, just give it back, you sleep with a stuffed penguin so just stop it!"

The group of girls turned to look at Tomi with curious smiles, except for Adeny, who stared daggers. Without looking at her, she handed the stuffy back to Stacy, who then ran out of the changing room crying.

"Why did you say that?" Adeny asked angrily, stepping towards Tomi.

"You were being cruel, I wanted you to stop."

"No, the penguin," Adeny said. Then turning towards her friends, she said, "I used to sleep with a stuffed penguin when I was little." She turned back to Tomi, who knew the truth. "How did you know that, about the penguin? You've never been to my house."

Tomi shook her head slowly. She'd imagined being in Adeny's bedroom, and imagined her sleeping with her arm around a stuffed penguin. *But I only imagined that*, she thought. *Why would I say that out loud?*

She felt vulnerable and exposed, ashamed she'd let even a sliver of what she did at night out into the world. *What would they think of me if they knew I imagined being in their homes, their bedrooms?* she thought, her stomach pounding with anxiety.

Adeny glared. "You're such a weirdo. Freak girl." Adeny turned to head into the gym, her friends following behind, one asking if she really slept with a penguin stuffy.

Tomi stopped her imaginary adventures that night, and didn't imagine herself flying or spying on her classmates again.

This feeling she had in the car with John wasn't quite the same. The other kids didn't really know why she was ashamed then. They didn't know *how* she knew about the penguin. But that feeling of being exposed was so familiar.

"So, that was quite the picture," John said, finally breaking the silence and interrupting Tomi's memory. "Are you going to tell me how you did that?"

John was sounding lighthearted, and smiled as he looked at Tomi and back to the road, but she could see he was hiding discomfort. Like he'd been kept out of an inside joke or secret.

"Maybe we can just talk about it later? That was just a lot and I have a bad headache," she said, turning to look out the passenger side window.

"Sure, sure," John said as they drove in silence home. When they got there, Tomi took a sleeping pill, crawled into bed, and slept through until morning. When she did wake up, she found coffee made in the kitchen and a note from John that he was out golfing. When he returned, they didn't talk about what happened at PSI.

Chapter 2

"Close your eyes and let the mind expand. Let no fear of death or darkness arrest its course. Allow the mind to merge with Mind. Let it flow out upon the great curve of consciousness. Let it soar on the wings of the great bird of duration, up to the very Circle of Eternity."

Hermes Trismegistus

When John returned from golfing, they ordered some takeout and ate in separate rooms, Tomi watching a movie while John worked on his laptop at the kitchen table. Life went on like normal. Neither brought up PSI and what happened that day. On Monday morning John woke up and went to work.

Tomi lay in bed, reliving and trying to make sense of what had happened at PSI. A part of her wanted to forget and move on, but under the surface, she felt something else. Deep inside she felt an agitation, a restlessness that had always been there, but was becoming harder to ignore.

In the past, Tomi at times had restless leg syndrome, which many assume means your leg won't stop moving. For Tomi, it felt more like something deep in her limbs just *needed* to move, like her nerves were demanding movement. If she stretched and flexed, she would get temporary relief, and then it was a race to fall asleep before the feeling returned.

Eventually she was prescribed a medication to suppress that physical restlessness, but what medication could calm a soul that needs to stretch and flex?

Tomi let these thoughts swirl in her mind for a time, and eventually made her way downstairs. She made herself toast and coffee, sat down at the table, and heard the doorbell ring. She knew immediately who it was, and wished she'd thought to get dressed. She pulled her housecoat tight and answered the door.

"Good morning, Thomasina," Ib said, his American accent betrayed as he pronounced her uncommon name. While Ib smiled, Barry stood beside him with a guarded expression on his face. Ib asked if they could chat.

She invited them in and served them coffee at the kitchen table. "Thomasina, this is a beautiful home," Ib said politely, looking around at the large country kitchen. John had done well, first in the Agency, and now as a contractor to the IC. John always wanted the finest, while Tomi had less interest in material wealth. This home was their compromise, not extravagant, but certainly privileged.

"Please, call me Tomi," she said.

"Tomi, I listened to the audio recording of your remote viewing session," Barry said, uninterested in continuing small talk. "It was impressive. You let the images come into your mind, and they were so accurate. And then of course there was the Mickey watch. You didn't speak about it in the session. When did you see it?"

Tomi thought. Parts of the session felt fuzzy. "I don't remember seeing the watch. Seeing Mickey. I had my eyes closed and was sketching. But I don't remember really seeing it. Or drawing it."

Barry didn't look satisfied with that answer but nodded. After a moment, he pulled a small recording device from his pocket.

"I want to ask you about this part, at the end of your session." Barry pressed play on the recorder.

"There's…like water in the middle. In between these buildings…like a little river…I'm getting closer…like I can touch…[gasp]."

Tomi's face reddened. Parts of the session were fuzzy, but the water - it really felt like she had touched the water, had felt it on her fingers. And when she did, it was terrifying.

She'd always had a fear of slipping into insanity. Like there's a cliff just off to the side of her, and one day if she shuffles too far in one direction, she'll fall off. And won't be able to return. Feeling that cool water when she dipped her fingers in made her feel like she shuffled too close to that cliff. It scared her.

But she couldn't ignore that it also excited a feeling deep within her. A proximity to something more divine. Some meaning beyond daily life.

"What did you see here?" Though Barry's face was serious, she could feel he was asking from a place of curiosity. She could see he did this work not for prestige, but because he was dedicated to uncovering some truth.

"I, uh, I saw a little river," said Tomi. "We saw from your drone picture after, the little waterway that goes between the buildings."

"Right." Barry paused for a moment, thinking about how to elicit the response he was seeking. "What I mean is - and Tomi, you're under no obligation to us, you came in for a one-time experiment. We just want to understand this better. What I'm asking is, were you seeing images or forms in your mind? Or - and it sort of sounds like this – is it possible you felt like you were really there? Present in that place?"

Tomi thought. She was such a private person and would keep an experience as strange as this one to herself. But she was also curious about what had happened. And beyond curious, she was stirred. After that session, she felt an energy growing within her. It felt transformative. She looked at Ib, who smiled gently, as though he was just as happy whether she answered or not.

"Yes," Tomi said finally, surprising herself with her surety. "It felt like I was really there."

"I thought so," said Barry. "And when you said you were getting closer, it felt like you were moving."

"Yes. Floating," she said, and experienced a pang of longing to feel herself floating, weightless, again.

"Did it feel like you could interact with your surroundings?" Barry asked.

She paused. She decided to be honest, but saved the detail of feeling the water on her fingers.

"Yes, I think so," she said.

Barry gave his head a slow shake. "Amazing. Most RVers just see shapes and images. What you're describing is sort of a level up. Almost out of body. Tomi, I think something special happened. We would like you to consider coming in again for some follow-up experiments."

She knew this was coming. And though she left on Saturday feeling exposed and confused, she'd felt the urge to do it again. To find out if she just had a weird, one-off experience, or if she possibly had her grandmother's gift inside of her, and hadn't noticed. Or hadn't wanted to notice.

"I'm not sure," she said. "Can I think about it?"

"Of course. Whenever you are ready. Here's my card," said Ib. She had expected more of a pitch, but appreciated him accepting that she needed time to think and process. He gave a smile as he placed his card on the table. It was the first time she really paused to look him clear in the eyes. He seemed happy and lighthearted in his demeanor, but she was struck by a deep sadness behind his eyes.

Ib and Barry stood, thanked Tomi for the coffee, and headed towards the door. As Barry stepped out the door, Ib said, "Barry, you go ahead to the vehicle. I just want to have a word alone with Ms. Newton."

"Sure Ib. Thank you for the coffee, Tomi, and I hope you'll consider it," said Barry, heading towards the vehicle parked on the street. When he was out of earshot, Ib turned to look Tomi in the eyes.

"You see, when I was a child, I was really interested in ghosts, and psychics, and everything paranormal. I would get all kinds of books about poltergeists and bigfoot and such from the library. My father did not approve. He was a biologist. More than that he just loved science. And if science couldn't answer something, or hadn't answered it yet, it didn't exist to him."

Ib paused for a deep breath. Tomi felt her face and gaze soften. She expected he might talk about payment to get her to come in, not about his father. This vulnerability was unexpected.

"As I got older," Ib continued, "he gave me a harder and harder time. He said I should be studying real things, not fantasies. Well, I wanted to please him, so eventually I gave up on those things, and I went into the sciences. Well one day, I stumbled upon some journal articles about ESP. And that was it for me. I thought, if I could also be a man of science, and use science to prove that it's not all fantasy, well, I'm not sure what I thought would happen. I don't know, maybe that he would respect me."

He nodded and smiled gently again.

"I'm not sure I ever proved anything to him. But when I went home on Saturday, well, I thought that maybe you might. Somehow, I think that maybe you could. I mean he's dead now, but posthumously," he said with a smile and laugh, suddenly lighthearted Ib again.

She didn't know what to say. Like finding a lost item you'd forgotten you even owned, she realized it was a long time since someone had believed in her. Tomi hadn't realized how much she desired assurance.

Ib stepped out the door and paused. "Please consider it. And thank you for the coffee."

He started towards the street, but paused when Tomi said, "Dr. Johansen? Thank you for sharing that."

"Call me Ib," he said with a smile, his overgrown hair being tussled by the wind, the portrait of an eccentric academic.

I'm not going to call him, she had thought. *I'm not going to do it.*

She loved her grandmother, but her grandmother also scared her. All this spooky stuff scared her. But it was beyond just the spooky factor. She'd always had a feeling that if she engaged, if she gave in to this other world, if she found that she *was* like her grandmother, she would start losing her grip on the world she lives in.

How do you have accurate visions about different places or times, then remember to go pick up washer detergent? she wondered.

Besides, she saw the way people acted around her grandmother, Esther. What they thought of her. Even Tomi's own mother.

Esther was her father's mother. Her father had died in an accident when Tomi was only a baby. Tomi's mother made sure that she had a relationship with her father's family, even if she looked concerned whenever she dropped Tomi off with her grandmother. In time Tomi realized that when her mother would look at her and tell her to call her if she needed her, she was really questioning if her grandmother could be responsible enough to care for her.

As the day went on, deep in her gut, *I'm not going to do it* started to feel like *I need to do it, just to find out.* There was so much she didn't know about her grandmother. As the day went on, a feeling grew in Tomi that returning to PSI might be the path to understanding more about her grandma.

That evening, when John came home, she was expecting to discuss the visit and the offer with him. Yet when he asked her about her day, she lied. *Uneventful,* she had said. It surprised her. Yes, there was a growing universe of things being left unsaid in their relationship, but she couldn't remember blatantly lying like that before.

John had no follow-up questions. He was distracted, starting to gather things from around the house. He explained that he was needed in the D.C. office, and would be flying out in the morning.

Tomi was surprised again that she felt a sense of relief. She wouldn't have to lie tomorrow about where she'd been when she returns to PSI.

The PSI office was different on a weekday. When Tomi stepped inside, she was suddenly disoriented. Her experience there had felt so intimate, it surprised her to see unfamiliar people inside, going about their work. Before she had a chance to change her mind and back out the door, Barry stepped out of one of the office doors, stopping in his path when he noticed her standing in the entrance.

"Oh, hi Tomi," he said tentatively, as though he hadn't expected her to actually return.

"Hi," she said, feeling suddenly more comfortable seeing a familiar face.

"Dr. Johansen isn't here right now, but - well, have you decided?"

Tomi gave a slow nod, her body accepting the role before her voice had a chance to weigh in. "Yes. Well, I would like to give it a try anyway."

Barry's face turned to a smile, a look she hadn't seen before. "Great. That's great. Well hey, we have a bunch of paperwork then, let's talk to Chris and get you started."

Barry wasn't exaggerating. For research purposes, there were extensive forms about her health history, her family's health history, her mental health now and in the past, medications, her education, interests, and on. And with each form a consent to sign. Then a lengthy Non-Disclosure Agreement. *There's a reason they call it Legalese*, she thought, *because this is definitely not written in English.*

"The NDA, you can take that and read it, or show it to a lawyer if you want," Chris explained. "Basically, it says don't tell anyone about your work here, now or ever. I mean of course you can tell your immediate family that you are working here, but you can't tell them any details of what you see, our experiments, our operations, et cetera. I don't know why it takes them eight pages to say that, but that's what it is."

Easy enough, she thought. She grabbed the pen and started to sign, scribbling slightly when she was startled by a voice behind her.

"Det er fantastisk!" Ib said loudly, clearly pleased to see she had accepted his offer. "This is fantastic. It's great to see you here, Tomi."

Tomi's remote viewing work at PSI started out with similar experiments to the one she had done that first day with John and his colleagues. Dr. Johansen and his team were continuously running experiments as they worked towards publishing their research.

Unlike the first session where she felt vulnerable and exposed in front of John and his colleagues, Tomi grew to enjoy the remote viewing sessions more and more. If she got something correct, even something uncanny, the staff there didn't look at her the way John and the others had looked at her. These were people who *believed* in psychic abilities, or at least allowed for the possibility. People who thought the paranormal just might be *normal*.

Rather, she started to feel more out of place in her daily life. One day after a particularly deep session, she stopped at the grocery store on her way home. She bumped into a neighbour who stopped her to chat about the spring weather and their gardens. Tomi was disoriented by the juxtaposition, as just hours ago she was investigating a remote location as a psychic spy, and now must think of anything at all to say about the weather. *It's like PSI is Hogwarts and outside of it I'm surrounded by muggles*, she thought.

At PSI, she had found a place of belonging, filled with people who really saw her, all of her. Over time she felt more confident, and started to feel a deeper sense of purpose in her life. One day John even commented that she seemed happier, and that it was good to see.

It was the only time he said anything positive about her work at PSI. When John had returned from D.C., she sat him down and told him about Ib and Barry's visit, and her deciding to try more remote viewing.

John made a *hmm* sound, and in the end said she should do it if it makes her happy. It was the right answer, but she could feel his deep reservations about it. She didn't think he was against her working or learning something new - he had been encouraging her to find something new to do, some new volunteer role or hobby, in hopes of it helping the depression and listlessness that she often experienced.

No, it's because it's too weird, she thought. What if people he knew or worked with found out? John was surrounded by very serious people focused on national security. What would it do to his reputation if it got out that his wife was a psychic?

John liked it even less once she started doing "real world" exercises.

After a few months of participating in RV research, Ib and Barry called her into Ib's office. Ib explained that while he and his team are focused on pure research, there aren't many research dollars available for studying ESP, or anything that might be called paranormal. Instead, PSI funded its research through contracts with the military and intelligence community.

"You see," Ib explained, "Stargate Project ended years ago, but parts of the national security community continued to use remote viewing to gather intelligence, though this fact was classified. PSI is one of the contractors used for this purpose."

"I see," Tomi said, though she had already assumed this to be the case, since John's firm had been evaluating PSI for that purpose.

Barry then explained that in remote viewing research - not just at PSI but back in Stargate Project as well - the best RVers would work to get to over sixty percent in accuracy.

"That's sort of the line that divides the upper tier of RVers," he said. "And lately you've been scoring well over that."

Tomi flushed. "So, that's good then?"

"That's fantastic," Barry said kindly. "And with that, you are eligible to start participating in real world exercises. This is when someone contracts us, usually from an intelligence agency, or military intelligence, to perform remote viewing to gather intel. Of course, this work is far more delicate and requires maximum discretion. But, you might be able to contribute to national security, if that appeals to you. Do something real. And maybe change a few minds, too. What do you say?"

Unlike the first time these two offered her a job, her decision was immediate. She'd grown more confident, but also had become more and more intrigued by this other world she was visiting.

"Absolutely, I'm in," Tomi said, leaning back in her chair.

"Fantastic," said Barry. "Chris will get started on getting your security clearance."

She had been excited to tell John about this development. His career was in intelligence, and it is a world she mostly wasn't privy to. *We would both be working in Intelligence*, she thought. *That has to count for something.* They had grown so apart, and she thought this work might bring them closer.

"I don't know. Do you really want to get mixed up in all that? The research is one thing, but-," John had trailed off, unsure how to articulate the problem. "I mean I guess, if you think you want to, I support you, of course" he finished, forcing a smile.

He didn't attempt to smile that day in early September when Ib and Barry came to pick her up, along with the General and the man in the suit. Though John was used to a military or intelligence escort picking Tomi up - they often liked to have eyes on the whole process, to ensure no information was provided by PSI staff before the session - having a general show up at their door was too much. Though John said the right things, Tomi felt the energy he gave off said *this is my world, and you don't belong in it.*

It seemed to Tomi that the General had this effect, making everyone tense and intimidated. The day the General picked her up, she stepped into PSI and found that this place that had become so comfortable to her felt colder, tenser.

When they stepped into the office, Tomi saw two other remote viewers she had worked with sitting silently on the couches waiting to be called into the session. Even Ib, normally lighthearted, had a more serious demeanor around the General, as he addressed Tomi as *'Ms. Newton'* and invited her to take a seat.

The general and the man in the suit weren't the only visitors, as there were two other men in suits standing towards the corner of the room. The general and the man in the suit joined the other two men in a whispered huddle.

Inside the Director's office, Ib, Barry, and Chris were going over the session procedures.

"Are the rooms all ready?" asked Ib.

"Yes, I'll just put the envelopes in there and we are ready to begin," Chris said.

In Chris's hand were three sealed envelopes, labelled *A, B,* and *C.* One contained a blank 3 by 5 card. Inside the other two, the cards read:

```
The planet Mars.
```

```
Time of interest approximately 1 million
years B.C.
```

Chapter 3

"Karin calls the other reality she perceives during her experiences the 'fourth dimension.'

'It's what we call illusion, but it's not illusion. It's not illusion. It exists. It's there. That's where they live... You don't use language when you're in this other experience. You use color, and you have vibration and everything else.'

Space/time in this dimension, she says, is 'irrelevant.'"

John E. Mack

Dr. Johansen sat deep in his desk chair and let out a long, slow breath. In the span of a long career, there are few days that really stand out, from beginning to end, in a way you know you will remember. *Every detail*, thought Ib. *I need to remember every detail of today.*

He turned on his desk lamp and arranged the fresh printouts. Barry had already run the transcription program and made a copy for him. The program wasn't perfect, but they would edit the transcript later. For now, he just had to see it in black and white. He had to understand what had just happened.

Ib swigged the last of the cold coffee in his mug, pulled a bottle of Glenmorangie from his desk - there to keep him company when working alone into the night - and poured generously into his empty coffee mug. He took a sip and felt it flow back into his mouth. The slight burn was welcomed, helping him confirm he was truly awake.

He began to read.

```
Method of site acquisition:

Sealed envelope.

The sealed envelope was given to the
subject immediately prior to the
interview. The envelope was not opened
before or after the interview as
instructed by the parties requesting the
information.

In the envelope was a 3 X 5 blank card.

Researcher's Note: two other sessions were
conducted simultaneously in the same
facility. In the other two sessions, the 3
X 5 card in the sealed envelope contained
the following information:

The planet Mars.

Time of interest approximately 1 million
years B.C.

Selected geographic coordinates, provided
by the parties requesting the information,
were verbally given to the subject during
the interview.
```

Ib leaned back, flipping to the next page and the start of the transcript.

He took another drink. When he started the day, he had no idea just how strange - and strangely wonderful - it would be.

Of course, any day that you are contracted by the type of people there today - a four star general and three stoic suited men from Lockheed - everything becomes far more tense. Despite a little tension, everything went as planned. They collected the remote viewers. He, Barry, and Chris led the sessions. Ib briefly reviewed the initial results with the client, who had watched both sessions. The client seemed to find them mildly interesting, but were so tight-lipped, it was hard to tell if they were satisfied or not.

They are satisfied now, he thought. He was sure of that.

Ib started to read the transcript, wishing he had been the monitor for her session.

MON:	All right now, using the information in the envelope I've provided, exclusively focusing your attention now, focus on: 40.75 degrees north 350.54° East
SUB:	......I want to say it looks like ah...I don't know, it sort of looks...I've kind of got an oblique view of a...a pyramid or pyramid form. It's very high, it's kind of sitting in a... large, depressed area.

MON:	All right.
SUB:	It's yellowish, ah...okra coloured.
MON:	All right. Move in time to the time indicated in the envelope I've provided you and describe what's happening.
SUB:	I'm seeing severe, severe clouds, more like dust storms, ah...it's a geologic problem. Seems like a, ah...Just a minute, I've got to iron this out. It's really weird.
MON:	Just report your raw perceptions at this time, Tomi, it's still early in the session.
SUB:	I'm looking at, at a...after effect of a major geologic problem.
MON:	Okay, can you go back to the time before the geologic problem?
SUB:	.........Um, total difference, it's ah...before there's no ah...I don't know...oh hell, it's like mountains of dirt appear and then disappear when you go before. I see ah...large flat surfaces, very

	ah...smooth...angles, walls, they're really large though. I mean they're megalithic.
MON:	All right. At this period in time now, before the geologic activity, look around, in and around this area and see if you can find any activity.
SUB:	......I'm seeing ah...It's like a perception of a shadow of people, very tall...thin, it's only a shadow. It's as if they were there and they're not...not there anymore.
MON:	All right. Can you go back to a period of time when they are there?
SUB:	.........Um.........(mumble) It's like I'm getting static like on an old TV. It's breaking up, just fragmentary pieces.
MON:	Just report the raw data, don't worry about putting things together.
SUB:	I just keep seeing very large people. They appear thin and tall, but very tall. Ah...wearing some strange kind of clothes. But I just see fragments.

Ib sat back in his chair and drew a deep breath. She had no idea. She hadn't opened the envelope. Even if she had, hers was blank. *If she really was remote viewing Mars,* Ib thought, *if she somehow subconsciously did follow the instructions in the other envelopes as Barry believes, well*…his thought trailed off.

Ib thought about his clients. They didn't look surprised when she described these tall people. *Why not?*

They had almost been out the door without knowing about Tomi's session. Ib had told them that they would draft and send a full report. The clients were about to leave the office and head to the airport to fly back to wherever it was they'd come from. Ib had no idea where that was. These clients didn't share any information that wasn't absolutely necessary.

Ib had been looking forward to them leaving. These men gave him the creeps. Just as they were gathering their belongings, Barry had walked slowly out of the third interview room, clearing his throat tentatively.

"Uh, Dr. Johansen, could I show you something? Before everyone leaves?"

Ib looked around. This was peculiar, but the clients seemed unphased, looking back to Ib as if to say, 'get on with it'.

Ib and Barry took a step away.

"Ib, something strange happened in the session with Tomi," Barry whispered. Ib and the clients had not reviewed Tomi's session. She was the control session. The two other remote viewers were given the proper envelopes, while Tomi's was blank, something that Ib often insisted on as part of his research.

"She was the control," said Ib flatly.

"I know. I double-checked, and Tomi had the control envelope. It was blank. I hadn't known what was written in the other two envelopes until I opened them to add the information to the transcript. And well, after I read the other cards in the envelope, I started to wonder..."

Barry trailed off as he held up the iPad in his hand, and opened the video of Tomi's session. Each session was recorded, both in audio and video, for research and transcription purposes. This also allowed the clients to watch the two active sessions by video in another room. Nobody had thought to check on the control session.

Barry scrolled the video to the middle and clicked play. He let it play for fifteen, perhaps twenty seconds before pressing pause.

"I think before they go, they might like to see the video of the session," Barry said.

Ib paused for a moment, then nodded. He stepped towards the front of the office again, while Barry connected his iPad to the projector.

"I'm sorry gentlemen," Ib had said, "but if you have a bit of time before your flight, you might want to see the video of the control session."

Ib looked back down and continued reading.

MON:	All right, now holding in this time period, I want you to move from your physical location in space to another physical location, but in this same time period. Move now to: 45.45 degrees north 353.22 degrees east
SUB:	......I'm deep inside of a cavern, not a cavern, more like a canyon. Um, I'm looking up, up the sides of a steep wall that seems to go on forever. And there's like ah...a structure with it...it's like the wall of the canyon itself has been carved. Again, I'm getting a very large structure.
MON:	Do the structures have insides and outsides?
SUB:	......Yes, they're very, it's like a rabbit warren, corners of rooms, they're really huge...I feel like I'm standing in one and it's just really huge. My perception is that the ceiling is very high. That's it.

MON:	All right, I'd like to move you now to another location nearby. All right, move from this point in time to: 45.86 north 354.1 east
SUB:	They have ah…appears to be the end of a very large road and there's a marker. I keep getting the Washington Monument overlay, but it's bigger. It's like an…obelisk. They're masters with stone.
MON:	All right, let's move into a little different place, very close. Move from the point you are now, in this time, to: 34.6 north 213.09 east
SUB:	There's a cluster of squares up and down. Um…it's like they're square anyways. They're all flush…flush with the ground and it's like they're connected…the material is very white or reflects light.
MON:	What's your position of observation as you look at this thing that reflects light?

SUB:	I'm...ah...sort of elevated...the sun is ah...the sun is weird...it's tough, the images are sporadic.
MON:	I realize that. I notice you're nulled out a little bit, and I want you to stay deep and recapture your focus here. When you're ready, holding the focus in time, moving now to: 80 degrees south 64 degrees east Take some time and get deep.
SUB:	I see pyramids......can't tell if it's overlay or not...because they look different.

"Fucking pyramids," Ib whispered to himself. *She must have thought she was in ancient Egypt,* he thought.

He was also impressed. She was recognizing potential overlay and working to refocus. Analytic overlay is something even the most experienced remote viewers have to watch out for. They might see an image, and instead of focusing just on what they see, the brain tries to make sense of it by retrieving an image they've experienced previously. If a remote viewer sees a triangle, their brain might show them a picture of the Great Pyramids. The subject needs to actively recognize and clear away the overlay.

She has developed so fast as a remote viewer, he thought.

When they watched the session, Ib was transfixed with Tomi. He focused deeply on her closed eyes and waited on every word.

When she said: "I think it knows I'm here," Ib's mouth opened slightly, and a deep chill ran down his spine, making his body shake.

He looked around at the faces of his clients. He thought they would find so much of this ridiculous. It was slight, but he saw the change in their usually stoic faces. They didn't find it ridiculous.

He realized that this is what they were here for.

MON:	Okay. Do these pyramids have insides and outsides?
SUB:	......Um hmm, they've got both...and they're huge......It's really, ah...it's interesting what I'm seeing.
MON:	Okay, I think instead of directing you to move, I'm going to ask you to go ahead and explore what seems interesting.
SUB:	It's from the storms.
MON:	Say that again, Tomi?

SUB:	These structures. They're like shelters from storms.
MON:	All right. Could you go inside one of these and find some activity?
SUB:	……Different chambers…sort of stripped of any furnishings…a strictly functional place for sleeping…or hibernation of some form…I just…keep getting raw inputs of storms, savage storms, and sleeping. Or meditating.
MON:	Can you tell me about the ones who hibernate or meditate here?
SUB:	…………Ah, very…tall again, very large…people, but they're thin, they look thin because of their height…and they dress in…oh hell, it's like a real light silk, but it's not flowing, it's cut to fit. I see three of them. They are sitting…hibernating…but not sleeping. Meditating.
MON:	Can you move closer to one?
SUB:	…It's, ah, its skin, I can't quite describe it…it has a shimmer……They're ancient

	people. They're ah...they're dying, it's past their time or age.
MON:	Tell me more about them.
SUB:	...They're very philosophic about it. They're looking for ah...a way to survive and they just can't. Can't seem to get their way out...so they're hanging on while they look, or wait for something to return, or something coming with the answer...
MON:	What is it they're waiting for?
SUB:	......They're ah...evidently it was a...a group, or search party of them that went to find a new place to live. It's like I'm getting all kinds of overwhelming input from the...corruption of their environment. It's failing very rapidly, and this group went somewhere, like a long way to find another place to live.
MON:	What was the cause of the disturbance to their environment?

SUB:	.........I see a picture of like a...oh hell, it's almost a warp in a...oh god, this is difficult...
MON:	Just the raw data of what you see.
SUB:	...Okay, I get a globe...it's like a globe that goes through a comet's tail or...it's through a river or something, but it's very cosmic...like space pictures...oh...oh god.
MON:	Tomi?
SUB:	I think it knows I'm here.
MON:	What makes you think that? Is it looking at you?
SUB:	No......it's still hibernating...meditating. It's just...I can feel its presence...I can hear it talking to me. Not hear it...I don't...
MON:	Can you ask it if it knows who you are?
SUB:	.........Yes. It says it's known me for a long time. There's like......a familiarity here...but how...

MON:	Can you ask it if you can help in any way?
SUB:	...............All I get is that they must just wait. Says...says I will help another time...
MON:	Can you ask it about the search party? When they left, how did they go?
SUB:	............I get an impression of a......I don't know what the hell it is. It's like the inside of a large boat. Very rounded walls and shiny metal.
MON:	Can you ask it where the party went? Can it show you?
SUB:	.........I get impressions of a very different place. Volcanos and plants. It's very different, there seems to be a lot of vegetation, where the other place did not have it......I'm just...confused...I'm ready to end this session now, please.
MON:	All right, start to come back now to the sound of my voice, into present time to right now, the 7th of September, 2023. Come back to the sound of my voice.

	Move now back to the room, here in the present.
	END OF INTERVIEW

Chapter 4

"Dr. N: How do you manage to hold each other with no bodies?

S: (with a sigh of exasperation at me) We envelop each other in light, of course.

Dr. N: Tell me what that is like for spirits?

S: Like being wrapped in a bright-light blanket of love."

~ Michael Newton, *Journey of Souls*

Tomi heard her phone chime. She reached over to see it was another missed call from Barry. She had been ignoring calls from Barry and Ib for most of a week, days that had been spent largely in bed.

Not that John had noticed. She had come home after the session - *THE session*, thought Tomi - to find John at the kitchen table working on his laptop. He said hello, but didn't ask her how it went. He was upset. She could tell. He hadn't looked up from his computer when she came in. He was avoidant. If he had a message, he would say it by saying nothing.

Tomi said she had a headache and was heading up to bed. He muttered to feel better, and that was the last they'd said to each other.

He'd fallen asleep on the couch. When he got home from work that day, Tomi had taken a long bath so as to avoid him. She could do avoidant, too.

Tomi put her phone down and buried her face in her pillow. Of course, things had already been moving into the territory of strange - or unbelievable - since her first visit to PSI nearly six months ago. She had already been feeling an internal conflict between what she thought she knew about reality and what she was experiencing there.

But this session had been different. Next level strange. When she was at PSI she felt a sense of safety, even a sense of sanity, among her colleagues. Even when she talked to the being, that moment when she realized it was aware of her presence, she still felt a sense of security being in that space, having Barry by her side.

But now at home, she was alone with her thoughts, alone with her memories of it. Alone wondering if any of it had been real or if it was just her brain making up pictures and stories.

But it felt real. And if it had been real, who or what had she been talking to? *And why did it say it had known me?* she wondered.

Hiding in bed, none of it had to be real. And if she avoided calls from Barry and Ib, it continued to not be real.

The doorbell rang. Tomi's body tensed up. She lay there perfectly still, even though she was upstairs and whoever was at the door couldn't possibly see her.

It rang again. Then her phone chimed again. She waited a few seconds, but curiosity won out.

It was a text from Kirsten. "C'mon Tomi, let me in, I see your car here."

Tomi had been ignoring Kirsten's messages also. The doorbell rang again. This time Tomi took a deep breath, got up, and headed downstairs towards the door.

Tomi put the kettle on and placed a tea bag in the teapot. Her grandmother's teapot, elegant and ornately painted with lines of gold.

"Where have you been, Tomi? Is everything okay? Something with you and John?"

"Oh, well that's one thing," Tomi said. Kirsten had shared relationship struggles with her in the past, but Tomi generally kept that to herself. Today she felt an openness that surprised her, as though that session had started to break down her walls. "Honestly, since that day we went to PSI, I feel like I'm losing it a bit. Losing my grip on reality."

She expected Kirsten to tighten up as most people do when someone says they think they're going crazy.

"Oh, I've been there," Kirsten said with a wave of her hand. "You're not actually losing it."

"What do you mean you've been there?" asked Tomi.

"Well, I had the sense you didn't want to talk about it, so I haven't brought it up, but that day, what happened there, well it was bananas Tomi!" Kirsten said with a kind laugh.

Tomi didn't know what to say. Of course Kirsten was right, but 'bananas' didn't make it feel okay.

"I mean, you looked really shocked. And uncomfortable," Kirsten said. "But really Tomi, it was amazing. I mean to see what you did, yeah, it was amazing. You have a gift."

Usually, Tomi would feel exposed, vulnerable from someone talking about her like this, but with Kirsten she was instead feeling seen. Validated.

"Maybe. Maybe it doesn't feel like a gift sometimes," Tomi said.

Kirsten nodded and smiled. The kettle started to whistle. Tomi got up, poured the boiling water into the teapot, grabbed two mugs, and sat down at the table with Kirsten.

"Can I make a suggestion?" Kirsten turned to angle her body towards Tomi. "I wonder if maybe you're going through a little ontological shock from it. I know it was months ago, but it can take time to catch up to you."

"Ontological shock?"

"Yeah, it's when something happens that makes you question your whole worldview. Like, for example, doing some crazy psychic shit," Kirsten said with a laugh.

Tomi laughed with her, already feeling lighter. *Of course that's what I'm feeling*, Tomi thought. *Though Kirsten doesn't know the half of it.*

"I think you might be right," Tomi said. "Actually, just knowing there's a name for it helps. I've never heard it before. Did you learn about that in college?"

"No. Well yeah, actually, but not originally. Can I share something like, extremely personal?" Kirsten asked, leaning closer.

"Of course," Tomi said. She hadn't had a friend to share like this in a long time and was realizing just how much she needed this.

"Okay, well now you're going to think *I'm* crazy. Jeff told me not to tell anyone. I don't think he believes me. And maybe you won't, but that's fine." Tomi gave a look to say *of course I'll believe you.* Kirsten smiled, but Tomi could see she was legitimately struggling to share. "When I was a kid, well, I come from a family that has had UFO experiences."

"Oh," Tomi said with a bit of surprise. She had no idea what Kirsten was going to share, but it certainly wasn't this. "Wow, well that's interesting."

"And abductions," Kirsten continued. "My brothers when they were kids. My father too. And me."

Tomi nodded, waiting for more, and realized she should say something.

"I believe you," Tomi finally said. An image of the being - person she had called it - flashed in her mind. But it wasn't a person, wasn't a human at least, she could see that. *Why wouldn't I believe her after that,* she thought. *And what are the chances she tells me this two days after that encounter?*

Kirsten looked encouraged. "Thanks. Most people don't, and I understand that. It was weird though, we all experienced it, but we didn't really talk about it as a family until we were all older. I remember my brothers talking about some people being in their room at night, but my parents just thought they were having bad dreams. Years later my brothers did a regression, you know, through hypnosis, and they were able to remember it clearly, going on the ship, everything. When they told us, my father, well he broke down crying," she said, wiping a tear from her eye.

"Sorry, it was just, thinking of my dad crying gets me every time," Kirsten continued. "He was really emotional, and he admitted that he had been abducted too. But he remembered it, and it was just like what my brothers described. And he just never told anyone about it."

"He must've been so scared, holding that in," Tomi said.

"Yeah. And guilty. It actually runs in families, abduction does, we learned. And he felt like it was his fault his kids were abducted too." Kirsten sipped her tea, then let out a laugh. "I know this sounds so crazy."

A week ago I was with a being in a pyramid who told me it knows me, Tomi thought. *Talking to me telepathically.*

"It doesn't sound crazy. Well it totally does," Tomi said with a laugh, "but it doesn't to me. So, your brothers and father shared, what about you?"

"Well, I went to the same hypnotist to see if anything happened to me," said Kirsten. "She did a regression, and it all came back. I'd been abducted a few times. I even remembered seeing my brothers on the ship. They did tests and stuff. I don't want to get into it too much today. You've got enough ontological shock going on without me freaking you out!"

They both laughed again. Tomi felt lucky to be sharing this moment with Kirsten. She was a little younger, long blond hair without a single grey strand, skin still tight around her eyes. But seeing her now, looking into her eyes, Tomi saw that she had a striking depth to her. *Old soul, young body.*

"My father did a regression too, and remembered more," Kirsten said. "Anyways, afterwards, not that day but a while after, it really caught up to me, like it rattled me mentally. Mentally and spiritually. I did some therapy, and that's how I learned about ontological shock."

Tomi nodded. She hadn't been a religious or spiritual person for a long time, and hadn't thought about what these kinds of experiences could do to your spiritual beliefs. Tomi's family had gone to church when she was younger, but she had always felt more spiritual when she was with her grandmother than when she had been at church. It had been a long time since she had felt anything spiritually. It just wasn't a part of her life. John was an atheist, and it wasn't something they ever talked about. *But what do I feel now?* Tomi wondered.

"And I've always been a spiritual person," Kirsten continued, "and I've always sort of questioned, or struggled a bit with reality. Like, accepting reality. I know that sounds weird. I just always felt like there was something else, just off to the side, like just past your peripheral vision. Just…something there that shouldn't be, some other reality. But if you didn't look at it, just ignored it, it wasn't there. But with the abductions, well you can't ignore it after that. Sorry, maybe that was too much to share."

Tomi gave Kirsten her most understanding look, which wasn't hard. She knew exactly what Kirsten was talking about. She couldn't tell Kirsten, or anyone else, about her recent experience at PSI because she had signed an NDA. But even if she could, she's not sure she would have the courage to share it, like Kirsten just had.

"I think you're really brave in sharing this with me," Tomi said. "I really appreciate it. It's actually already helped a lot."

Until now, the memories of the session two days ago would enter and exit her mind. As soon as they would arrive, she would try to push them out. At this moment, she could feel the memories of it entering, but this time she wasn't scared. She let it play out in her mind for a moment.

I've known you for a long time, it had said. Nothing *looked* familiar, but something *felt* familiar.

"This hypnotist you saw," said Tomi, "is she here? I mean local?"

"Yeah, we still keep in touch," Kirsten said. "She became a bit of a family friend."

"Does she do past life regressions? Do you think you could get me in?" asked Tomi.

Kirsten picked up her phone and started typing.

"Absolutely," she said. "One sec – oh my god! She had her session today cancel, she's at her office and was about to leave, but she could do it if we went there now!"

"Oh-ah," Tomi stammered. She hadn't expected this to happen so quickly. Something inside of her, this new Tomi that was emerging, told her to go with it. "Okay, let's do it."

"Great, I already told her we were coming. You're going to love her. I can't believe she's available right now, what a crazy coincidence," Kirsten said.

"So, you want to do a past life regression. What motivates you to do this?"

Tomi tilted her head to think. Marja (pronounced as Maria, she had clarified) held Tomi's gaze with a kind smile that said *there's no hurry, time has no meaning to me.*

Before Tomi knew it, they had set off to Marja's office, though office didn't seem the right word for it. It was in a small 1970s office building, and Marja had the first door upon entry. It was a single room with built-in white bookcases on one wall, draped windows on another, and opposite the bookcases was a bed. The bed was high off the ground, similar to a hospital bed, but dressed with a homey quilt. Beside the bed was a seat, and in the middle of the room were two chairs where Marja and Tomi sat and talked before the session.

Tomi wasn't sure how to respond to Marja's question. This had all happened so fast, and before she knew it Kirsten was gone and she was here in this room with Marja, who was kind but intense. She had long, perfectly straight white-blonde hair, designer rimmed glasses, and she wore an impossibly white women's business suit. *She's so put together and professional*, thought Tomi, not what she was expecting.

"This is okay, if you don't exactly know or want to say," Marja said, sensing Tomi's struggle to answer. Tomi tried to place Marja's accent - Eastern European? - but she wasn't sure. She had a kind voice, and her accent somehow made it sound kinder. "Is there a question you want me to ask? Anything specific you want to find out?"

"Hmm - yes, there is," replied Tomi. She didn't need to be specific. "I want to know if I knew a certain individual in a past life. I don't have a name to share, but if you ask me, I'll know who you're talking about."

"No problem, I will ask this," said Marja.

Marja explained in detail how the session would go. She asked many questions about Tomi's health, her mental health, her life experiences, and took copious notes. Tomi appreciated Marja's thoroughness, but was impatient to get going.

Marja explained that sometimes, we have traumas in this life that can be healed by connecting to a past life. And that sometimes traumas in past lives can impact us in this life.

"This session," Marja explained, "is not just about being curious about your past lives, but about healing and learning, so that we can grow in this life. Are you ready to begin?

Let's use the bathroom now so that it's not a problem later, then when you're ready, make yourself comfortable on the bed."

Tomi hopped up onto the bed and began to settle in. She looked at the small table beside her, and Marja sitting beside the bed.

"This water," Marja said, pointing to a plastic water bottle, "is for you to take. I blessed this water yesterday, and that blessing charged the water and will help you remember and heal from your past lives. And these crystals, they are here to share their energy. If you want to pick one to hold onto through the session, you can."

Tomi looked at the crystals and wasn't sure. Just six months ago she didn't imagine herself going through a past life regression, let alone believing in healing water and crystals. But she was here now, and the past few months had completely thrown into question what is real and what wasn't. She looked them over, and picked up a clear crystal.

"Clear quartz," Marja said with a smile. "Good choice. This crystal will help to remove negative energy, and regulate your energy flow. Now, get yourself comfortable, and let me know when you are ready to begin."

Tomi settled into the bed and closed her eyes. She pulled the quilt up a little bit. She listened to the music in the background, a sort of meditation music with long, low tones.

"I'm ready."

"Great. Remember, you are safe here. And if you ever need to stop, you just tell me." Tomi had felt uncomfortable when she first got into the bed, to be laying down and having someone seated right beside her. But now, with her eyes closed, Marja's voice was soothing.

First Marja took Tomi through a series of breathing exercises. Then a series of visualizations, suggesting objects such as a car or a tree, and spending time examining what Tomi saw. Eventually she had Tomi visualize hiking through a forest path and coming to a stone staircase.

"With each step you take down the staircase, you will pause and take a deep breath. And with each step, you will get more and more relaxed. At the bottom, when I count to zero, you will enter into a deep state of relaxation, a state of hypnosis, where you can easily remember your past, in this life and in others. You will be able to remember, but you won't really be there. Nothing can hurt you, and you are safe to just observe." Tomi listened to Marja's words, and could see this stone staircase in fine detail, curving down so that she couldn't see what was at the bottom. "Ten. Take a breath, and see the steps in front of you. Nine."

Tomi wasn't sure how long these exercises had gone on, but she found herself in a deep state, losing track of the feeling of her physical body. It was similar to her remote viewing experiences, but even deeper.

"Five. Good, take a breath. Four. At the bottom of the stairs, you see a door. Three. What does the door look like?"

Tomi's mind's eye was sharp. When she remote viewed, most of the time it was making sense of lines, shapes, and colours - except for those rare, intense times. But in this state, she could see so much detail. Such rich colour. This stone staircase was cut into rock, so there was a rock wall on each side of her, with some sort of beautiful vine growing up the walls. The staircase was shaded with foliage, but she felt like just past the door was sunshine.

"The door, it's a big heavy door," Tomi said gently. "Dark wood. It has that rounded top, like an old, old door. I can't see what's behind it. There is a big iron handle on it."

"Oh, it's beautiful," Marja said sweetly. "One. Now on your next step, you will enter a deep state of hypnosis. And you will be at the bottom of the stairs and can open the door. When you do, you will call up a past life. The one you need to see today. Zero. Now open the door. What do you see?"

Tomi imagined her hand reaching for the big cast iron handle, and was surprised that the heavy wooden door put up no resistance, gliding open as though someone was pulling it from the other side.

"I see a barn," Tomi said. "Not a big new one, it's old. I mean the materials aren't old, but the look of it is old."

"Yes, I understand. Is this your barn? Your farm?"

"No. But I live here," said Tomi.

"Oh, you live on the farm?" said Marja, genuine curiosity in her voice.

"No, I live in the barn. I sleep in the barn. And I work here," said Tomi, her voice a little deeper, scratchy.

"I see, so you work on the farm, but you don't own it. Are there more people here?" asked Marja.

"Yes," Tomi replied. "There is the family. They live in the house."

"Oh, there is a house?"

"Yes. It's up a little bit of a hill from the barn. It's beautiful. It's a very old style," said Tomi, "but it looks very new."

"Do you ever visit the house?"

"No, I don't go in there."

"Why don't you go in there?" asked Marja. "Is the family not nice to you?"

"No!" Tomi's voice, though soft, was raised to indicate the question was ridiculous. "No, they aren't nice to me. Well, the young kids are, they sometimes visit me and play in the barn. But the family…they think I'm less than them."

"Why do they think that?" asked Marja.

"Because I'm dumb," said Tomi sadly.

"No, don't say that, you're not dumb."

"That's what they say about me. Like I have some kind of learning disability," said Tomi. "But I'm big! I'm a man, and a big man. I'm strong."

"Do you know your name in this life?" asked Marja.

"Benjamin," said Tomi, with confidence.

"And how old is Benjamin?" asked Marja.

"I'm…maybe twenty? Maybe a little younger?" wondered Tomi. "I'm…not sure I know exactly how old I am."

"And do you know when and where this is?" asked Marja.

"It's…England. Northern England. But I don't know when. Like, I think a few hundred years ago? But I'm not sure of the date. I don't think I know in this life what year it is," Tomi said.

"I see, well that's okay. What work does Benjamin do for this family?"

"I work. I work on the farm. I lift things. I dig. I carry things. I feed the animals. I do what they tell me to do," said Tomi.

"And they pay you for this work?" asked Marja.

"No," said Tomi flatly. "There's no pay. I think just getting to live here, and they feed me. That's my pay."

"So the family feeds you," said Marja. "Do you go to the house for meals with them?"

"No, someone brings it to me," said Tomi. Her voice carried a sadness. "The woman who works in the kitchen. She's nice. She brings some extra sometimes, when she can. I'm big and they don't give me enough food. I'm always hungry. It's hard to sleep when I'm so hungry."

"That doesn't sound nice," Marja said sadly. "Do you have a family?"

"Yes. I did. But I don't see them anymore," said Tomi.

"Where are they?" asked Marja.

"They're not too far away," said Tomi, sounding surprised by her response. "On a farm. But not like this one, just a tiny one. We were much poorer. We had a little house."

"Tell me about Benjamin's family," said Marja.

Tomi paused, taking in the scene she saw in her mind, trying to make sense of it.

"My mom was nice. Quiet but nice. Loving," Tomi said. "My father wasn't as nice. And I have brothers."

"Oh, that's nice. Are these brothers older?"

"No, they're younger," Tomi said with a pause. "But they pick on me. They can be mean. They don't want to let me play with them."

"That doesn't sound nice of them," Marja said. "Why do they treat you this way?"

"Because I'm dumb," Tomi said. "I think they're embarrassed by me."

"I'm sorry they were so mean," said Marja, compassionately. "How did you end up on this big farm away from your family?"

"I think…my father sort of gave me to them. He didn't want me," Tomi said, sounding pained. "Because I was the oldest."

"Why didn't he want you because you were the oldest?" asked Marja.

"Because…" Tomi paused to collect the story, "…because I should get the house. And the farm. Because I'm the oldest. But he doesn't want me to have it. He wants it for my brother. So he gave me to them. I'm not dead, but it's like I'm dead."

"I'm so sorry this happened to you." Marja's kind voice soothed the experience for Tomi.

"Thank you," Tomi said.

"Before this session, you said you wanted me to ask if the person you were thinking of knew you in this life," Marja said. "Did you know this person?"

"No. Not in this life." Tomi felt certain of that.

"Okay. Now I want you to go forward. Go to the day you most need to remember," said Marja. "Go forward to the day that you die."

"It's…I was in the barn," started Tomi, her voice growing soft.

"The barn you sleep in, on the big farm?" asked Marja.

"Yes," said Tomi. "And the two little girls were down there playing with the chickens. And I was helping them catch them so they could pet them."

"That sounds really nice," said Marja.

"It was nice," said Tomi, her face starting to scrunch up. "But then the one girl moved. The little one. She ran to a fence. And started climbing under. And there was an animal in there. A horse? No, a donkey. And it was mean. The girl was climbing under the fence."

"Oh my, what did you do?"

"I yelled," Tomi said. "I kept yelling. I ran to the fence yelling. And her sister was screaming, I think because I yelled. And I reached over the fence and grabbed her. Grabbed her arm and yanked her up over the fence. But she hit the fence post. Her legs, they got scratched. And I grabbed her too hard. Her arm was hurt, and she was crying."

"It sounds like you did the right thing! You saved that girl," said Marja.

"Yes, but…it didn't feel like it," Tomi said. "The girl was crying and her sister grabbed her and they ran back to the house. I felt so bad. I tried to say it was an accident, but they were gone. So I got back to work."

"And then what happened?" asked Marja.

"The man came down," said Tomi solemnly.

"The father?"

"No," said Tomi. "He's like the manager. He managed the farm. He told me to go with him. He had me walk in front of him. We walked past the field and towards the trees…I'm so scared."

"It's okay, you're just watching, nothing can hurt you here," Marja reassured.

"We got to the little stream that was on the other side of the trees. I loved this place," said Tomi, making a slight smile. "I would come and bathe here, it was so beautiful."

"And what is this man doing?"

"He told me to stand there," Tomi said. "I tried to say something, that it was an accident, that I was trying to help her, but he didn't listen. He had me facing away from him. I could see the sun in the sky. Then he hit me. The back of my head, with a rock. And it's over."

"Yes, it is over. It's over," said Marja. "You don't have to feel that pain ever again. That sounds like a very difficult life Benjamin had, but in this life, Tomi's life, you don't have to feel any of the pain you felt in that life. That life is over, and you've learned and grown from it. That was you, that was your life, but it's not this life."

"No," Tomi said. "No, that wasn't my life."

"Yes, it was, it was you that lived it, but it's over now," said Marja.

"No," Tomi insisted, in her soft, groggy voice. "No. I didn't live that life. It's a memory they gave me. When I came into this life, it's like they uploaded other lives into me."

"Oh?" said Marja, both surprised and intrigued. "Why did they do that?"

"Because we learn from our past lives. They give us wisdom," said Tomi, with a tone of authority. "Because I didn't have any past lives on Earth. This is my first time here."

"Tell me about this hilly island."

Though Marja had been surprised to hear that this was Tomi's first life on Earth, she knew not to question it, and instead follow where the subject needed to go. Marja asked her to ignore those memories of other lives on Earth, the ones that weren't really hers, and go back to her life before coming here.

It's an island, Tomi had said. *It's an island but it's like a huge hill, like the slope of it is so high. Impossibly high.*

"Where are you? Are you on Earth?" asked Marja.

"Oh no," said Tomi, her voice sounding confident. "I mean, the grass is green and the water around the island is blue, but this is very different than Earth. Earth is so heavy, human bodies are so heavy. But here everything is light."

Marja watched Tomi's face move around slightly, and gave her time to look around at what she was seeing.

"It's…it's different though," said Tomi. "It looks different. Sometimes it looks like a hill on Earth, but other times…well it's like it can move and stretch, making the hill really tall, and you can squish it down, too. Almost like when you see video games rendering, like the place can take different shapes. Fold in on itself."

"This sounds like an interesting place," said Marja. "Do you see anyone?"

"No, I don't see anyone right now," Tomi said with a pause, taking in the scene. "I'm up at the top of the hill, in the long grass. And the grass is so soft! Down at the bottom of the hill there are big rocks, then water. At the bottom on the right is a little village. And down the hill, kind of built into the hill, are little doors. Little houses built into the hill. They almost look like hobbit houses! And there's flowers and butterflies, and the long grass is swaying in the breeze.

Rhythmically. Like it's a metronome, keeping time with the universe."

"It sounds so beautiful," said Marja earnestly. "What happens in this place?"

"It's so beautiful. It's…sort of a meeting place. It's a place where beings meet. Like, a bit of a magical place." Tomi paused and smiled. "My god, I feel so at home. I'm so light!"

"Tell me about your body," Marja prompted.

"I don't have one!" responded Tomi, sounding liberated.

"You don't have a body?" asked Marja, surprised.

"No! I have like…an essence. I'm made of energy." Marja watched Tomi's face raise into a smile as she described herself. "I'm a shimmer. Like if someone was here, they might see a little shimmer floating around, and that's me! It feels so magical."

"How long have you lived here?" asked Marja.

"A long time," Tomi said, drawing out the word *long*, her voice sounding almost childlike. "Such a long time. I'm not sure the time makes sense in Earth time. But this was my home. Is my home."

"Before the session, you wanted me to ask you if you knew a certain person in this life," Marja said.

"Yes. Yes, she was here," Tomi said longingly. "She was a shimmer, too. That was a long time ago."

"You say 'she,' this was a female?"

"Not in this life," said Tomi. "But her soul, I see as more feminine. Souls can be more masculine or feminine. But not like girl or boy, I mean like the divine feminine and masculine. And feminine souls will have lives where they're male, and vice versa, and all along a spectrum. You need to have those different experiences."

"Yes, I see," said Marja. "You speak of their soul; you know this person's soul?"

"Yes," Tomi said with certainty. "She's in my soul cluster, my soul group."

"Yes, I understand," said Marja, familiar with the many people who in hypnosis, or in a near-death experience, describe a group of souls, like a family or close friends. "This soul cluster, what do you do together?"

"We are learning," said Tomi. "It's almost like a class. We support each other, but we challenge each other too. When we review and learn from a life, we can say *hey, could you have done better here?* That kind of thing. And sometimes we have lives together, or we make plans to meet in lives together, helping each other towards whatever our goal was in that life."

"Yes, it's a beautiful relationship, this soul cluster," said Marja. "So this other soul, you planned to be together in this life on the hilly island?"

"Yes, that's right," Tomi said.

"And what did you two do together there?"

"Oh, it was great," said Tomi, smiling. "We could just float around. We would chase each other, and when we would catch each other, we would wrap up like a hug."

"Wow, that sounds so nice," said Marja. "As an energy being you can hug? What is that like?"

"Peaceful," said Tomi with a sigh. "It felt like home. My god that feeling of home, it's so deep. I miss it so much."

With her eyes closed, still in a deep state of hypnosis, Tomi began to weep.

Marja gave her a few moments to let her emotions flow, then asked, "What is making you cry?"

"It's just…this feeling. Like I've felt so out of place my whole life here on Earth, and now I see why. I belong here in *this* place."

Tomi's crying stopped.

"This current life, the one you are living now, you say it is your first on Earth," said Marja. "Why did your soul go to Earth if it was so happy in this place?"

Marja watched Tomi's face tighten while she considered the question.

"There was a call," Tomi said finally.

"A call? What kind of call?" asked Marja.

"There was a call put out to the universe. That the Earth needed help, and needed wise souls to go there," Tomi explained.

"And your soul heard that call and went to Earth?"

"No. No, not the first time," Tomi said. "The third time."

"You heard three calls?" asked Marja.

"Yes. This third one was so desperate," Tomi said. "I didn't want to go, Earth is beautiful but it's so heavy, life there is so hard."

"So, you answered the call and came here," Marja said. "For what purpose did you come to Earth? What are you to do here?"

"I don't…I don't know exactly," said Tomi. "We are to help in some way, the souls who came because of the call. It isn't clear. But…love. I feel it's about love."

"Is this place, this hilly island," Marja asked, "is it a place Tomi can go back to?"

"Yes, anytime," Tomi said with a smile. "I go in my dreams. It's always there for me."

"This is good," Marja said. "So from now on, you can always think back to this place, or meditate and go there, and feel those good feelings. Now it's time to start to come back to the present, back to your body. I'm going to count up, and when I get to ten, you will be back and aware, and you will remember what you saw today. One, feel your toes, two, start to move them."

Tomi didn't want to come back, she wanted to stay on this hilly island forever, but she could suddenly feel her toes vibrating slightly, and couldn't help but move them.

"Seven, start to hear the sounds around you," Marja continued.

Tomi was already feeling present, aware of her body. She felt heavy, her muscles weak against the pull of gravity.

"And, ten. You can open your eyes. Welcome back."

Tomi sat up on the side of the bed and smiled at Marja. Marja handed her the bottle of water.

"You remember what I said about this water?" Marja asked.

"Yes, I do," said Tomi. "Marja, that was…well that was amazing. But that was really weird, wasn't it?"

Tomi could feel no judgement from Marja, even though she questioned herself. *First life on Earth?* Tomi thought. *Implanted past life? Energy being? Where did that come from? Had she made that all up?*

"Tomi, it isn't weird at all. But it was special. Have you heard of Dolores Cannon? *The Volunteers?*" Marja asked.

Tomi shook her head.

"Well, I got to study and learn from Dolores." Marja pointed at a picture of herself with a woman who looked like a kindly grandmother. "When Dolores did past life regressions, she saw a pattern. She noticed a certain number of people would go to a past life, and instead of it being on Earth, they might be flying around on a flying saucer, and they're an extraterrestrial. Seriously!"

Marja let out a laugh, and placed Tomi's hand between both of hers.

"Some would be living on some other planet," Marja said. "And yes, some were energy beings, sometimes just living out in space. Oh, and some would have memories of Earth, like you, but say they were sort of uploaded, rather than lives they had lived. Sort of like borrowing some wisdom for your mission on Earth."

Tomi wasn't sure what to make of any of this but felt reassured by Marja.

"Now, people with these experiences, Dolores called *the volunteers*. She said there were three waves of souls who volunteered. The first came after The Second World War, when the nuclear bombs were dropped. Each wave is a little different. And you are part of the third wave." Marja squeezed Tomi's hand and smiled. "So, you came here for a purpose. Earth called you here for a reason, and you need to figure out what that reason is. And for many that's hard. Many volunteers struggle. They find Earth too hard or violent, or their bodies too heavy. Or they always feel like they're meant to be somewhere else. But no, you come from somewhere else, but you're meant to be here."

"This call, to come to Earth, what…who made it?" asked Tomi.

"If I say to you," said Marja, "that the Earth is a living being, can you understand that?"

Tomi thought for a moment, and was surprised how easily her mind accepted it. Somehow it made perfect sense to her.

"Yes, I understand."

"So," said Marja, "do you think maybe the Earth itself made this call? A plea for help, sent around the universe?"

Tomi smiled and nodded. Marja stood up and moved towards the door. When Tomi stood up, her body felt heavy, and her mind tired, but she also felt a sense of peace she hadn't felt in a long time. *Ever felt?* she wondered.

Marja opened the door, and Tomi stepped through, surprised to see Kirsten balled up and asleep on a chair in the hall. Tomi touched her foot to wake her.

"I didn't realize you were waiting here. That must have been a long time, you didn't have to do that," Tomi said.

"Yeah, no problem. And hey, I got a nap," Kirsten said, Marja smiling kindly. "How was it?"

"Really good. Really interesting. I think I'll need a while to take it in." Tomi turned to Marja and thanked her.

"My pleasure," said Marja. "Now, I will tell you, *don't be afraid of shining a light. Don't be afraid of being powerful. Don't be afraid of being more special.* Dolores said that. I want you to take that with you."

On the drive home, Kirsten gave Tomi the space to sit quietly and consider her experience. Tomi appreciated that, appreciated this bond she had with Kirsten. She leaned her head up against the passenger window and watched people and buildings and signs and crosswalks zip by. Along with a feeling of peace, she felt certain that she was following a path that was leading her…*where?* she wondered. Although her purpose was still fuzzy, for the first time, she felt sure there *was* a purpose.

Kirsten pulled the car into Tomi's driveway and offered to come in and be with her if she needed that. Tomi declined; she needed to process. And even though she had been laying down and almost asleep for several hours, she was exhausted.

She thanked Kirsten, hugged her across the console of the car, and went inside. She realized it was getting dark, and that John would be home by now.

Instead, she found the house empty, and a note on the counter that he had to head into the DC office, and that he would call later. Tomi felt a sense of relief to be alone in this moment.

She climbed into bed, put her phone on silent, and decided she would call PSI in the morning.

Chapter 5

"The [UFO] Phenomenon is not looking to be ineffable, just wonderful. Fantastic, as in a manifestation of fantasy. It is as if we are being urged to dream a little more daringly, to imagine the possibilities of which we are capable. They have baited a hook, which we imagine to be a worm, and we take the bait."

Peter Levenda

"That was an eight martini session, Tomi," Ib said with a smile. "Back in the days of the Stargate Project, they used to call the really wild, really intense remote viewing sessions *eight martini sessions*, since it took them going to the bar and drinking eight martinis to return to reality."

Tomi laughed. "I think they knew what they were doing."

"The point is that we should never have just let you leave after that session," Ib said, his tone shifting to apology.

"And that's on me," said Barry.

Instead of calling the next day, Tomi decided to take a few more days to process her past life regression. She felt like she was becoming more in tune with the way her body, her energy responded to these experiences. When she felt ready, that she'd processed enough and her energy had returned, she decided to drop in to PSI. She felt sheepish coming in, having ignored them for days, but found that they were the ones feeling sheepish.

"You know, you were the control, so we didn't have plans to keep you around. I went to find Ib, but he was in a closed-door meeting with the clients, and when I got back, you were already gone." Barry then added: "And understandably. A definite eight martini session. Anyways, I apologize for not handling that better. You may have noticed I'm a bit better at handling data than I am with people."

Barry tried for a smile. *I have noticed that*, thought Tomi, but despite Barry's deeply serious nature, she had grown in affection for him. He reminded her of her uncle, who she rarely saw smile, but who she always knew was in her corner.

"Oh, that's totally fine Barry," Tomi said. "I'm sorry I didn't say anything. I just felt panicked and left. And I'm sorry to you both for ghosting you."

"Don't be," Ib responded quickly. "I sense that the session was a shock, and shock takes time to dissipate. We're just happy to have you back. And we owe you a martini. Or eight. There's a little bar just down the street, they make a terrible martini. Shall we?"

Tomi said she couldn't turn down a terrible martini, and the three locked up PSI, with everyone else having left.

When they arrived, Tomi looked around and wasn't surprised the martinis were terrible. The inside was dark, a sports bar from the days before sports bars were packed with flatscreens. Ib went up to the bar to order, while Barry and Tomi found a table in the darkest corner, away from the few people inside.

They sat down, and Tomi smiled awkwardly, realizing she had never really chatted with Barry about anything but work. She knew she would have to break the silence.

"So, Barry, do you have a Ph.D. like Dr. Johansen?" she asked.

Barry just shook his head. She thought she was going to have to think of another question to try to get him talking, until he suddenly spoke.

"No, I really have no business working for an organization like PSI," Barry said. "But Dr. Johansen is an outside the box thinker, and he brought me in."

"What do you mean, you have no business at PSI? You sure seem like you know what you're doing," she said.

"Well, that's because I do know a thing or two," he said, with the outline of a smile that pleased Tomi. "What I mean is that I'm not an academic. I'm an amateur historian. A researcher and writer. I got a college degree, then worked for a small newspaper, but my real interest was researching the CIA, and so I wrote a few books on some of their most secret and bizarre programs. I wrote a book on the history of MK Ultra, for example, which was a program where the CIA basically used psychedelic drugs to see if they could master mind control to create assassins or disable enemy soldiers."

"I think I've heard about that, "Tomi said. "And wow, that's amazing! So was the book published?"

"It was, it was published by a small publishing house, which went under shortly after it was released. So it didn't go too far," Barry said with a shake of his head.

"Oh, I'm sorry," said Tomi, as Ib joined them, carrying a tray with six martinis.

"It's a start, right?" Ib said, handing them each a glass and sliding the rest to the edge of the table. "Sorry, I don't want to interrupt."

"I was just telling Tomi about how we came to work together," Barry said. "So after the book on MK Ultra, I wrote about Stargate Project and remote viewing. And I was hooked on this one. I was still working full-time, so when I had a vacation from work, or a long weekend, I would head across the country to interview people who had worked in the program."

"So you are the remote viewing historian, basically," Tomi said.

"You could say I wrote the book," Barry said with a small lump of a laugh. "I did write the book, of course. And well, it wasn't a best seller, I self-published it. And somehow Ib here found a copy, tracked me down, and convinced me that since my book concluded with questions about the efficacy of remote viewing, I should come and work with him and help answer those questions."

"And here he is, thankfully," Ib said, lifting his glass. "Skål! Cheers," he said. Tomi had become so used to his accent, she sometimes forgot he had come from abroad.

"And what about you, Ib," said Tomi. "I remember what you told me about your father, but how did you come to study remote viewing?"

Ib sipped his martini. "Well, I had been a professor back home, and I was one of the few academics who would study ESP or psychic abilities. Not as my main work, of course, but here and there I would get to slip something in, a class or a small paper. But even that was sort of the kiss of death for your career. As a person of science, a serious academic, you're not supposed to even consider those things."

"A very scientific approach," Barry said sarcastically.

Ib smiled and continued. "Tomi, do you read science fiction at all?" Ib asked. "Phillip K. Dick?"

Tomi shook her head.

"Well, he once gave this incredible speech, where he declared we live in a computer simulation, and that other worlds exist right beside ours. That his stories are actually from these other worlds. Fascinating," Ib said with a look of wonder. "Anyways, in that speech he said that it's a common theme in his stories that a dark-haired woman would show up at the protagonist's door and tell him his world is delusional. Anyways, I loved that line, and sort of wished that would happen to me. You know what?"

Tomi paused, then answered, "no, what?"

"One day a dark-haired woman showed up at my door and told me my world was delusional," he said, pausing for a long sip, dragging out the suspense the way a good storyteller can.

"I had a visit from the Board Chair of the Perceptual Studies Institute. She told me that our material world, time, our accepted reality, none of it was real, and she wanted *me* to prove it," Ib said, pointing to himself. "The board at PSI had read some of my work, had quietly vetted me, and wanted me to run the Institute. I mean I was flattered, but I didn't know much about remote viewing specifically, so I said I would think about it."

"Wow, how long ago was this?" Tomi asked with surprise, somehow imagining Ib studying remote viewing since his teens.

"Just over a year ago. I'm still a newbie, as they say. That's why I needed this guy", Ib said, pointing his thumb towards Barry.

"I spent two days basically combing the internet," Ib continued "reading articles, watching documentaries. Then I found Barry's book and read it straight through. Anyways, I thought yes, this is something that can be provable, if done right. And that's what I hope to do. Even if in the end we conclude that no, it isn't real, it doesn't work, at least we did our scientific duty in asking the question."

Tomi nodded, and they exchanged their empty glasses for the on-deck martinis.

"Well, cheers to you both for doing the work. I sure hope you prove something soon, so I don't feel quite so crazy," Tomi said with an awkward laugh. "And Barry, I would love to read your book."

"I can bring a copy for you tomorrow," Barry said. "Actually, there's a case in the book you might find interesting. You know, when you were viewing, you were interacting with the being, and felt like it noticed you, right?"

Tomi nodded. Her body tightened thinking of that moment of awareness, of contact between her and the being.

"You might have heard of him, Ingo Swann? He claimed that he was hired to do some remote viewing of the back side of the moon," said Barry. "In his viewings, he found alien bases there, and he saw alien beings in those bases."

Tomi was floored. *Who is asking them to do these viewings?* she wondered. *Why?*

"At one point," Barry continued, "the being noticed him. But in Ingo's case, the beings were not friendly. He felt a hostile intent."

"Huh. I didn't feel that," said Tomi. "At all. I mean, it was shocking, but I felt a sense of peace from the being. But wow, that case sure does sound familiar."

"If you like that story," said Ib, a martini-inspired smile on his face, "wait 'til you hear about the sexy, scantily clad extraterrestrial woman he encountered in a supermarket afterwards!"

The group shared another round while Ib and Barry told Tomi more about the history of remote viewing. Afterwards, they ordered two Ubers, with Barry and Ib heading in a different direction. Before they parted, Ib said quietly: "I'm not supposed to tell you, but be ready any day now for a session. The people from last time are coming back, and they specifically want you."

She got into the back seat of her Uber, and chatted with the driver on her way home, a significant drive across the city. She learned that he worked in construction full-time, and drove for Uber in the evenings, as he was working on sponsoring his family to immigrate. She wished for him to be successful so he could be with his family again soon. She thought about how detached, frivolous studying ESP, consciousness, must feel with most people's daily struggles, their daily lives. *Even if Ib proved it was real, would most people care, or have the time to care?* she wondered.

Eventually the conversation moved to a comfortable silence, until they were a few blocks from her home. She noticed he started looking in the rearview mirror more and more.

"Ma'am, is there supposed to be another car following you home?" the driver asked.

"No. Why?" She turned to look out the back window, and could see headlights, but couldn't make out any details.

"The car, the one behind, it's just that it's been with us since I picked you up," he said, sounding concerned. "I noticed it as it's gone late through a couple of lights, like it was keeping up with us."

She turned and looked back again. As they drove through an intersection, she saw the right turn signal come on, and the headlights disappear down another street.

"Oh, maybe not, sorry to alarm you. Maybe just a bad driver," he said with a laugh.

Yes, it's nothing. Bad driver, Tomi thought. Still, a chill ran down her spine.

Tomi looked out her second-floor bedroom window and saw Ib, Barry, and the man they called the General, along with the same suited man from last time, getting out of a large black SUV. She had been waiting for them to arrive, having woken with a feeling that today was the day.

She had been looking out her window frequently the past few days, since the Uber ride. Tomi couldn't get that feeling of being followed, or watched, out of her system. Yesterday morning, she saw a dark sedan parked two houses down. Then later in the day, it was parked two houses down in the other direction. She told herself she was being paranoid.

Tomi moved quickly down the stairs, and opened the door just before they rang the doorbell.

"Good morning," said Tomi cheerily.

Ib's greeting matched the seriousness of the group. "Good morning Tomi, our client is hoping you will be able to come in for a session today."

The General and the suited man remained stoic.

"Of course, I'm ready," she said. She motioned towards the vehicle, and the group took her queue and headed back to the SUV.

Ib and Barry sat on the back bench, Tomi sat in a seat beside the suited man, while the General sat in the passenger seat. A driver with dark sunglasses and a dark suit started the vehicle and pulled away.

As the SUV moved forward, she looked towards the dark sedan that was parked on her street. The windows were tinted, and she couldn't make out if anyone was inside. Out of the corner of her eye, she thought she saw the General turn his head to glance at the sedan, but she wasn't certain. She rode in silence watching the back of his head, as he stared straight forward in silence.

When they arrived at PSI, Tomi was surprised to see that only one interview room was prepped, and there were no other remote viewers there. Barry came up beside her and said quietly: "They wanted as few people here as possible. They only wanted you."

Tomi looked around and realized there were no PSI staff other than Barry and Ib. Through the window looking into the conference room, she noticed several men in suits. *They're here to watch me*, she thought, immediately trying to put them out of her mind.

Tomi entered the interview room, sat cross-legged on the couch, and began some breathing exercises. She wasn't bothered that there could be people watching her right now. Instead, she felt a deep excitement about the possibility of reconnecting with that being. *Was it really the same being, the same soul, from her past life regression?* she wondered. *It said it had known me a long time.*

Barry entered the room and started getting the equipment ready. Tomi heard some voices from outside the room. Clearing her mind, she listened deeply and was surprised she could make out the conversation.

"I want you to tell her what we're looking for. All information is valuable, but we have one clear goal here today," she could hear the General say.

"I understand your priorities, and we will work towards that, but stating the purpose beforehand corrupts the process," Ib said. "It will invalidate any data. As I assured you-."

"Hey Tomi," Barry whispered, unintentionally interrupting her eavesdropping. She opened her eyes to see a little smile on his face. She hadn't seen him smile in the first few months she knew him. She realized he was one of those people who let few people in, but once they do, you're in for good. "If you reconnect with that being, maybe you can ask it about Atlantis. I mean if they had pyramids and if they headed to Earth, well I've always wanted to know if it was real." His smile broadened and he winked.

"Sure, no problem," she said with a smile, turning to look towards the door in time to see the General turn and head towards the conference room. Ib came into the room, whispered into Barry's ear, gave Tomi a smile and nod to say *it's time*, and followed in the direction of the General.

Barry turned on the AV equipment, then pushed an envelope across the table towards Tomi.

"The date is September 29th, 2023. I am the monitor for this session, Barry Class. Session is being held at PSI. Subject has been handed a sealed envelope. The envelope contains instructions for site acquisition. The envelope will not be opened before or after the interview, as instructed by the parties requesting information."

He looked kindly at Tomi and nodded to her. "Ready?"

She nodded, and laid back on the couch, pulling a throw blanket over her, and continued breathing exercises to get into a deep state of relaxation.

On a 3 by 5 card, enclosed in a sealed envelope on the table, was written:

Planet Earth. Geographic area: Airspace above Nepal.

Approximate time of interest: 12,500 years ago.

"Okay Tomi," Barry's voice gentle and calm, "I want you to train your attention to the instructions provided in the envelope. When you are ready, I want you to go to these coordinates: 28.3948570 degrees North, 84.1240080 degrees East."

There was silence in the room. At first nothing came to Tomi.

"Remember," Barry said, sensing she was struggling, "don't force it. Just keep your mind clear and let the raw data come to you."

The darkness she saw with her eyes closed started to give in to greens and blues. "I see green. So much green. Big green hills. I see a river. The sky is blue to one side, but to the other I see darkness. A storm rolling in. There's lightning."

"Alright, what is your perspective?" asked Barry, wondering what angle or placement she was viewing from.

"I'm…I'm looking from above. Like I'm high in the sky, looking down on the mountains," Tomi said.

"Take a look around," instructed Barry. "Is there anything drawing your interest?"

Tomi scanned the vision in front of her. It wasn't like moving your head or eyes around to see; rather, she found it like opening a zoom lens to get a wider field of view. When she was really deep, it felt like she could see all around her, a 360-degree view.

She noticed a flash above her, like a glint of light reflecting off metal.

"Yes. Above me, high in the sky, there's something flying. I'm going to get closer to it." Tomi paused. "It does look metal. Shining metal, like stainless steel. It's round, it…I mean I don't know how else to describe it. It looks like a classic flying saucer."

"That may be overlay," Barry reminded her. "Can you get closer?"

"Yes. I'm floating, just beside it right now," Tomi said. "It's not moving, just hovering in place. It's a circle. It really is like two saucers put together, so it is wider towards the centre. I see three lights on the bottom. I don't see a window or a door. It's like the outside is seamless, one piece. And it's silent. Behind it I can see the storm in the sky. The storm is closer now. It's heading in this direction."

"Alright, don't worry about the storm, it can't hurt you," Barry reminded her. "Do you think you can enter the craft?"

Tomi thought about how to enter the craft. A voice spoke to her, in her mind: *yes, we want you to come in*. The image in her mind quickly shifted, and she was inside the craft.

"I'm inside," she said. "It's so much bigger inside than I thought. Impossibly big. Everything seems to be that shiny metal, with no seams. There are doors, so there are other rooms, but this room seems bigger than the outside of the craft. There are walls…but, when I focus in on them, it's like the wall disappears and I can see outside. It's not like a window, it's not permanent. It's like I can see through the metal wherever I focus. I can see the storm outside."

"Okay," said Barry, "can you see any activity? Do you see any life?"

"Yes. There is one in front of me," she said. "It's standing in the middle of the room, facing towards where you can see the storm. There are others on board, I think, but not in this room. The being is tall and thin, like the one from before, but it's not the same one, it looks a little different. I don't know but I sense it's female. And she's wearing sort of a hat. Like a helmet. Wait. She's turning towards me."

In one quick motion, the image of the being in front of her flipped around. She could see facial details more clearly than last time.

"It's like…I'm seeing this in HD. I see so much detail," Tomi said, sounding amazed. "She's wearing that tight suit, like the one before."

She looked into the being's eyes. They weren't human. They were big, much bigger than a human's eye compared to its face. They looked more like a cat's eye. The being had a form similar to a human – bipedal - but very tall and thin. Its skin was pale, a dull creamy green, almost blue, and when Tomi focused in, it was as though a shimmer ran across its skin.

"They are so tall," she said. "Like eight or nine feet tall. But thin, kind of lanky. Wait…she's talking to me. She's not moving her mouth. I can hear her in my mind."

Hello, it is so nice to see you again, it said without moving its small, tight mouth, the words appearing in Tomi's mind.

Are you the one I met before? Tomi asked in her mind's voice. *On Mars?*

"What is it saying?" Barry asked after giving Tomi a moment.

Yes. That was me. It was my soul body. But a different physical body. That body is long gone, the being said.

I did a past life regression, Tomi said. *Was that you - your soul - on that hilly island with me?*

The being looked at her, and though its expression didn't change, Tomi felt like she smiled.

"Tomi?" Barry said.

"Yes, we are just getting acquainted," Tomi finally said.

"Does the being have a name?" Barry prompted.

You can call me Ete, the being said. The words were in Tomi's mind before she even posed the question.

I'm Tomi, she replied. *Can I ask: if your body is gone, if this is a new life, how do you remember meeting me?*

"Its name is Ete," Tomi said. She realized she somehow knew both the spelling of the name, and the pronunciation. "Like Eddie, but E-T-E."

"Can you ask Ete what it is doing there?" Barry asked Tomi. "Where are they travelling in the craft?"

We remember, Ete said. We don't forget. *Humans don't remember. They forget it all when they are born. You must sleep beside the river of forgetfulness, as humans say.*

Why do we forget? Tomi asked.

That's the way humans are made, Ete said.

"Tomi, what information are you getting?" Barry asked, trying to regain her focus. She remembered that the clients were watching this, and chose not to relay this information. She focused.

Why are you here? On Earth, in this craft? Tomi asked.

We live here, Ete said. *We came to Earth and made a home.*

You live here on Earth with humans? Tomi asked.

Humans live here on Earth with us.

She could feel a sense of playfulness from Ete.

"They live here. On Earth," she said. "They moved from Mars when it was no longer hospitable."

"Alright, where on Earth do they live?" Barry asked.

We live underground. The sun here is too strong for us. And we also live to the side. Again, Ete answered before Tomi even asked the question in her mind. Tomi's mind felt overloaded trying to communicate both orally, with Barry, and telepathically, with Ete.

"They live underground because the sun is too strong," Tomi said to Barry, struggling to keep up with both ends of the conversation.

What do you mean, to the side? she asked.

There are other places, other levels of reality right beside this one, Ete said in Tomi's mind. *We can go in and out. Think of it like a pocket of this reality. Or this reality a pocket of that one.*

"They can also go in and out of another reality, beside this one," Tomi relayed, not really grasping what it meant.

"Alright, how do they travel between these realities?" asked Barry.

You are saying there's a whole other world? asked Tomi. *Like a different dimension?*

Yes, said Ete.

And humans can't see it?

Most don't think they can, said Ete. *But if you stop and think about it, Tomi, haven't you always known it was there?*

Tomi experienced a flash of images and memories, but jumbled. She pushed them aside, her mind overwhelmed and unable to make sense of them.

How do you travel back and forth? Tomi asked.

This time, instead of hearing or seeing the response in words, she saw an image that she interpreted as a vibration. It was as though she could see the vibration of each particle, each electron around her. She became suddenly aware of her own body's vibration. She realized the vibration was always there, but only now she really felt it.

"It's…vibration. I don't really understand," Tomi said.

"Can you get more information on how vibration helps them travel?" Barry asked.

Tomi thought about the general watching her, seeing her eyes closed, her lips moving, sharing this information. She felt protective of Ete. Deep down her gut told her not to share this with that man.

I'm glad that your people came to Earth. When I saw you on Mars, it sounded like it might be the end, Tomi said in her mind's voice.

The end is still coming. We are still dying. Earth prolonged our species, and it was time we needed, as there's still more to learn. But our species as it is doesn't have long to go, Ete said, the voice in Tomi's mind not conveying the sadness she expected.

I'm so sorry, isn't there a way to stop it? Tomi asked.

You assume we want to stop it, Ete said. *This is the way of things, our next step. There is no death in this universe, not really.*

"Tomi, what's happening?" Barry asked.

"Their species is dying," she said, her voice somber.

"Why? Is there some help they need?" asked Barry.

"No," Tomi replied. "They've accepted it."

"Okay, I want you to turn your attention to the craft. Do you see any controls?" asked Barry.

Tomi scanned the room in the craft. Everything was smooth. She saw no steering wheel or stick, no buttons, no levers.

"No, I don't see any controls at all. It's all smooth inside. Seamless."

So all this time, when people reported UFOs in the sky, it was you, your people, Tomi said to Ete.

Some of them, replied Ete. *Some were others.*

There are others? Like you? asked Tomi.

There are others. Some like us, some very different, said Ete.

How many others? wondered Tomi.

Many. The universe is abounding with life, Ete said.

A vision of particles vibrating, moving, and dancing around entered Tomi's mind. She felt physically connected to this vision, as though she were related, connected to the particles. Her view started to widen, and widened rapidly. Suns and planets were spinning and whizzing by, and on each she got glimpses of life. Microscopic life, bizarre and beautiful plants of so many different colours, creatures with fur, some naked, some bipedal, big and small, some without form, some terrifying.

All of it so beautiful and magical, Tomi thought. She saw these galaxies, this universe begin to fold into itself, layer upon layer, and with each layer, there was more and more life. An unbelievably abundant universe flashed through her mind.

That was so beautiful, Tomi said. Tears escaped her closed eyes.

It's what we're made of. And you're made of. All of us, Ete said. *It's not your fault you can't see that it's all around you. You're limited to what the physical human body can perceive.*

But you can perceive it all? asked Tomi.

We can perceive more, replied Ete.

"Tomi, are you okay?" asked Barry, noticing a tear dropping down the side of her face and into her hair.

"Yes. I just saw something…something beautiful" Tomi said. "I can't really describe it."

"Okay, can you ask it how the vehicle moves, how it is controlled?" prompted Barry.

"Ete," Tomi corrected him.

"Yes, *Ete,"* Barry said, correcting himself. *"Can you ask Ete how the vehicle is controlled?"*

Are any of these others…bad? Hostile? Tomi asked. She knew she needed to answer Barry's questions, but wanted to ask her own before losing the thread of the conversation. That vision was so fast and was full of beauty, but she felt like there were pits of darkness.

You need darkness to see the light. Ete's words entered her mind just as she thought about that darkness. Tomi realized it wasn't just a conversation. Her thoughts were being shared.

You can read my thoughts, said Tomi.

Yes. There are no true secrets in the universe, said Ete. *To your earlier question, some are hostile, yes. We try to protect you. And others do, too. We watch over you. Of course, you need to learn on your own, as a species, so we rarely intervene.*

You protect us, Tomi repeated back. *I can sense that. Why? Why do you want to protect us?*

We feel sorry for humans, Ete said. *You have no idea of your potential. No idea who you really are. One day, you will understand that vision I showed you. You will understand that we are all made of the same stuff. The same essence. There is no separation. And one day humans will realize that if they hurt another, they hurt themselves.*

"Tomi, I need you to report back what you are experiencing," Barry said.

"There, um…there are others. Other kinds of beings, here on Earth. Or visiting Earth. And these ones, Ete's people, protect us," Tomi said.

"What do they protect us from?" asked Barry.

There are others who have their own agendas with Earth. With humans. Ete's words filled Tomi's mind before she even relayed Barry's question.

Do you have an agenda? Tomi asked.

We all have agendas, Ete replied. *We have an agenda with humans. We want to guide you, prepare you to ascend, as a species. We protect you, as we can, to give you time to take the next step. If you can avoid your own destruction first.*

"Tomi?"

"They protect us from others. Hostile ones," Tomi said, struggling to put so much of this into words. She also questioned how much of this conversation was just for her and how much to share with her audience. "And from ourselves. Because we can destroy ourselves."

"Okay, can we go back to the craft and how it works?" Barry asked.

If you came to Earth a million years ago, Tomi said, *you've been watching humans this whole time?*

Yes, replied Ete.

So you know everything about us, Tomi thought, imagining the major events in human history, the rise and fall of civilizations, all of the wars and destruction they might have seen. *My friend wanted me to ask about Atlantis, I mean he was joking, but-*

That's not what it was called, interrupted Ete.

Atlantis? So it was real? What was it called? asked Tomi.

You will know the name one day Tomi, but not today, replied Ete.

"I'm asking about Atlantis," Tomi told Barry. "It was real. It had a different name."

"Tomi, please go back to focusing on the craft and how it operates," replied Barry, his voice becoming more impatient.

What happened to it? asked Tomi.

I will show you, Ete replied. In an instant the walls of the vehicle were gone, and she was in the sky, looking down on a horrible, apocalyptic scene. The sun was dampened by dark, thick clouds. Flashes of lightning broke the darkness, with pieces of a comet raining fireballs from the sky. Below her was a majestic cityscape, much of it already flooded, and what wasn't flooded was roaring with flames. Her view zoomed out, and she saw the most horrible, civilization-killing mountain of water hurtling in the city's direction.

Tomi was horrified by the scene. She yelled in her mind's voice, *Can't you do something? Help them?*

We did, Ete said calmly. As she spoke, the scene broke, and they were back in the craft. Tomi looked around and saw through the walls that they were back over the green, mountainous place again. She could also see that those dark, rolling clouds were getting closer. *This was an event we could not protect them from,* Ete continued. *And we don't usually intervene, but we did save some of them.*

Where did they go? asked Tomi.

"I could see the city, there was massive destruction, and a huge wave destroying it," she said. "It was horrible."

"Okay," Barry said, hoping to get her on track. "Please focus on the craft. What can-"

At that moment, Barry was interrupted by a banging sound, and Tomi could hear raised voices outside of the interview room.

Tomi tried to ignore the sounds around her. She was safe, Barry was here. She tried to focus on Ete, not wanting to lose this connection.

"Why the fuck is she asking about Atlantis?" She thought it was the general's voice. "How to operate the craft. That's what we want. Get her on track!"

She was losing the vision.

"Okay, Tomi, I want you to ignore any noises you may have heard," Barry said calmly. "I want you to take a few moments to breathe, get centred, and direct yourself back to the same time and place."

Tomi regulated her breathing. She could feel Ete's presence before the vision came back. The scene was the same, Ete standing in the middle of the room in the craft, with a helmet on, facing her. Over Ete's shoulder, through the walls of the craft, she could see the storm clouds closing in.

"Okay, I'm back," Tomi said.

"Great. Now I want you to ask about the vehicle, how it's operated," Barry said.

How does this vehicle fly? Tomi asked. *There are no controls that I can see. How do you operate it?*

You already have everything you need to control it, Ete said. *You will be taught how to control it, Tomi.*

"Ete says I will be taught to control it," Tomi said. "To fly it."

"That is great, please report back as you go," said Barry.

You will learn to fly it, Ete said, *but not today. Not this time. In just a few moments, this craft will crash.*

Tomi looked again at the storm closing in on their position. *What? No. No! Is it the storm? Is it my fault? I've distracted you, I can go,* she said, panicked.

It's okay Tomi, this is always what happened. Many years from now, some people will dig this craft up, Ete said calmly. *Those men who want you to ask me how to operate it, those men have it, and they want to use it. Their interests are in violence. One day you will learn how to fly it, but never when those men might learn as well.*

"Ete says she will never show me how to control the craft if those men could learn also," Tomi said. "Says they are violent. She won't help them. Barry, she says their craft is going to crash."

Go now, Ete said. *We will speak again.*

At that moment she could see the inside of the craft suddenly flip, and Ete's body being hurled towards a wall.

Tomi's eyes burst open, and the horror of the crash was replaced by the view of white commercial ceiling tiles. She sat up straight, sucking in a breath.

"Tomi? Tomi, breathe, just sit back and relax," Barry said.

Tomi stood straight up, pushing through the wooziness as her body adapted to suddenly being upright. She opened the door and stepped out of the interview room, to see the General and the other men collecting their belongings and heading towards the door. Ib followed, trying to convince them to stay for a moment and review the data.

"You knew!" Tomi tried to shout, scratching out of her dry throat. The General turned to look at her. "You knew that they would crash, you sent me in knowing that's where they would crash. That they would die. What the fuck?"

The General let her words hang in the air for a moment, before looking at Barry, then to Ib, and back towards Tomi. "I will remind you of your clearances and the requirements of your NDAs." He scanned their faces again. He turned and exited the door with his group following closely.

Tomi looked at both Barry and Ib, mouth open, and repeated, "What the fuck?"

"So that's all they wanted," Tomi said, reviewing the session with Ib and Barry over martinis. "They only cared about how to fly the thing. I mean, Ete is talking about peace, and protecting us, and these guys just want to get to the part where they can figure out how to make it blow something up."

Both men nodded along to show they felt her anger was justified.

"And they knew it was going to crash there, because they dug it up," she continued. "They knew they were going to die, and sent me to see it."

"FUBAR," said Barry. "Fucked up beyond all recognition. But he was right, Tomi. About the NDAs. You can't talk about this to anyone. You know that, right? These aren't the kind of people you mess with."

Tomi nodded and drank from her glass. She thought about the car from the other night.

"I'm sorry, Tomi." Tomi looked at Ib, and saw sincere sadness in his face. "I'm very sorry. Barry is right. These aren't people you want to mess with. And I'm very sorry that I got you involved in this. That you had to see all of that. I'm truly sorry."

Tomi held his gaze and smiled gently. "I appreciate that. But the fact is I wanted to do this. I feel like I'm on to something. I don't know what exactly. But I want to continue."

Tomi raised her martini to clink glasses with Ib.

"Before the session started," Tomi said, "I could hear him saying to you that he wanted you to tell me what the goal was today. I guess that goal was how to operate the craft?"

Ib nodded.

"I heard you say you'd assured him about something, but I missed the rest. What was it?"

Ib looked down at his glass, and back to Tomi. "I was telling him that in remote viewing, the more something is being hidden, the more it's like a beacon, like a lighthouse. What people want to keep hidden just wants to be found."

"There are no secrets in the universe," said Tomi.

Chapter 6

"D: So now the DNA is being allowed to change again? (Yes)

How will people notice that in our world today?

M: Well, some people won't notice, but those that are aware will feel well connected to "All" that is. Their senses will be heightened. They'll become lighter...more transparent.

D: Will people around them notice this?

M: Some will. Some will just keep sleepwalking.

D: I was thinking if they were becoming more transparent it should be noticeable.

M: They'll just become invisible.

D: Eventually?

M: Yes. But they'll still be there. It's like changing channels on the TV.

D: But if they become invisible, those around them won't see them anymore? (Yes)

Where will they be?

M: On a different channel.

D: Another dimension? (Yes) Will they be aware of it? (Yes)

They'll know something has happened? (Oh, yes.)

But the other people won't? (No)"

Dolores Cannon, from The Three Waves of Volunteers and the New Earth

Home had started to feel like an uncertain place for Tomi.

When she was at PSI, she was surrounded by people who believed in her, in her abilities, and that what she was experiencing, as impossible as it seemed, was actually possible. When she was with Kirsten, she felt it too - secure in her sanity.

But at home alone, she was living on a margin. Her recent experiences told her that the very nature of reality, of the universe, was fundamentally misunderstood by everyone around her. But home, with her furniture, the television, pictures on the walls, water and electricity bills, and the presence of John - so rational and so certain of his world - felt so at odds with this new paradigm she was experiencing.

It was a liminal and lonely feeling, which felt a little less lonely when she remembered a line from Alice in Wonderland, a book she would read with her grandmother when she would have a sleepover: "It's no use going back to yesterday, because I was a different person then."

Amen Alice, thought Tomi.

And then there was the question of what to do about John. He had returned from DC, and they talked a bit about his time away. She told him that she had been brought in by the General again, but of course, she couldn't tell him more. Not that he wanted to hear more. Though he wasn't vocal about it, it was obvious that he was not supportive of this new direction her life was taking.

John was avoidant and could continue on that track for an impressive amount of time. In the past, it was up to Tomi to bridge a gap between them, sort out their feelings, and repair whatever was broken.

This time Tomi didn't have the urge to bridge that gap. She didn't want to go back to the way things were. Her eyes were opened, and she finally felt a sense of purpose in her life. How could she explain any of her experiences to John in a way that he would understand, let alone support?

Still, she knew they would have to have a real conversation at some point.

While in the past she would have prioritized a conversation - this was her marriage, after all - she was instead focused on peeling back further layers by learning more about "the phenomenon," which she learned was a catch-all term for UFOs, extraterrestrials, and all kinds of high strangeness. Tomi scoured the internet for answers, finding herself going down a rabbit hole that had few clear and reliable facts to rely on, but all kinds of stories that made Tomi feel less alone.

Knowing that she had that second place, outside of this home, that she could go where she would not only find acceptance, but also some answers, was a grounding feeling for Tomi. PSI was her oasis at this point. Which made it even harder on her fragile mental health when she learned she would not be allowed back.

It was a Monday morning, and John had already left for work when Kirsten came to the door. Tomi had already been up for a few hours, deep into a podcast series on the history of UFOs, and had forgotten they had made plans for a visit.

When Tomi got to the door and saw Kirsten, she remembered they'd planned to go out for coffee. Kirsten was wearing a long cotton dress made of horizontal strips of multicoloured fabric - *something like Joseph's Technicolour Dreamcoat,* Tomi thought - with an indigo patterned shawl wrapped around her shoulders. *She is so unique and beautiful,* Tomi thought, looking down and seeing a yoghurt stain on her black t-shirt.

"Oh my God, you look amazing," Tomi said. "I'm so sorry, I lost track of time. I'm not showered or ready to go out at all."

"Thanks, and hey that's no problem," Kirsten said, stepping in and wrapping Tomi in a hug. She stepped back and looked Tomi in the eyes. "Are you doing okay? Your eyes look really tired, what's going on? I hope it's not the hypnosis session that's got you up?"

Kirsten had been out of town for a few weeks, and this was the first time seeing each other since they had their conversation about ontological shock, and Tomi's session with Marja. They had planned to finally catch up today.

"Oh, well, that and a few other things. That ontological shock sure does linger," Tomi said, trying to smile.

"Why don't you go take a nice hot shower, and I'll make some tea," Kirsten said, pointing Tomi upstairs towards the shower, indicating it was more of an instruction than a suggestion.

Tomi brushed her teeth and peeled off her stretchy pants and stained t-shirt, realizing it had been three days since her last shower.

She looked at herself in the mirror, and felt she looked older than she should. *These sessions really do a number on me*, she thought.

She washed herself, then just leaned against the shower wall, letting the hot water run down her body. The podcast she had listened to had considered the question: why is the universe so perfectly tuned to facilitate life?

What universe would be so perfectly tuned to allow for hot water showers? wondered Tomi.

She pulled her hair up, put on some fresh clothes, and came down to find Kirsten at her kitchen table, where there was a place setting for Tomi, along with tea and an omelette. A small bunch of flowers picked from her garden were placed in a drinking glass at the centre of the table.

"I figured if you're not showering, you might not be eating, either," Kirsten said. "Also, you hide your vases well."

Tomi laughed and sat down, giving a look of thank you to Kirsten before picking up her fork.

"How are you so put together," Tomi asked Kirsten. "I mean with what happened to you and your family. What you know, what you've experienced. Doesn't it make you question everything?"

Kirsten smiled and laughed. "I've had a lot of moments like you're having, believe me. I certainly recommend lots of therapy. And a good friend of course."

"Of course," Tomi said with a smile, feeling particularly grateful that Kirsten, with her kindness and her experiences, would come into her life just at the right time. "How do you relate to people who haven't had your experiences? Don't see, I don't know, how much more there is to the world around us?"

"Hah, like Jeff? Yeah, that's not really working out. But not just because of this. Honestly, sometimes it's nice to be around people where you can just forget about that stuff and enjoy life. Jeff was that. I mean who knows what all is going on in the universe, but whatever it is, it created these flowers," Kirsten said, stroking the petals of a daisy. "And you can look at their colours and smell them. You know, you need to find a way to enjoy the beauty around you. The beauty of life."

"Yeah," Tomi said, nodding, not sure how to put everything that's happened out of her mind, even for a moment. "I think that's something I have to learn. And I'm sorry about you and Jeff."

"Oh, don't be sorry, and I got you out of it! Here's something else I think about sometimes. I'm in on a secret that most people aren't. Most people are walking through life thinking everything is as it seems. But me, I'm in on a big secret," Kirsten said, with a deep laugh. "I feel kind of privileged that way."

Tomi smiled at this.

"So, you know that I've been going in and doing remote viewing at PSI," Tomi said. Kirsten nodded. Tomi paused and considered how much she could say, and realized it was almost nothing. But she needed someone to have some understanding of what she had experienced, someone outside of the people at PSI.

"Well, I've done some sessions…some for the government." She realized she was speaking slower and quieter, as though pacing and volume would make breaching an NDA a little more acceptable. "And they got, well, weird. I'm really, really not supposed to be saying anything, but…Well, I got into really deep states, and connected with…with an alien, I guess. Well another being, anyways. They live here on Earth."

Kirsten allowed a long pause, holding Tomi's stare. She finally broke eye contact, reached for the teapot, and poured tea into Tomi's, then her own mug. She raised her mug to blow on her tea and smiled. "Well, we really are two spooky chicks, aren't we?"

Tomi laughed and nodded.

"Well, I can see why you looked the way you did when I got here this morning," Kirsten said. "That sounds like a lot, Tomi. I'm glad you shared that. And don't worry, I won't tell anyone."

Kirsten smiled. "So, I'm single now. Is the alien cute?"

The two laughed and had their tea, a welcome moment of reprieve from Tomi's rabbit holing. For a few minutes, Tomi enjoyed conversation, her omelette, and the sun shining in through the kitchen window.

Then the doorbell rang.

"I'll get rid of whoever it is," said Kirsten, laughing and rushing off to the front door. Tomi sipped her tea, and could hear a male voice. After a moment, Kirsten returned to the kitchen with Ib.

"I'm so sorry to barge in, Tomi," said Ib, stepping tentatively into the kitchen. I just hoped we might get a chance to chat. But I see you have company."

"Come, have some tea," Kirsten said, opening multiple cabinets, forgetting where she had found the mugs. "We were just chatting about spooky stuff."

Tomi turned her head to look at Kirsten. She felt a sudden pang of worry that Kirsten would let out that she had broken her NDA, even if it was just a few details.

"Oh, I love spooky stuff," said Ib, taking a seat at the table and thanking Kirsten for pouring his tea.

"Bigfoot? Nessie? Poltergeists?" said Kirsten, in a playful nature that Tomi admired.

"Some of my favourite subjects," Ib said.

"Mine too! What's the weirdest or spookiest thing you believe in? Like legit believe in," Kirsten asked Ib.

Ib sat back with his tea and considered the question. Finally, his face got more serious, and he said: "Elves."

"Elves!" said Tomi, smiling with a sense of surprise. "Like, for real?"

"Sure," said Ib, "why not? You know in Iceland, still to this day, they will divert roads around certain boulders to not upset what they call the 'hidden folk.' Icelanders are pretty smart and modern people, yet many do believe."

"Yeah," said Kirsten. "I've heard that they do that. And that it's common to believe in them there."

"Yes. And it wasn't so long ago people believed in them where I'm from," Ib said. "In Denmark we have *nisser*. They are a kind of elf, that we believed in from way before Christianity came. The nisser watched over the house or the barn. When I was a kid I would visit my grandmother's farm, it was an old farm her family had lived on for generations. Anyway, there was a tree beside the barn, and under the tree was a big flat rock, and sometimes she would leave things there, leave little gifts. Oatmeal, whenever she made oatmeal, she would put a little dish out there."

"That's so interesting!" said Kirsten.

"When I would ask her about it, she said her mother taught her to do that because they share the farm with the nisser, and it's best to keep them happy. If you don't, they might even hit you on the side of the head, or even mess with your animals." Ib leaned in and his voice grew a little quieter, a natural storyteller ready to get to the good part.

"One day I asked her, I said grandma, you don't really believe in nisser, do you? And she just smiled and hummed as she stirred a pot on her big cast iron wood stove she still cooked on. And I realized yes, she really believed. Well, she really inspired me, opened me up to at least imagine that such things are possible. So yes, I will say nisser are the weirdest thing I believe in. Who's to say, right?"

"Wow, that's super interesting, Ib," said Tomi. "And you're right, who's to say what's a weird thing to believe in." She gave Ib a knowing look.

"Indeed," he said, drinking the last of his tea. "Now I wonder if I might chat with you in confidence for a just few minutes, Tomi."

"I feel like I'm being called into the principal's office," Tomi said, as Ib closed the door behind them.

"Well, it is an office, I suppose," Ib said, scanning the walls of John's office. It had a large, handmade dark walnut desk, with matching built-in bookcases behind the desk. Ib glanced around at the pictures on the walls of John with various political and intelligence figures. He stopped on one, a younger John with his arm around a young man in Air Force blues.

"Hm. There's something familiar about this one," he said.

"Ib, what's going on?" asked Tomi.

"They're shutting us down, Tomi," Ib said, turning away from the picture to look Tomi in the eyes. "Or more accurately, they're shutting you down. I'm sorry, Tomi."

"What? Who, the General? Why? Can they do that?" Tomi tried to hold back tears, not wanting to cry in front of Ib. It wasn't just about losing the job; PSI had become a refuge for her in a world that no longer made sense.

"I'm afraid they can," Ib said. "If we don't stop working with you, they will pull our security clearances, so we won't be able to take on government contracts anymore. That's the way we fund PSI and our research. If we don't have the contracts, we can't continue at all."

Tomi held her jaw tight trying to repress tears. She finally felt that she could loosen her jaw and speak without also letting out a flood of emotions.

"I just…thought we were on to something," she said sadly. "I'm not sure I know what the questions were, but I felt like we were heading towards answers."

"So did I," Ib said softly. "I don't know what they're afraid of, but we were given this message in no uncertain terms. I'm very sorry, Tomi."

Tomi was looking down, processing this, when she realized Ib had stepped closer. She met his eyes. He looked around the room, then spoke softly.

"You are right," he said, "I don't know what the questions are, either, but I want answers, too. They said we couldn't work with you at PSI, but what if we continued this investigation? Unofficially. Not at PSI. We could do it here."

Tomi's heart raced. These sessions where she had met Ete had been overwhelming, and at times terrifying. The thought of doing it again made her anxious, while the prospect of getting closer to the truth - whatever that meant - made her heart beat with anticipation. Ib reached into his pocket, and again scanned the room.

"You keep looking around," Tomi said in a near whisper. "Why?"

"Oh," Ib said with a boyish shrug, "it's silly. I'm sure they aren't listening or anything. I'm just…nervous."

"What are you nervous about?" asked Tomi.

Ib pulled a folded, sealed envelope from his front pant pocket. His voice was below a whisper now. "The last time they were at PSI, they provided another envelope and set of coordinates, in case the ones we used weren't successful. Normally we shred these if they aren't used. But I kept this one. We could use it to see if you can connect with Ete again. We could do it today."

Tomi took a deep breath to calm her nerves. She was surprised that Ib had stepped out of line in this way. She could tell that breaking rules was not in his nature, and yet here he was with this envelope. This meant a lot to him.

"On one condition," Tomi said. "I want Kirsten to be there. I need someone in my life who understands what I'm experiencing."

Ib opened his mouth and bobbled his head, considering the request. "Tomi, we signed NDAs."

"Yes, and we're not working for PSI on this anymore, are we?" she said. "So it doesn't really matter. And you can trust her. I trust her."

Ib wasn't sold on this logic, but understood why she would ask.

"Okay, Kirsten can sit in," he said. "Let's do it."

Tomi smiled, and headed towards the door. Ib followed, giving one more look at the photo on the wall on his way out of the office. He held in his hand the leftover envelope, unused by the General. The 3x5 card inside read:

Planet Earth. Geographic Location:

Central Alaska, approximately 62 miles below surface

Time of interest: Present Day

Chapter 7

"The mushroom said to me once, this is what it's like when a species prepares to depart for the stars. You don't depart for the stars under calm and orderly conditions, it's a fire in a madhouse, and that's what we have, the fire in the madhouse at the end of time. This is what it's like when a species prepares to move on to the next dimension. The entire destiny of all life on the planet is tied up in this. We happen to be the point species on a transformation that will affect every living organism on this planet, and its conclusion."

Terrence McKenna

Tomi hydrated, used the washroom, and laid down on the couch in her basement. They chose the sparsely decorated sitting room in the basement for that reason - a bland space that wouldn't be distracting for the subject.

Tomi pulled a folded blanket from the top of the couch and flipped it out so it would fall evenly over her body. She looked at Kirsten, then Ib, smiled, closed her eyes, and started to focus on her breathing. Kirsten had pulled a chair up to Tomi's side, and reached over to hold her hand, while Ib was seated a few feet away beside the coffee table, where he'd placed his recording device and the unfolded, sealed envelope.

After giving Tomi time to get into a relaxed state, Ib led her through further relaxation exercises until she was in a deep enough state to remote view. Ib pressed the record button on his device.

"This is Doctor Ib Johansen on September 25th, 2023. The subject is laying on a couch in their basement. Also present is the subject's friend. The method of site acquisition is instructions written on a card, which have been presented to the subject in a sealed envelope. The envelope was not opened prior to the session. Tomi, when you are ready, I want you to first focus on the instructions in the envelope. Then I want you to navigate to these coordinates: 63.6300 degrees north, 146.7161 degrees west."

Ib listened closely as Tomi breathed quietly. One of the challenges for a moderator is knowing when to let the subject take in information, and when to interrupt that silence with another prompt. After a few minutes, Ib broke the silence.

"Tomi, you don't need to make sense of it, just tell me the raw data, what are you seeing?"

"It's just, it's…it's nothing. It's darkness. I feel like I can get a bit of texture sometimes. It feels like something is there, it's just very dark. It feels dense."

"Okay," said Ib gently, "focus again on the instructions in the envelope. Point yourself towards the area and time of interest again."

A few minutes went by, but this time Tomi broke the silence.

"Okay, suddenly it feels like my vision opened up," said Tomi. Kirsten watched her face closely, noticing small movements, as though Tomi was looking around.

"It's just so much brighter now," Tomi said. "And open. Wherever I was it was dense and dark, and this feels open and light."

"Great, Tomi," said Ib, "can you see what the source of the light is? Where is it coming from?"

"I can't quite…" said Tomi, her face scrunching slightly in frustration. "It's like it's coming from all around. It's not a bright light, it's a sort of low glow…It feels so soothing."

"That sounds nice, Tomi," said Ib. "Can you get a sense of where you are, your surroundings?"

"Yes…The light felt bright at first but it's because it was so dark before. Now I see it, this low light. Low glow. It's a big, big open space. I'm looking around but I…almost can't make out up and down."

"What is your perspective," asked Ib. "Can you see where you are viewing from?"

"Okay, yes," said Tomi, sounding unsure despite answering in the positive. "I'm on the ground. But it's like the ground eventually just curves up and becomes walls. And I mean big walls, this place is huge…and I don't see a sky. It curves up and makes a ceiling, too."

After a pause, Ib prompted her. "So, you're inside somewhere. Can you sense if you're inside some kind of building? Or craft?"

"No, neither," said Tomi. "It's like a cave, a giant cavern. I think I'm underground. It's like it's carved out of rock." Tomi paused to listen. Sometimes the information was visual, sometimes it came as words, and still others it was a feeling, a hunch. Posing a question and waiting for your body to feel the answer. "Yes, I sense this is deep,

deep underground! But it's such a big space. I'm starting to get impressions of smaller spaces, smaller rooms, off to the sides. Or maybe hallways."

"Great," said Ib," is there one that is catching your interest? Would you like to move towards one?"

"Yes…There's one, there's like an oval doorway. Well not a door, it's an opening. I'm moving in that direction," she said. "I just…I don't understand the light. It comes from everywhere and nowhere. It's…it's the walls. The walls are giving off this light. But not like a lightbulb on the wall…like the whole surface of the wall is glowing. It's beautiful and feels nourishing. It's a low glow, and it feels like it's all around you because the walls, floor, and ceiling are all one. It's glowing all around."

"That's very interesting, Tomi," said Ib. "Have you come to the entrance to the side room?"

"Yes," she said. "Yes, I'm moving through the entrance. The dividing wall is smoothed, there are no hard edges. But all of it glowing."

"What do you see as you step in? How big is the space?" asked Ib.

"It's a smaller room," said Tomi. "The image is coming to me slowly."

"That's okay, Tomi," said Ib. "Take your time. We can reset if you need."

Tomi took several long, slow breaths. After a few minutes, she said, "long. The walls aren't quite straight. But long. Like it's a long room that kind of goes like a snake, so you can't see from one end to the other. All the walls are smooth and rounded here too. It's…darker in here. Not darker exactly. The light is still there, from all around the walls and ceiling…but the light is darker. It was kind of golden in the last space. Here it's kind of…inky. Like a dark blue…purple."

Kirsten silently mouthed *indigo.*

"Indigo. That's the word," said Tomi. "It's such a dark light. It's beautiful. Okay, I'm seeing something sort of along the walls. This light is so beautiful but it's almost distracting…it sort of takes longer for the details to come."

"That's okay, take your time," said Ib. "Take your time, what are these things you are starting to see? What shapes?"

Tomi was silent for a few moments, processing the information. Kirsten had her hand resting softly on Tomi's, letting her friend know she was safe. For the first time in this session, Kirsten felt Tomi's hand jerk slightly.

"They're here," Tomi said, in a whisper. "That's what I see along the walls."

"Tomi, who is there?" asked Ib.

"The same beings, they are here," she said. "Ete's people. They are sitting. There are several of them. Seven. No, six. They are still so tall even when they are sitting."

"What are they doing while sitting?" asked Ib.

"They are sitting, shoulder to shoulder, in a line," said Tomi. "They are meditating. Yes…they spend a lot of time meditating. They are such a spiritual people."

The corners of Tomi's mouth pulled up into a slight smile.

"Can you sense the purpose of this meditation?" asked Ib.

Tomi paused, waiting to feel the answer to this question. "They are watching."

"Okay," said Ib. "What are they watching?"

"They are watching…oh, many things. I feel like I'm getting little glimpses, images. I think I'm seeing what they are watching. It's fast. Too fast for me to make sense of. I think I saw a forest. I see people, many kinds of people. Stars. Dangerous stars…sorry, these flashes…"

"That's okay," said Ib. "Can you make sense of any more of these flashes?"

"War. I see a mushroom cloud, but I feel like it's ancient, a long time ago," she said, her voice carrying her confusion. "It's horrible. And some sort of landscapes…I can't make sense of. I want to stop these flashes,"

"Can you stop them?" asked Ib.

"Yes," Tomi said, relieved. "They stopped when I asked. I'm looking at the beings again, this soothing light. Wait…one opened its eyes. It's looking at me."

Tomi was quiet for some time, and Ib gave her the space to take in what she was experiencing. Finally, he reminded her to report what she was seeing.

"Tomi, what are you experiencing? Is the being communicating with you?" Ib asked.

"Sorry, yes…it was just looking at me," she said. "And then it closed its eyes again. There are six of them, and seven of these stools. I think it wants me to join them."

"Can you move your perspective to where it wants you?" asked Ib.

"Yes. I just…I don't feel it physically, really…but it's almost like I can feel that I'm sitting down. This stool, it's like it makes you lighter. Like the stool is floating. I'm floating," she said.

"That is interesting, Tomi," said Ib. "What are you experiencing now that you're there? Do you recognize any of the beings?"

"I just feel…very light, "she said, with soft joy. "I don't hear words, but I feel very connected to them. It's as though when they meditate, it isn't alone. Not solitary. It's collective. Like each of them is entangled together. And sitting here I feel like I'm a part of it."

"And do you recognize any of the beings? Are they communicating with you?" asked Ib.

Who are you? Have we met before? Tomi was used to the being speaking first. She wasn't sure her message would get across.

Immediately, she had brief visual flashes. There were many images, but she recognized two of them being her meetings with Ete.

"I saw flashes of my previous meetings," Tomi reported. "Some of this is so clear, so vivid. It's like the group of them meditating are helping the connection somehow."

Are you Ete? Tomi tried to ask.

Yes, Tomi, Ete said, the words appearing in her mind. *It is so good to have you here.*

She sensed that the words were coming from the one that had opened its eyes. *You have a new body,* she said, remembering their last meeting where Ete explained she was the same soul in a new body.

Tomi could see a visual of this new version of Ete, male this time, and young. She knew that they lived long physical lives, much longer than humans. It was strange to be receiving information this way, she kept getting visuals, but with them came a depth of information. She felt like she couldn't process it all.

"The information is coming differently this time. It's more of an understanding I have, instead of words," Tomi said.

"What sort of information are you receiving?" asked Ib.

"It is Ete, in a new body," she said. "Male this time. He's young, I feel like around 20 if he was human, but he's actually much older."

When you are born, do you always remember your past lives? wondered Tomi. She couldn't imagine carrying around all that information.

Yes, but it's not heavy. We don't carry it. Ete's words swept into Tomi's mind, not like a beam of information from one to another, but as though the words hung like a cloud over the group of them seated in meditation.

A visual took form in her mind of a bright white light energy shooting in all directions, throughout the cosmos. She could see it flowing in waves, and within those waves, she could feel a vibration, a high vibration. And for what felt like a fraction of a second, she felt that light energy sweep into her body, producing flashes of lives, some hers, some not, some on Earth, and some far away. For just a moment a vision of the hilly island filled her, along with a feeling of incredible lightness, and an incredible longing.

As quickly as the experience came, it was gone. Tomi felt both relieved, as the massive download of information was overwhelming, but also nostalgic for times and spaces she didn't know she missed. Tears welled in her closed eyes.

So it's everywhere? Tomi asked. *The information. And not just past lives, there was so much information. It's everywhere, and you can get it anytime?*

That's correct, Ete replied. *Our bodies are something like an antenna for a radio signal, to put it in human terms. Your bodies are, too.*

"Tomi, what are you experiencing?" Ib asked.

"It's…well, how to describe it," Tomi said. "They showed me how they can know their past lives, like the information lives all through the universe. Ete said their bodies are like antennas. Our bodies too."

If our bodies are like antennas too, why can't we remember? Tomi asked Ete.

But you can, Ete replied. Tomi felt like Ete knew what she would ask even before she did, but enjoyed humouring her with conversation. *You've remembered yours, haven't you, Tomi? Or at least parts of yours. Imagine the human antenna being blocked by a brick wall. It might catch bits of information, but the reception would not be good.*

What is the brick wall? Tomi asked. *What stops us from receiving, from seeing it all?*

Again, flashes of images and information came into Tomi's mind. She saw a double helix, and knew it was human DNA. She saw hands working on it. She saw waves again, flowing around a human body.

It's our DNA, she thought. *It's there in our DNA, but it's turned off. And…someone did that. When? Why?*

That's right, Tomi, said Ete gently. *I know this is a lot, but there's a lot you need to know. Humans have souls, you know that now. Everything in the universe is conscious, but not everything has a soul. When homo sapiens were ready, your DNA was changed to allow a soul. To become hosts. That's when you transcended from homo sapiens. It's when you became human.*

It was seventy thousand years ago, and your people did it, Tomi thought. She didn't know how, but she knew the answer to her question.

Homo sapiens were struggling, Ete replied. *They saw in humans a species complex enough to allow for spiritual learning and growth. Life doesn't just automatically come with souls. A species needs to have its antenna turned on, so to speak. Why do you think your species was an animal, just like any other for most of its history, then all of a sudden you weren't? How do you think that happens without intervention? Homo Sapiens are animals built for survival. It's the quest of the soul to grow that makes you human.*

Tomi was overwhelmed with all of this information. She struggled to know how to respond or what to ask next, and chose to question one word. *Who is the "they" who saw that in humans?*

Some higher being perhaps? The universe itself? God? We don't know.

Tomi's mind's eye could again see the light energy flowing through the universe, a bright white, thick energy, reaching through the cosmos and hugging the earth. *Souls entering human bodies,* she thought. She felt like her body was vibrating with this energy, as though she could remember the journey here. She thought about asking about God, then felt she didn't need to.

"Tomi, can you report what you are seeing?", asked Ib.

"So much information. It's overwhelming," she said. "They got a message to change our DNA a long time ago. And this gave us souls."

"Oh…okay," said Ib. "Can you ask more about this? Who gave them the message?"

"The universe?" said Tomi. "It's hard to explain, so much of the information is visual, or a feeling."

"Can you find out how they did this? And why?" asked Ib.

How did you change our DNA? How did you change homo sapiens? Tomi put the question deep into her mind, and waited for the response, unsure what form that response would take.

We didn't change homo sapiens, answered Ete. *The sapien animal didn't change. What changed is that your animal bodies had a passenger. A soul from the other place, an inside influencer, both one and separate, in unison and in tension. Here, this might help to explain it.*

Tomi waited for an image or scene to enter her mind, but instead, she felt her body. It was like she could feel the vibrations of every atom, each electron buzzing. *The material me; the human animal,* thought Tomi. She then started to feel a higher vibration, not something inside her body, but like a mirror of her body, made only of light energy. The difference in vibration from one to the other felt like hitting a low key on a piano, and then hitting a high key. Together, they make a chord.

She began to see images, scenes from her own life, where she chose to follow the body over the soul. Over and over, her choices in relationships, her home, her work and hobbies, over and over choosing physical comfort and security over what might make her soul grow. What might make her soul known. It was as though most of her life she only heard the lower note.

Tomi then saw flashes of her time with her grandmother, and it was as though she could hear the chord again. She could see she had once been more aware of her soul, but had lost it.

I see, I understand, Tomi spoke into her mind. As she did, her awareness of her body's vibration lessened. *So the human challenge is getting them to work together, the human...machine, and a spiritual consciousness?*

Yes, said Ete. *Get the two to harmonize on this plane, and that's the key to transcendence. But how can you harmonize when one doesn't even acknowledge the other?*

"They changed the DNA, but it didn't materially change humans. It made us hosts for souls. Before it was just the human brain, and after it was both the brain and the soul," said Tomi, not sure if she was making sense in conveying what she was experiencing.

"Okay," said Ib, pausing to consider what to even ask next. "Is this manipulation, this change in our DNA, is it something we can see, that we can confirm scientifically?"

So even if the human animal didn't change, you did something to our DNA, said Tomi. *Wouldn't our scientists be able to tell that our DNA has been changed? Or what parts of the DNA turn on the spirit, so to speak?*

Tomi didn't hear laughter but felt it. It wasn't unkind, but more like the amusement a grown-up has at a child's curiosity.

Your scientists are learning a lot, said Ete, *but still have much to learn. Your scientists call the majority of your DNA junk. If they don't know what it does, they assume it does nothing. Much like the universe itself.*

"Our scientists can't tell. There's still much for us to learn," reported Tomi.

What do you mean it's much like the universe itself?

Most of what makes up the universe, humans can't see or perceive, said Ete. *You humans call this dark matter or dark energy. Your scientists assume that if you can't see it, it must be dark, rather than so bright it would blind a human eye. Tomi, the universe is even more majestic than you can know.*

I believe it, said Tomi. *I used to think of space as being so cold, dark, and empty.*

Oh but it is, said Ete. *It must be. Without darkness, there is no light. No void, no plenty.*

I understand. No hate, no love, added Tomi.

There are no opposites, said Ete. *Only one and the same.*

"Can you ask more about the souls, Tomi?" asked Ib, imagining the reaction from the General to this line of inquiry. "Where do they come from? What is the purpose?"

*Ete, where do the…*before she could ask the question, a vision invaded her mind. She was in a place she had never seen before, but felt so familiar. It wasn't quite a feeling of coming home, but perhaps like going somewhere you love, like returning to a beloved school or workplace after a time away.

She was in a room, in that there were walls, but it felt like she could walk through the walls if she wanted; nothing was hard here. Everything was soft and light. Tomi realized she wasn't alone, and saw figures emerging. Now it really felt like returning, not just to that beloved place, but returning to people you love and miss. She could feel the loving energy flowing from them.

This is my group. The words entered Tomi's mind, though she was unsure how she knew this. *It's my soul cluster. My class. This is the place we come back to, in-between lives. We get together, we give feedback to each other on how they did in their lives, and they give the same to us. We encourage and push and challenge each other to do better in our next lives.*

Yes, you remember now, said Ete.

The vision fizzled, as though a billion particles detached from one another, and just as quickly reattached into a new picture. She was no longer in the classroom. This room was darker. It was circular, and it was as though the walls were one continuous video screen, though she saw no electronics. There were two beings there. *These are guides,* Tomi thought. *They show me possible lives, and help me pick the right one for my mission. My goals.*

Yes, you remember this, too, said Ete.

The walls lit up with glimpses of her life, this life, here on Earth. It was as though someone had a camera focused on her for her whole life. The moments were flashing so quickly, and were flashing in three hundred and sixty degrees. She could see all around her but couldn't process all the scenes.

There she was, her eyes closed, laying on her grandmother's couch, her grandmother beside her. Her mother's funeral. Her and John in bed, giggling and teasing each other. And she saw unfamiliar scenes. John, hurt on the ground in a forest. Kirsten, but as a child. A gunshot. Blood. *Stop*, she thought.

She was immediately back underground, in meditation with the six other beings.

Ib watched Tomi take a deep breath. He knew she was deep into this one, and wanted to allow her to take in all that she could, but was wanting to at least have Tomi share reference points so they could debrief later.

"Tomi, what have you learned about the souls?" Ib watched her slowly become aware again of his voice. She was in a deep state. "Tomi?"

Tomi smacked her dry mouth open. Her words were becoming less pronounced, like talking to someone just as they are falling asleep. "It's, uh…wow, how to explain. We go to a place, an in-between place. And we have a group of souls. Like a class. Earth is a classroom for us."

Ib looked to Kirsten as though she would have some guidance. Kirsten shrugged.

"Uh…Can you say more?" asked Ib.

"The souls, we learn from each other," she said slowly. "And we pick our lives based on what we want to learn. And when we're done, we go back and do it again. We live these lives as part of some learning process. I don't know what for."

"Do…do we do this forever?" asked Ib. "What is the purpose, or outcome?"

Tomi breathed, and focused herself on being present with Ete. *Does this go on forever, Ete, this cycle of lives?*

This is a hard one to understand, said Ete. She could feel Ete trying to make this information comprehendible to her. *I can sense when you are saying* forever, *you're imagining that as a line from beginning to infinity. That's not your fault. You humans only understand time as the present. You don't see that everything that will come to pass already has. And still will.*

Tomi thought she understood what Ete was saying, but couldn't wrap her mind around what it really meant.

You humans, Ete continued, *you often feel so isolated. Lonely. Disconnected. We think this is because you only experience the present, where the universe, and everything in it, is expanding. Everything is pulling apart. You don't remember the times we were closer, all was one, and so you don't see that we are always all one.*

Tomi wasn't sure she really understood, but started to think back to moments where she felt more connected. Where she felt at one, with…what, she didn't know.

But to further answer your question, said Ete, *souls are working towards greater understanding, towards further transcendence. There are other levels beyond what you and I have seen, where truly advanced souls go.*

And what do the souls do there? asked Tomi.

As we understand it, when they get advanced enough, they create the universe, said Ete.

What do you mean? asked Tomi. *Hasn't the universe already been created?*

An image came into her mind, a beam of pure energy in a straight line. *Time,* she thought. As she remembered what Ete had just said about time not being linear, the beam broke off into what seemed like a million points of light energy, and between each of them she could see the interconnections, like drawing a multi-dimensional shape, but the number of dimensions keep expanding. The line, the beam, had formed into a shape of pure interconnected light. *It's so beautiful,* Tomi thought. *But how can the universe already have existed before the souls built it?*

The image faded and she was again underground, sitting in meditation. *I believe,* said Ete, the words conveyed with a feeling of playfulness, *it's what you humans might call a classic chicken and the egg scenario.*

"It's, uh…oh boy, this is hard to explain," said Tomi, struggling to put this experience into language, especially while trying to maintain her connection to Ete. "So, as souls we are learning, and we transcend to higher places, and we also build the universe. Like, we've already built it, or we're building it all the time, because time isn't how we see it."

Kirsten and Ib both looked at each other and nearly caused the other to laugh, realizing the other also couldn't follow that train of thought.

"Um, okay," said Ib, looking at Kirsten with a shrug, unsure of where to go next. "Tomi, why is this relevant? Why are they telling you this?"

Why are you showing me all of this? asked Tomi.

There's still more I need to show you, said Ete, *so much more. The stars are changing, Tomi. It's a time of transcendence, and there's much to do.*

Tomi saw herself shooting into space, as though she were launched as a satellite above the Earth. She saw the Earth rotating, with the moon circling it. Zooming out, she saw the Earth speeding through space, in orbit around the sun. Her view zoomed out again, and she saw the sun spinning through the Milky Way galaxy, and then galaxy upon galaxy on the move, every planet and sun and asteroid all locked in a great cosmic dance.

Her vision zoomed back to the surface of the Earth, as though she were laying on the ground, watching the stars zipping through the sky in their great procession. She looked towards her feet, and watched as a massive black stone obelisk emerged from the ground, stretching into the sky. She watched as the stars slowed and began to hold their place behind the obelisk. After a pause, it was as though the whole planet – the whole solar system – shifted into a new space, like clicking to the next setting on a dial. The stars shifted in the sky behind the great obelisk.

I see it, Tomi said. *The stars are changing. A new time is coming.*

This new time may bring transcendence for humans, said Ete. *The human experience is living a life of uncertainty about the soul, about what happens after death. Humans only get glimpses of it, and so you have many religions, and many ideas and beliefs, but no certainty. But you see, life on Earth would be very different if humans knew with certainty that their soul, their consciousness, would carry on. That there are other dimensions they may experience.*

I suppose it would be very different, said Tomi. She had never tried to imagine what life would be like if we no longer had or needed faith in life after death.

This is also why we could not make our presence truly known, said Ete. *Humans believe they are the smartest, most god-like creature in the universe. That has been the only experience for most humans. If we made true contact, humans would know that your species is not unique. Not the smartest or most advanced. It would be a fundamental change in your reality. Let me ask you, would a human still be a human with this knowledge?*

Tomi considered all of this. *A transcendent human, I suppose. What does that look like?*

With your help, we may find out, said Ete.

"Something is coming," said Tomi. "A change in the sky, a new age. A time of transcendence. For humans. We will learn about the others, all the other life, other realities. And the soul. Humanity will change. I will help."

Ib again gave a puzzled look to Kirsten. "How will you help, Tomi?"

What do you mean, with my help? asked Tomi.

I sense that the word transcendence *sounds pleasant to you,* said Ete. *Transcendence means* to climb to the beyond. *Imagine climbing a giant mountain, Tomi. It will be difficult. Many humans will resist this and will become hostile to change. It will be destabilizing. It will be chaotic. And this is just the human response to it. There are some other beings out there who will want to prevent this, keep humans as they are, isolated. It will be a whole new universe for humans.*

How am I to help? asked Tomi.

You know you came here to Earth for a reason, said Ete. *Let us show you something.*

The six beings rose from their stools, formed a circle, and joined hands. Kirsten could feel Tomi's hand tighten slightly in her own.

As they joined hands, they were immediately taken to another room. *But not a room,* thought Tomi, as she scanned up and down, from floor to ceiling. She could see they were underground still, though these walls looked very different, like different people made this place. These looked like rough-cut stone walls, as though massive hunks were chiselled off by giants. *And taken where?*

She continued scanning in wonder, at how deep this place must be to have ceilings so high, it was almost like looking up at the sky.

As she scanned down, she saw the capstone. A pyramid so massive, the capstone stretched high up to the sky. The outer walls of it were smooth, and looked almost seamless, the black stone seeming to almost shine.

"Oh my god," said Tomi. "I'm here on Earth to help in this transcendence, somehow. They took me someplace, underground again but the cavern is so huge, and there's the most enormous dark pyramid. There's no weathering, it looks like it was just built."

What is this place, asked Tomi. *It's incredible!*

It is incredible. But it's also complicated, Ete said, sending Tomi a feeling of urgency. *Tomi, there is much I need to show you still, but we will be interrupted momentarily, and before that happens, I must give you this instruction: find your grandmother.*

Tomi was confused. *What do you mean, find my grandmother? What interruption?*

Find your grandmother, Tomi. Tomi's vision of the pyramid, the cavern, the circle of beings, felt like it suddenly sped away out of view, and was replaced by darkness.

"Find my grandmother," Tomi said. "Ete said I need to find my grandmother."

"Your grandmother is dead," a male voice said, deeper than Ib's and farther away. *John.* Tomi's eyes shot open, she began to raise her head, then flopped back down, dizzy from the sudden start.

Ib jumped out of his chair, and took a step back, startled at the interruption, while Kirsten continued to hold Tomi's hand, and put her other hand on Tomi's forehead, easing her back on the couch.

"Transcendence? Underground pyramids? Tomi, what the fuck is this?" asked John. Tomi opened her eyes again, and turned her head on the pillow to look at him. His face was red and scrunched up. *Not angry,* she thought, *embarrassed. And deeply disturbed.*

"John," said Tomi, her voice weak and dry, "we were, well, it's hard to explain. I thought you would be home late today."

John stared at Tomi, as though he had stepped into another dimension and couldn't comprehend what he was experiencing. Finally, he gave his head a little shake, and looked at each of them. He looked down, as though the floor was grounding him. He held up his phone.

"I got a text from a blocked number," John said. "Telling me I needed to get home ASAP."

Chapter 8

"Quantum mechanics describes nature as absurd from the point of view of common sense. And yet it fully agrees with experiment. So I hope you can accept nature as She is - absurd."

Richard P. Feynman

"Tomi, really, what the fuck was that? I watched for maybe a minute, and it was completely insane," said John. They had moved into John's study. Tomi had asked Ib and Kirsten to leave, so she and John could talk.

"I know, I know it all sounds crazy," Tomi said. "I couldn't tell you about any of this because of the NDA. You understand that."

John looked at Tomi. She had seen many looks on his face, and had learned to read his emotions, barely noticeable with his stoic nature. But this look was new: pity. She could see that he felt pity for her, his wife having fallen into a state of delusion.

"Tomi, you don't work for PSI anymore," John said. "Whatever happened there, you have to understand that whatever you thought you experienced was bogus. None of it was real."

Tomi was starting to feel crushed. When surrounded by Ib, Kirsten, and Barry, she felt perfectly sane, perfectly rational, someone on the trail of some larger truth. She felt like she had a clarity she had lacked all her life.

But here was John, the man she had lived with and trusted for years, and it felt like that was all being peeled back. The look of concern and pity on his face made her feel dizzy, like the ground she was standing on was starting to wobble.

"Tomi," John said gently, "it's time to get some help. You need to say goodbye to PSI and these characters. This isn't healthy for you. It isn't healthy for us. Tomi, I want you to come with me to the hospital. It's time to get some help, and get you back to reality, don't you think?"

John stepped forward, took Tomi's hand, and held it between both of his, hers so much smaller, nestled like a stone in his grasp. Tomi looked up at him, her face suddenly looking perplexed.

"What do you mean I don't work at PSI anymore?" she asked. "How did you know that?"

"You told me," John said, with a shake of his head.

"No, I didn't," Tomi said, with growing certainty.

"See? You don't even remember," he said. "Come on, Tomi. Come with me and we'll get you some help. All of this is absolute nonsense, and it's time to get you looked after."

"I know you've never liked me having this job," Tomi started.

"It's not just the job, Tomi," John interrupted, before she could continue. "You've been talking in your sleep these last few months. All sorts of nonsense like this. Pyramids and islands and beings. Not to mention what it does to you, you come home and barely function for days."

Tomi paused, and looked down. She could not argue with that. Yet at the same time, she felt more alive than she ever had. She took a deep breath. She was so disoriented. The session had taken everything out of her, then the sudden interruption, and now being accused of being crazy and needing to be admitted to hospital. But Tomi knew she was right; she could feel it deep inside. A sudden determination welled up inside her. She wasn't crazy. She needed to keep going.

"I know it all sounds crazy, I know that," said Tomi. "But I promise you John, if you had the experiences I have, you'd understand. When you actually go down the rabbit hole as I have, when I started to investigate this stuff, well, now I feel like a right fucking idiot. Not because it's ridiculous or crazy, but because it's been there all along. This phenomenon. It's there all around us and we just pretend it isn't. I don't know, maybe Ancient Aliens fucked it for everyone."

John rolled his eyes back and started to interrupt, but Tomi put up her hand to say she wasn't done.

"It's there in history, it's there in religion. And folklore," she continued. "And so many UFO sightings and experiencers. And the billion shitty videos and pictures. I mean it's right there to the side of us, all the time, always has been. And I just don't know how to get on with normal life when I can see it now. And I don't want to. There's a whole other reality, another universe, right beside me and it's terrifying and wonderful and it suddenly feels more real than this desk."

She put her hand on his large wood desk for emphasis and stability. John just stared back, gathering his thoughts. Tomi's eyes were drawn to the picture on the wall, the one Ib had been so interested in. She pointed.

"Who is in that picture with you?" asked Tomi. John continued staring, catching up to this change in subject.

"What?" he asked, sounding exhausted by this conversation.

"That picture," Tomi pointed. "Who is in that picture with you?"

John turned his head to look at the picture. He turned back to Tomi.

"Tomi, are you ready to come to the hospital with me?" John asked plainly.

Tomi exhaled. "No. For the first time, it feels like I'm on the right path. And I'm not crazy."

John nodded silently. Tomi thought he was holding in tears, something she hadn't been able to do this whole conversation.

"I am going to go and work out of the DC office. They need me there, and I think I need that space. From this. From us," he said.

Tomi nodded, surprised to be feeling a sense of relief, an emotion she tried to keep hidden.

"Tomi, you call me when you're ready for help," John said kindly. Tomi nodded. John turned and walked towards the front door, grabbing his work bag and jacket.

"I'm sorry I wasn't the right path for you." The words stung like a bee, as John opened, then closed the door behind him.

She went up to her bedroom to watch his car pull out of the driveway, and off into the early evening. She then flopped face first onto her bed, her face squished into the pillow, muffling her cries.

A few minutes later, the doorbell rang, and her phone lit up with a text from Ib: "We are still here. Barry is on his way. You need to pack a bag."

Barry and Ib were sitting in the back corner of Rory's, martinis with one sip out of them. After what John had said about receiving a text telling him to check on his home, they knew Tomi's house wasn't safe. They started to assume PSI was being monitored as well. And likely their homes, too. Somehow this distant corner in Rory's Tavern seemed the most secure place for them to regroup.

They were waiting for Kirsten and Tomi to arrive, who they had left at Tomi's to pack a bag for a destination that had yet to be decided. They couldn't talk about it at her house, anyways.

Ib was scribbling thoughts into his notebook, hoping that the act of writing would somehow generate a plan forward. He was in it now. After going to Tomi, continuing to pursue this, he knew his time would be limited at PSI. It was only a matter of time before the board was informed. The Rubicon had been crossed.

Barry was staring deeply into his laptop. He was behind, unsure of all that had transpired in the session, so he immediately copied the recording over to his laptop, ran the auto transcription application, and was reading it over.

Finally, he took his eyes off the screen, sunk back into his chair, and flopped his head back, staring up at the ceiling.

"Well, you know who would be pissed off if the recording ever got out," Barry said, now looking at Ib, "absolutely fucking everyone."

He said the last three words slowly and with emphasis, then started to laugh. Ib smiled. "Yes, I suppose so," he said. "Perhaps a few religious leaders would disapprove."

Barry looked back at the screen. "Probably," he said. "Although doesn't it sort of affirm them, too?"

Ib nodded thoughtfully, then replied with a tone of sadness, "I suppose there's very little I can be certain about these days. I'm not sure I understand what Martians and UFOs have to do with souls and reincarnation."

"Yeah. I don't know." Barry considered this for a moment. "Do you know who Robert Bigelow is? Bob Bigelow?"

Ib shook his head.

"He's a billionaire," Barry said. "What you'd call an eccentric billionaire. He's used some of his money to set up organizations and studies about UFOs, as well as studies about consciousness and the afterlife. He's probably spent more money studying both than any other individual. When I first learned about him, I thought it was strange, these two interests together. Well, maybe he's on to something."

While Ib considered this, Barry looked back at the transcript on his screen.

"I suppose reading this over, and the previous sessions, you could also make a case for a simulation. That this whole thing, the reality we know, is a simulation. Maybe it really is the Matrix," Barry said, widening his eyes to show he was saying that at least partly in jest. "Or the prison planet hypothesis."

Ib tilted his head to one side. "I don't think I know that one."

"It's the idea that Earth is a prison. Or like a farm. And we are the cattle, or the playthings or slaves of one or more advanced alien species. I never liked that idea. But Ete has said there are more than one species of others. If that's true, who knows how many competing agendas there are."

Ib nodded. "If that's true. That's the key there, isn't it? I mean, what if we're wrong about remote viewing? Is it possible it's just something coming from Tomi's subconscious alone? Or Ete. Even if it's a real being, a real connection, how do we know what Ete is telling Tomi is true? Perhaps she's being deceived for some purpose."

Barry nodded along. "My intuition tells me that neither is the case. But also, both could be true. May be more likely to be true."

Barry paused and considered his words for a moment. "I think I'm going to put my trust in Tomi."

"You're right," Ib said, lifting his martini as though taking a drink sealed the deal. "I'm not sure I trust Ete. I definitely don't trust the General and his crew. But I'll put my trust in Tomi. And you."

"As your countryman said," replied Barry, "you just need a *leap of faith*."

Ib smiled. In his peripheral vision, he saw Tomi and Kirsten approaching the table, Kirsten pulling Tomi's rolling suitcase, and Tomi holding an old Florsheim shoebox with a ribbon wrapped around it and tied on top.

"The weirdest thing happened," said Tomi, as they sat down at the table, Tomi placed the shoebox on the table in front of her. "I opened up a small closet downstairs to get my suitcase, and as I opened the closet door, this box was hanging off the shelf inside the closet, and fell on my toes when I opened the door."

"Ouch," Ib said.

"No. Well yeah," Tomi said, "it did hurt, but what was weird is that this was my grandmother's box. It's got some of her old letters and cards and things. I took this from my mother's house when it was cleaned out, put it in that closet when we moved here, and haven't touched it since. And today it falls off the shelf. After Ete tells me to find my grandmother. How spooky is that?"

"So spooky," agreed Kirsten. "And clearly not a coincidence. I suggested she bring it in case it can give us any clues on what to do next."

"Spooky," agreed Barry, with a sombre tone. "And you're right, Kirsten. There is a difference between coincidence and synchronicity."

Tomi unlaced the ribbon around the shoebox and pulled off the lid. Inside was a jumble of old letters, postcards, a few old display spoons from different countries, and a tattered old copy of Timaeus.

Tomi pulled out some of the letters and spread them out on the table, then paused before picking one up. "I haven't looked at these," she said, in a confessional tone. "My grandmother died when I was young. And I never really got to say goodbye to her. I was really close to her. I've just never had the heart to actually look at this stuff."

"That's okay, whenever you're ready," said Kirsten. "Or we can look at them if you want."

Tomi nodded. Kirsten picked up the book, and started flipping through the pages to find any markings or writing. Ib and Barry both picked up an envelope. Barry started to lift open the flap, but stopped when he noticed the return and destination addresses on the envelope.

"Um, Tomi," said Barry, his tone causing the others to stop and listen, "this letter is sent by Ray Jarmark. And it's addressed to Esther Baptiste. Tomi, is Esther Baptiste your grandmother?"

Tomi nodded slowly, realizing that *of course* Barry would know about her grandmother. He wrote a book on remote viewing. *Of course he would have heard her name*, she thought.

Barry put the envelope down, put his hands to his face, and rubbed his eyes and forehead. When he stopped, he looked at Tomi and nodded. "Well this all makes a whole lot more sense."

"Well, I certainly know the name Ray Jarmark," said Ib, looking at an envelope. "I don't know as much about Esther, but you're right Barry, this does make more sense now. Tomi, why didn't you say anything?"

"I…I don't know," she said. "My mother taught me when I was young to not talk about my grandmother. She said it was because her work was top secret. But now that I'm saying it out loud, maybe my mom just didn't want me to talk about her because she was so…different."

"Well," said Ib, "this is remarkable."

"It sure is," agreed Barry.

"Okay, I'm out of the loop here," said Kirsten. "Who is Tomi's grandma?"

"And who is this Ray guy?" asked Tomi. "I don't know who he is or who he was to my grandma."

Barry gave Tomi a playful look and shook his head. "Tomi, I loaned you my book what, two months ago? You haven't read it, have you?"

"Oops, no, I forgot, I'm sorry Barry. I will read your book."

"No problem, I'm teasing," said Barry. He picked up the envelope again. "Many years ago, the American government set up Stargate Project, which was a funded study into remote viewing, with a particular focus on its military and espionage applications. The contractor on the project was the Stanford Research Institute, or SRI. Anyways, Ray Jarmark worked at SRI and was one of the mainstays of the project, and really one of the pioneers of remote viewing. He probably knows more about it than anyone."

He flipped over the envelope, pointing at the address block. "Esther Baptiste - Tomi's grandmother - well she was one of the remote viewers in the program. One of the psychic spies. From my research, she was one of the best, and was said to possess unique psychic abilities."

Kirsten looked at Tomi, at first seriously, then with a smile. "Okay, yes, that does make sense."

"Unfortunately, she didn't do it for that long, so we didn't get a lot of data on what she was capable of." Barry looked at Tomi. "You know, I'm glad that you didn't read the book, because I didn't warn you that the book covers the disappearance. That might have been triggering."

Tomi looked around the table, then back to Barry with a confused expression. "Disappearance? What disappearance?"

"Well, you know," said Barry. "Her disappearance. Sorry, maybe I shouldn't have brought it up, I imagine it's hard to talk about."

Tomi furrowed her eyebrows even more. "*Her* disappearance. You mean my grandmother?"

Barry nodded.

"I don't know what you mean," said Tomi, clearly struggling to understand his words.

Barry paused, looking Tomi in the eye to determine if she was being serious. He could see that she was. He spoke gently, in case he really was the first person to tell her.

"Tomi, your grandmother disappeared. She went missing and was never found," he said. "Just before the end of Stargate Project. You really didn't know that?"

Tomi looked to Ib, then Kirsten, seeing their faces both incredulous and solemn.

"No," said Tomi, shaking her head, "no, she died. When I was a kid."

Barry nodded. "She did. Well, she was eventually declared dead. But they never found her. The details are fuzzy, it was a long time ago I wrote that book, and I didn't get into detail about the case. But yeah, one day she didn't show up to SRI. They didn't think much of it, a couple of days go by, and they go to check on her. They realized she wasn't at home. Eventually the police were notified, and there just wasn't a trace of her. And eventually the case went cold. I'm so sorry Tomi, I just assumed you would have known that."

Tomi was trying to stretch her mind back to when she learned her grandmother had died, but couldn't produce the memory. She just remembered that she had.

"Oh my god. I feel so dumb right now. How could she not tell me?" Tomi looked to Kirsten, her eyes red and holding on to tears.

Kirsten reached across the table and took her hand. "She was my father's mother. My father died when I was really young, so of course he couldn't tell me. But why didn't my mother tell me the truth?"

"You were young," said Kirsten. "Maybe she was just trying to protect you. Maybe she thought if you knew she was missing you would be worried forever. Or run away and try to find her. She probably had her reasons, but I agree, it's shitty. I'm sorry you're learning in this way."

Tomi looked down at the table. This day had already been so exhausting, she wasn't sure she was able to begin processing this information. She finally said softly, "Guys, I'm just so tired. I'll want to know more one day, Barry. And don't feel badly. Thank you for telling me. But right now, I just need to know where I'm going, and I need some sleep."

"Yes, let's get you some rest," said Barry. "I've got a plan I'm forming. First off, give me your phones."

At first nobody moved, then realized he was serious. They took their phones out.

"Okay, I'm going to put the Signal app on your phones," said Barry. "Tomi, from now on, you send no texts, no emails, no phone calls. Ib, Kirsten, we only talk to Tomi, and we only talk to each other about this – situation - through this app. It's encrypted, so if they are tracking Tomi - which I'm sure they are - then it'll at least make it harder for them."

Everyone nodded in agreement that they understood.

"Kirsten, can Tomi stay with you for a day or two?" Barry asked. "I doubt they would be monitoring you Kirsten, but regardless I suggest speaking as little as possible, and not at all about, well, about any of this."

"Of course," said Kirsten, looking to Tomi and smiling to reassure her.

"Ib, over the next few days," said Barry, "you should keep going in to work. Keep up appearances, just act like everything is normal."

"Normal. Sure, what's not normal here?" Ib said with a laugh.

"And can you and Kirsten work out a safe location for Tomi?" Barry asked Ib. "Somewhere we can get her off the grid?"

Ib looked to Kirsten, nodded, and looked back to Barry. "Yes, we can do that. I already have an idea."

"Great," said Barry. "Finish your drinks, and Tomi, you get some rest. Take a day to rest and process. Tomorrow I'll get prepped, and I'll pick you up the next morning. Then we'll hit the road."

They all looked to Barry, waiting for him to say more, though he was distracted setting up their phones. Finally, Tomi asked, "Barry, where are we going?"

"Oh, well, you were told to find your grandmother. I don't think any of us know what that means or where to start," Barry said, picking up the envelope and showing it to Tomi. "So, you and I will head for Chicago. We're going to go find Ray Jarmark. Maybe he knows something that can help us."

Chapter 9

"But the day before he passed away, he wrote me a note: "This is all an elaborate hoax." I asked him, "What's a hoax?" And he was talking about this world, this place. He said it was all an illusion. I thought he was just confused. But he was not confused. He wasn't visiting heaven, not the way we think of heaven. He described it as a vastness that you can't even imagine. It was a place where the past, present, and future were happening all at once."

- Chaz Ebert, on the death of her husband

Her forehead resting against the window, Tomi closed her eyes, as watching the landscape whipping by was making her dizzy. Even if she weren't in this car travelling at highway speeds, instead sitting on a bench secured in concrete, she thought she would still be dizzy.

The past thirty-six hours had been a blur, and had thrown her whole life upside down. From waking up at home to hearing about the afterlife from Ete, from John wanting her committed to sleeping at Kirsten's to avoid being spied on, to being simply exhausted, Tomi felt disoriented on all levels. *Oh, and my grandmother didn't die as grandmothers do, but instead vanished 30 years ago,* she thought.

Tomi largely slept the previous day away, interrupted only when Kirsten tried to get her to eat. She had slept that dreamless, dark sleep, where when you wake up you feel like you had just closed your eyes. Instead of waking up to find that the previous days had just been a bad dream, she woke up to an encrypted message from Barry: *Be there in 15 mins. Wear a hat or hood. Go out the back to the laneway and don't look around.*

Right, she thought, *I need to sneak out. Because this is my life now.*

They had been travelling for some time, though Tomi wasn't sure how long, feeling so disoriented. She appreciated that Barry had let her rest while he drove, the drive quiet except for the sound of the vehicle, and the album *Nebraska* playing on a loop in the car's cassette player.

The car hit a small pothole in the road, bumping Tomi's head against the passenger window. Her eyes shot open in time to see the sign telling them they were entering West Virginia.

Tomi lifted her head and started to take in her surroundings, the car, Barry, and the overcast skies. Although she had been out of bed for several hours, she felt like she'd just woken up. She heard *Atlantic City* start playing again - third time? she thought - and looked at the tape deck in the console, an anachronism in 2023.

"What kind of car is this?" Tomi asked, realizing they were driving in an older vehicle she didn't recognize. Though they had been silent all this time, Barry answered as though they'd been chatting throughout.

"This, young Tomi, is a 1987 Saab 900 SPG Turbo, one of the finest vehicles to ever come out of Scandinavia," he said. "Now you would think that Ib would appreciate a classic Scandinavian vehicle, but apparently the Danes and Swedes have a bit of a rivalry."

Tomi saw Barry smile a little. She got a kick out of how serious he typically was, but then small things he was passionate about brought out a hidden childlike enthusiasm. She rubbed her fingers along some of the wood trim.

"I've had this car for years, actually," said Barry, "but I don't drive it often. I have it registered to my mother, so I thought it might be a bit harder to track us. You know, if anyone were trying to."

"Well, it's a cool car, Barry," said Tomi. "Don't you drive a Tesla?"

Barry gave her a quick sideways glance. "You just assume I drive a Tesla because you think I'm an old yuppie type who thinks I'll save the world by driving a hundred-thousand-dollar box of steel and plastic."

"Oh, um, no, I don't know much about cars, I-"

"I'm joking," interrupted Barry, smiling. "I do drive a Tesla, because I am an old yuppie. Though I'm quite aware I'm not saving the world with it. But, I live in a country that was built for the profits of the car and gas companies, and that's about as close as I get to sticking it to them, I guess."

"You've got them there," said Tomi with a laugh, suddenly feeling a little lighter and normal just sharing a chat with a friend.

"And I may just be a sucker for the name. Tesla is such a fascinating figure. You know," Barry said, tilting his head back slightly, which Tomi had learned meant he was going to get a little reflective or philosophical, "we go along in a direction, as a society, a technological and developmental direction, and when we look back, we assume it had been inevitable. Had to be this way. Of course we would invent the internal combustion engine, and of course we built the world around petrochemicals, right? We rarely think about what the world would look like if we had gone in another direction. Tesla is an example of where it really could have gone very differently."

"I don't know much about him," said Tomi. "He's the Tesla Coil guy, I assume?"

"That's right," said Barry. "He imagined a world with free wireless energy. Where you would send energy into the atmosphere for everyone to collect. Well, you can imagine what they did to him. No wires no copper, no copper no mining and processing, no money. So they destroyed him. And his ideas."

"The world sure can be pretty hostile to new or different ideas," said Tomi.

"And you, Tomi, you get to find that out firsthand, I'm afraid." Barry gave her a playful look. "Want to hear a cool theory? There's a theory that the great pyramids of Giza were actually power plants. Basically, there are these deep chambers that get filled up with water, and the water vibrates the granite pyramid, creating electromagnetic energy. And then the pyramid would act like a giant Tesla coil. I don't know if this is true, but it's a fun theory. It is true that they vibrate, they have a resonance. They're musical."

As he said this, she could suddenly see the pyramid - the dark, underground pyramid Ete showed her - vibrating. Singing. She thought about the walls in Ete's home and how they almost glowed.

Tomi sighed, knowing how rare these moments of levity were becoming before her mind would be consumed by whatever it was that was happening to her.

"Sorry about the music," said Barry. "I didn't really have time to plan a full setlist, and so this is the only tape that was in the car. I mean, if it's the only tape in the car, you could do worse than *Nebraska*."

Tomi smiled. "Barry, thank you for this. Risking yourself, driving across the country with me. Believing in me. I really can't thank you enough."

"Hey," said Barry, giving a kind glance and looking back at the road, "don't worry about it. I've studied this stuff for so many years, and now I'm finally experiencing it. Through you. Really, I'm in awe of you, Tomi. Being around you, and what you can do, well it's a bit like finding out that magic is real. That this," he knocked on the glass, then the dashboard, "this reality, well it's a fraud. A hoax. That everything we think we understand, we don't."

He paused for a moment, quietly steering through a curve in the road.

"And somehow," he finished, "it seems to make it all more worth living." He looked to Tomi again, who nodded quietly, tears welling up in her eyes.

"Somehow it does," Tomi said. "Like you're living for the long term now. Not next year, or when you're seventy."

"Yes. And think about all the things we'll get to see, how much more we'll understand. All the lessons I'll bring to some future life where I'm some reptilian being living in Zeta Reticuli," Barry said with a laugh.

Tomi smiled, then yawned, and they went back to travelling in silence. Tomi watched West Virginia go by in a blur, trying to get her mind to rest by focusing on the music coming through the tape deck.

Tonight down here in the valley, I'm lonesome and oh how I feel, As I sit here alone in my cabin, I can see your mansion on the hill.

Tomi stared out the window and began to daydream that she was in a cabin. Kirsten was there. A vision of them tucked away in a forest flowed through her mind. She could see herself outside at night, for some purpose. She saw a child, a little girl. Tomi shook the images out of her mind, feeling a little freaked out that it felt more like a memory than a daydream.

She focused out the window again, watching more forest go by. Suddenly she felt her heart jump, as she swore she saw a person, a dark figure, standing between two trees. *It went by so fast, it could have been anything*, she told herself. *And so what if a person was standing in a forest? People hike.*

She pulled a sweater out of her backpack on the floor of the car by her feet, bundled it up into a pillow, and rested her head on it. *I need to sleep for a week*, she thought.

Tomi felt the car come to a stop, and the engine turn off. She opened her eyes and lifted her head, surprised to see that the sun was shining bright. They were in a parking lot.

"Where are we?" Tomi asked groggily.

"Come on," Barry said, "time to use the washroom and stretch our legs."

She got out, seeing that they were in a parking lot of what looked like some kind of park or greenspace. She saw the washrooms, and her body reacted with a sudden urge now that the opportunity presented itself.

"Meet you outside the washroom!" she said to Barry, racing to make it in time.

When she stepped out of the women's washroom and saw Barry wasn't there, she started to look around, and realized she had raced right past a park map on a big wooden board. At the top, it read, *Serpent Mound State Memorial.*

"Better?" asked Barry. Tomi turned to see him wiping wet hands on his pants.

"Much," she said, realizing getting out of the car, getting to the washroom, and feeling the sun on her face had helped. "What is this place? And is it safe to be walking around, out in the open?"

Barry started walking towards the path to the entrance of the site, and Tomi joined him. "Well we need to stop sometime. We actually stopped for gas when you were sleeping. I thought about waking you, but, anyways, if we are being followed, there's nothing we can do about it. And I wouldn't think they would engage in a public place like this. Besides, if they wanted to take you in, they would have by now. My guess is they want to watch you and see what they can learn first."

Tomi was feeling lighter from Barry's reasoning, until the last sentence. The thought of being observed, or of being snatched up when they want, was unsettling. And realizing these were considerations not for some character in a book or a movie, but for her, Tomi, who up until recently thought her life was pretty ordinary.

"Anyways, this place wasn't far off our route, and I've always wanted to see this. It's the largest serpent effigy in the world. I mean huge, like over a thousand feet long, just built into the ground."

They came to a copper-coloured Ohio historical plaque.

"*Built on a spur of rock overlooking the Ohio Brush Creek around 1000 A.D. by the Fort ancient culture,*" read Tomi. "Wow, it's over a thousand years old!"

They continued down the path. "There's actually debate about how old it is and who built it. One study found it was 2300 years old and built by an even older indigenous culture. But regardless of who built it," Barry said, as they entered an open expanse of grass, parts of it mounded up into a continuous line, forming the body of the serpent, "the question I have is *why.*"

Tomi couldn't believe how big it was, how long the body of the serpent extended. She found it hard to make out the shape of the serpent from the ground, with the body curling and twirling.

"I had no idea something like this was here," said Tomi. "I've never seen anything like it. It's just remarkable." She stooped down to press her hand onto the earthen mound.

"All over the world," Barry said, "ancient people built the most incredible buildings and temples and effigies. Stonehenge, the pyramids, Gunung Padong, Nan Madol, Easter Island, Machu Picchu-"

"The Serpent Mound," Tomi said, her eyes closed as she rested her hand against the ground, feeling energized.

"The Serpent Mound," repeated Barry. "You know there's another one in Canada, and it's over 2000 years old. Mounds and megaliths. All over the world. Always mysterious. And some of them just seem so miraculous."

"They sure do," Tomi said, standing. "And you're right, we always ask how they did it, and when. Not much on why. Oh, like the Nazca lines that you can only see from the air. Why?"

"Speaking of which," Barry said, pointing, "let's go climb the observation tower so we can see this from the air."

They headed towards a metal framed structure, and climbed a tall set of metal stairs, then a second smaller set to get to the top platform. From there, they found a much wider view of the body of the serpent and the spiralling tail.

Barry took a deep breath, scanned the scene in front of him, and exhaled slowly. He stopped scanning when he saw something from a nearby treeline. A flash, like a reflection off glass. He wasn't sure, but he was sure that he saw a figure in the trees, wearing what looked like a dark suit with a black overcoat.

He blinked hard as he was unsure what he was seeing, and when he refocused, the figure was gone.

"This is just amazing," Tomi said, "I mean it's powerful from the ground, but you need to be up high to really take it in. Why make something that can only be seen from the sky way before we could fly? I suppose maybe creating it for god?"

Tomi turned to look at Barry, who was looking away from the great serpent, scanning trees.

"Everything okay?" Tomi asked.

"Yeah, everything is fine," Barry said, giving one last look around, seeing a few other sightseers, but not the dark figure. "I think it's time to go."

They descended the stairs and followed the path back to the vehicle. Barry decided not to mention the dark figure he saw, being uncertain of what he really saw in the first place. *Besides*, he reassured himself, *if they actually wanted to take her in, they would.*

Barry steered the Saab back onto the highway, and they continued on.

"When will we get there?" Tomi asked, watching the sun heading down below the treetops.

"It's going to be midnight or a bit later when we arrive," said Barry, pulling the sun blind down to block the bright, setting sun.

Tomi felt confused, realizing they were most of a day into this trip and she didn't actually know the plan. "What are we going to do when we get there? We can't just knock on his door in the middle of the night, right?"

"It's okay," said Barry, "he's expecting us. I called him yesterday. I met Ray before, years ago. I interviewed him for my book. I mean he barely remembered me when I called, but when I explained I was bringing Esther Baptiste's granddaughter to meet him, he didn't hesitate. I also told him our visit required absolute discretion, and so he's prepared for that, too."

"Oh, that's great, thanks Barry," said Tomi. She had put a few of her grandmother's letters in her bag, and pulled one out to read, realizing the setting sun would shortly make that difficult.

She found them hard to follow, as she didn't have the reply letters to give them context. Their relationship seemed to be friendly and professional, and mostly about sharing novel ideas. There was one letter she found most interesting, even if she didn't fully understand it.

Dear Esther,

By the time you return to SRI from your trip, I will be away for a conference and some travelling, so it may be some time until we cross paths.

First, I hope you found whatever it is you were looking for and are able to settle whatever it is that has been competing for your attention.

Second, I read over the transcript of your latest celestial journey. It was interesting to see the similarities with Ingo's viewing of the dark side of the moon, but what most interested me was the difference in your interpretation of their intent. When I return, I hope to hear more about how you came to the conclusion you did.

Next, as you know, I am always on the lookout for ideas and theories that might explain what our research is telling us, since our current science only recognizes reality as that which can be measured. Weighed, measured, or counted. When I return, I want to tell you about Susskind's Holographic Universe theory. Basically, the universe is actually 2D, just information, and we experience it as a projection, as a 3D hologram. How does that resonate with you?

You and I know how limiting human perception can be. Most people proceed through life without ever recognizing this

information field that we are uncovering. Of
course, we are just the latest in a long
line of humans who have understood it, from
shamans to buddhas to prophets to artists.

Yours,

Ray

Tomi folded the letter back up, put it in the envelope, and put it back in her bag. She stared out at the horizon, the sun no longer shining bright, and dusk creeping up on them. *What was it that she was looking for?* Tomi wondered. *And where had she gone?*

She was still digesting the news that her grandmother had gone missing. *All those years I could have done something, researched, tried to find some clues*, she thought, feeling a deep-down rage that her mother had kept this from her.

"Barry, how long did the search go on for my grandmother?" Tomi asked.

Barry tilted his head to one side, considering the question. "Officially, not too long, as I understand. I mean the case was open, but the San Francisco police kind of ran out of ideas. They interviewed everyone around her, but really didn't get any leads." After a pause, while he did a lane change to pass a slow driver, he continued. "Now, unofficially, I think the people at SRI continued to try to get answers, traded theories, and tried to figure it out in the background, but I don't think they ever got much further."

Where could she have gone? Tomi wondered. *And why would Ete tell me to find her? Even if she hadn't died when she went missing, she would be nearly eighty now.*

"I just wish I had known what really happened before," she said. "Like, I feel like maybe I could have done something, researched and tried to solve it. Tried to find her."

"Don't feel guilty about it," Barry said. "It does no good, and it was all beyond your control."

Tomi nodded, knowing she will need to remind herself of that again and again.

"I uh, I heard things weren't left well between you and John," said Barry. "I'm sorry about that. But you know, if you do reconcile in the future, perhaps he could help you. You know we've worked with his company as PSI. Well of course you know that, that's how we met you. But his company, they are very integrated with the Intelligence Community."

Tomi's mouth opened slightly, as she looked at the profile of Barry's face, while he looked forward at the road. This hadn't clicked for her yet. Of course John might have access to files, anything classified around SRI, or her disappearance. She wondered if he would help her.

"I mean very, very integrated," continued Barry. "They have access to a lot of secrets."

Tomi looked forward at the road. John could always say so little about a lot of his work, she never thought of him being so connected that way. She thought back to how naive she had been, thinking that she had broken some security rule by telling him her grandmother had been part of Stargate Project, when it turns out he probably could have access to that information, and so much more. She wondered what all he could have known.

"Do you think John knew that she went missing?" Tomi asked, thinking out loud. Barry didn't respond and kept his focus on the road.

They drove in the dark for several hours, the highway lights illuminating the road, but drowning out the stars above. She wasn't sure when, but at some point on the drive Tomi fell asleep again, until she was awakened by Barry.

"Tomi. Tomi, it's time to wake up. We're here."

She opened her eyes to find that they were parked along a city street, the streetlights illuminating low-rise apartments to one side, and a brick-clad pub on the other.

"This is where he lives?" Tomi asked, looking at the beautiful brick apartments with a vertical row of bay windows.

"No, he lives a few blocks away. I didn't want to park the car in front of where he lives. Come on, grab your bag," said Barry, opening the car door.

Barry looked at the map on his phone to get his bearings, and they walked several blocks down city streets with bushy, mature trees covering the sidewalks, each building unique and charming.

"These buildings are so beautiful," Tomi said.

"Old Town Chicago. A city known for its architecture. Here," Barry said, pointing across the street at a red brick three-story home with brown framed windows. "It's this one."

They paused and scanned around before crossing and approaching the house. They saw no one, walked up the eight concrete steps to the front door, and rang the doorbell. Barry turned around again, but didn't see anything suspicious.

The door opened, and they were greeted by a smaller, older man with thick round glasses and a kind smile. He welcomed them in and closed the door.

"Come in, come in. So, you are Esther's granddaughter. You know I met you once at your grandmother's house when you were little. You probably don't remember, but your grandmother was a good friend." Ray turned to look at Barry, and extended his hand. "Mr. Class, it is nice to see you again."

"Thank you for letting us come here," said Tomi, feeling relieved that he seemed kind and welcoming.

"Anything for Esther's granddaughter," said Ray. "Now, I am dying to find out why you are both suddenly arriving at my doorstep, but you must be tired from your trip. And I'm tired because it's the middle of the night. I'll show you to the guest rooms, we can all get some sleep, and start trading stories in the morning."

"I won't argue with that, and I'm so sorry we've kept you up so late," said Barry.

"Don't worry about it," said Ray, leading them up the stairs. "Now let's get some rest. Tomorrow, we get to work."

Chapter 10

"In our universe, we are tuned into the frequency that corresponds to physical reality. But there are an infinite number of parallel realities coexisting with us in the same room, although we cannot tune into them."

Steven Weinberg

Although she slept, it was unrestful, a night with a repeating dream, a dream that was more of a location than one with a plot. She saw large, empty, bland rooms, like an old office from the 1980s with the cubicles and chairs removed. The smell of moist, mouldy carpeting, the buzz of fluorescent lights.

Tomi opened her eyes, the buzz still in her ears, to see the sun streaming through a gap in the curtain. She looked around the room to see an unfamiliar bedroom set in front of dark red walls. She took a few moments to place herself: *I'm in Chicago, I'm in Ray Jarmark's house. Barry is here. John wants me committed, and he left. My grandma is missing. I might be in danger.*

Tomi got up, pulled a set of pants and a top from her bag, rolled on some deodorant, and got changed. As she opened the door to her room, she could hear that Ray and Barry were up, and talking downstairs. She was up on the third floor, and descended two flights to find them sitting in the kitchen drinking coffee.

"Good morning," they both said as she entered.

"I hope you slept well," said Ray. "There's some bread over there and a toaster, if you'd like something to eat. And there's coffee here for you as well. Your friend Barry was just starting to fill me in on your story. I have so many questions for you. But my guess is that your first priority is to ask me about your grandma. Esther. So why don't we start there?"

"Esther was a friend," Ray said. "She was an intuitive. She would joke that she was a good witch, though I'm not sure it was always a joke."

"How did you first meet her?" asked Tomi.

"I first met your grandma at a sort of spiritual conference in San Francisco, where she was living. I was immediately impressed by her insights, and the way she would connect one esoteric idea to another. It was as though she had a unique view of the universe, like her peripheral vision was wider." Ray raised one finger from each hand and held them up just outside of his peripheral.

"Does that sound familiar?" said Barry, looking at Tomi.

"It does. I realize I know so little about her," said Tomi, wishing she'd had more of the days she had spent with her. "How did she come to be this way?"

"That's a good question," said Ray. "Well, you probably know that she grew up in a devout Southern Baptist family. I think that was the basis of her faith, but it was never a seal on her faith. It didn't stop with the Baptist Church, it just kept growing, the more she learned and experienced. She didn't see other faiths or ideas as in competition with each other. She could see how they all fit together, found them all speaking the same truths. I mean, she was the kind of person who could have Jehovah's Witnesses show up at her door, and they would leave questioning everything," he said with a laugh.

Tomi smiled at the image. "Do you know anything about my grandfather? I really don't know much about him."

Ray nodded. "I guess you probably wouldn't. I'm afraid I don't know much either. I'm not sure if they had separated or if he had died by the time I met her. I do know that they were an interracial couple, which of course was harder and rarer back then. By the time I met Esther, your father had already passed on. You were so young. That must have been so hard for you, Tomi."

She nodded. Her father's face came into her mind, an image she wasn't sure was a memory, or if it came from an old photo.

"After I met Esther at that conference, I invited her to come to the Stanford Research Institute to try remote viewing. We did just a simple experiment to see if she could locate a member of our team, and well, the results were just remarkable," Ray said. "She was a natural."

"Like grandmother, like granddaughter," Barry said.

"Once we got her trained and part of the team, she had some real breakthrough sessions. There were a few times when Esther didn't just see things in some far-off location, but she seemed almost physically present. Even interacting with, and communicating with other beings."

"Hmm, that's not typical?" asked Tomi.

"Not typical, but possible. That's what we would call an eight-martini session," said Ray.

Barry and Tomi smiled at each other.

"We've had a few of those," said Tomi. "I have a letter from you to my grandmother, and you mentioned remote viewing the dark side of the moon."

"Yes," said Ray. "We did that one a few times with different remote viewers. Ingo Swann did it, and he found a lot of activity. Alien bases on the moon. He was spotted by them, by the extraterrestrials, and came away feeling that they had malicious intentions."

"You said my grandmother had a different conclusion?" Tomi asked.

"She did," said Ray. "She also saw these bases and activity, and also connected with a being there. She said they did have plans for humanity, they are interfering in some way, but she felt their intentions were good. Of course, Esther saw the good in everyone."

Tomi sat with that comment for a moment, wondering if she had walked through life as charitable with others as her grandmother had been. She was also amazed by the parallels between her and her grandmother's experiences. *What would her grandmother say about all of this?* she wondered.

"I remote viewed Mars," said Tomi. "And I connected with a being there."

"Oh, that old one!" said Ray. "Your grandmother did an investigation of Mars, too. But not present day, if I recall correctly, it was well in the past."

"One million years in the past," said Barry.

"Yes! She did that exact one," said Ray. "I remember it. She saw pyramids and megaliths. An obelisk. I don't recall her connecting with beings, but I remember her doing it and having an incredible session. The Air Force contracted that one. Or was it the CIA? It's a long time ago."

"It was the Air Force," said Barry, shaking his head, realizing it had been done before.

"How about that," said Ray. "They go to the same target, what, thirty years later? Makes you wonder what information they have that would make them do it again."

"Or what information they want, and still don't have," said Tomi.

Barry nodded. His voice got softer. "They were very interested in finding out how the beings operated their craft. Their spacecrafts. Our assumption is that they have one, or have multiple, but don't know how to operate them. To make them fly."

"That's what I was told, by the being," said Tomi.

"I mean it sounds outrageous, but it also makes the most sense," said Ray. "If they tried to find out thirty years ago, it makes you wonder how long they've had the craft. How wild."

The conversation came to a pause as they considered this. Ray poured himself more coffee.

"Ray," started Tomi, feeling her eyes starting to well with tears, "can you tell me about her disappearance? What happened to her?"

Ray took a deep breath, adjusting his thick glasses. "I don't know what happened, kid. It was like one day she just walked off the face of the Earth. We had missed each other at SRI for a while. I was away, she was away, and I was away again. While I was away, she was supposed to return but didn't. At SRI they thought maybe her trip got extended. After a few days, they went to check her apartment. Her luggage was there, so she had returned home from her trip. But *she* wasn't there. None of the neighbours had seen anything suspicious. She was declared missing, there were lots of us putting up posters, asking neighbours, that sort of thing. But we didn't have a clue where to search, really. And we didn't have any leads."

Tomi sniffed and wiped a tear, thinking about all these people out looking for her. *And I had no idea*, she thought. *I did nothing.*

"So, what happened?" she asked. "Everyone just gave up?"

"Well, eventually, yah," said Ray. "Technically the police didn't give up, the case was still open, but without new leads, the search hit a wall. Some of us continued to pursue it in the background, but eventually without anything new, well, people eventually just moved on."

"And she just disappeared," said Tomi. "How can that happen, without a trace?"

"Do you know how many people disappear, even today?" asked Ray. "Last I looked - and I look, because like you Tomi, I don't understand how in this modern world, someone can just disappear - over six hundred thousand people are declared missing each year, just in the US. Of course, most eventually return. Some turn up deceased after a body is eventually found. But around one percent are never found. That's around six thousand people a year in this country who disappear without a trace. They're Schrödinger's cat, not alive or dead. So where are they?"

Tomi and Barry both exhaled deeply, imagining that number of people vanishing.

"I mean think about that," continued Ray, "in the thirty years since your grandmother, you could populate a small city with Americans who have just vanished."

"It's terrifying," said Barry.

"Did anyone have theories about what happened to her?" asked Tomi.

"Sure," said Ray. "There was no shortage of theories. The Russians of course was a popular one. They were doing the same research, maybe more of it. So maybe they knew about your grandmother's abilities and didn't want us to have access to them. Or maybe they wanted her for themselves. I mean we were all spied on by the Soviets back during the Cold War, but this theory made no sense to me. After the Wall fell, I just don't see it."

"Domestic?" asked Barry.

"Yes, of course," said Ray. "Again, lots of theories. The CIA for whatever reason took her out. Or maybe took her in. There were some theories back then that you could use remote viewing for assassinations. If the remote viewer was gifted enough, the belief was that they could stop hearts. Again, that was a theory back then, and maybe some group wanted that ability for themselves and kidnapped her."

"I don't think she would ever do that, kill someone, no matter what they did to her," said Tomi.

"I agree," said Ray. "And then of course there were more exotic theories. Abducted by aliens, of course. In some of the spiritual circles she was in, they thought she had transcended material reality. Me? I just don't know, Tomi. I wish I did."

"You said that she had been away," Tomi said. "In your letter, you said she had gone to find something. Where did she go? What was she looking for?"

"I don't know where she went. She told me she was looking for something. She said something big, and that she would tell me when she returned," said Ray, his face looking forlorn.

"Do you have any idea what it was, this big thing? What she was on to?" asked Tomi.

Ray took a moment to consider his answer. "I think it will be easier to show you," he said.

Tomi and Barry followed Ray up the stairs, Tomi noticing the beautiful wood banister for the first time in the light of day, and the creaking of the wood stairs under her feet.

They entered Ray's bedroom, where he approached a big antique dresser. He opened the second drawer, pulled the whole drawer out, and placed it on his bed. He pulled out paired-up socks, placing them to the side. Then he felt the bottom of the drawer slowly, and the drawer bottom sprung open. Tomi could see several envelopes. Ray flipped through them, finding one marked "Buoy" in blue pen. He pulled the envelope out, dropped to his knees on the floor, and placed the envelope on the bed.

Tomi thought he almost looked like a boy at his bed about to say his evening prayers. She dropped down beside him to get a closer look, while Barry stood behind them, looking down.

Out of the envelope, Ray pulled some napkins. He unfolded them, revealing a faded drawing done with a ballpoint pen.

"We were having some drinks in a dive she loved," Ray said, turning his head to speak to Tomi, the napkins still folded in his hands. "Of course, I didn't know it, but it was the last time I would see her. It wasn't too long after that session, the investigation of Mars, and she told me that in her own time she had done more, that she had learned so much more. That she felt she was on to something. I don't know if she was RVing on her own or with someone assisting her, I didn't think to ask, but boy do I wish I had."

Ray looked back to the napkins, wearing regret on his face.

"So of course I asked her what it was she saw, what had she learned?" Ray continued. "She was a bit coy, which wasn't her style. She was usually so open, unless she couldn't say something, and then she would just say so. Instead, she sort of laughed and said oh it's too hard to explain. But that laugh, it wasn't lighthearted. I realized that she hadn't seemed quite herself, like she was carrying something heavy. Whatever it was, it was eating at her. So I asked again, I pleaded a little bit, come on, you have to give me something. It wasn't just curiosity. I felt a bit worried about her."

Ray fiddled with the napkins, unfolding them in his hands to reveal the first drawing.

"Eventually she said okay. She pulled a pen from her purse, pulled these napkins from the napkin holder on the table, and drew this," Russel said.

Tomi focused on the drawing, and saw that it was a landscape. It looked like towers, but bulging at the top, shaped almost like mushrooms. There were faint circular pen marks. On the right side of the drawing was a circle, but the pen wasn't faint there. This was emphasized. In the middle of the circle, she wrote *Entrance*.

As though Esther had spoken, Ray nodded to the silence. "The moon. The backside."

Ray put the napkin to the side to reveal the second drawing. On this one, there was a horizontal line, with what Tomi thought were some mountains, and hastily drawn trees, a vertical stick with a few inverted v's for foliage. Under the horizontal line was a wavy line, and in between some pen squiggles. *Dirt. Ground,* Tomi thought.

Below the ground, Tomi saw a large circle, the curved line not perfectly straight, but a bit wavy. Instead of continuing to curve, there was a razor-straight line at the bottom. That straight line was the base of a pyramid.

"Your grandma wasn't a great drawer," Ray said with a little smile, "at least after a few drinks and pen on napkin as a medium. But it appears to be a pyramid, to me.

"Look at those wavy lines coming from it," said Barry. "What is that do you think?"

Ray shook his head. "I'm not sure."

"Vibration," Tomi said. "Harmonics. Sound."

Ray looked at Tomi, and nodded, seeing that this picture wasn't a surprise to her. Tomi looked back at the napkin, and her breath halted for a moment.

Tomi had been so focused on the pyramid, she missed the face. To the right of the circle, her grandmother had drawn a face, an upside-down egg-shaped head, with big dark eyes. Her grandma had thoroughly filled in the eyes, and marked two small lines for a nose, and a small slit mouth. Beside it, she had written *short greys.*

Ray looked back to Tomi. "She didn't say where."

He placed it on top of the first napkin, revealing the last napkin drawing. This time it wasn't a picture of a place. It simply had several long horizontal lines, distinct and evenly spaced, starting from the edge of the napkin. After about an inch of straight line, those evenly spaced lines started to get wavy, then spiralled, until they all started to intersect.

Under each line, where they were still evenly spaced, she wrote the word *reality*. Eight times, *reality*, one for each line.

"She handed me these, and she said *that's all I'm going to say about it until I get back*. Soon after we called it a night, I went back to Chicago for a time, she went wherever she did, and that was it. I never saw or heard from her again."

Ray placed the napkins back into the envelope, stood up, and handed them to Tomi. "Something tells me that you will need these more than me," he said.

She looked at the envelope. "Why does it say *Buoy* on the envelope?"

Ray smiled. "It was the codename for the Mars remote viewing mission. I don't know why, but I labelled it that when I put the drawings in there."

"Ray," Tomi said, "in my Mars mission, I met a being. A being who I have met again in subsequent sessions. This being told me that I need to find my grandmother. That's what led us to you. Do you have any idea what this means? How I can do that?"

Ray paused to consider this. "I don't know what that means. Or how to find her. So, I suggest we see if we can call up this being - this Ete, as Barry told me this morning - and see if we can get some clarity. Shall we?"

Chapter 11

"My brain is only a receiver, in the Universe there is a core from which we obtain knowledge, strength and inspiration. I have not penetrated into the secrets of this core, but I know that it exists."

Nikola Tesla

"Okay Tomi, I'm placing this sealed envelope here on the table beside you. Now that you're in a deep state of relaxation, I want you to focus your mind on the contents of that envelope," said Ray.

They had eaten lunch, let Tomi relax for a while, then headed all the way up to the attic, where Ray had a plain sitting and meditation room. Barry sat in a chair in the corner, having asked Ray to be the monitor for the session.

"Please, I want you to run the session," Barry had said. "Otherwise it would feel like I'm trying to paint a picture with Michelangelo watching over my shoulder."

Ray humbly agreed, and they decided to use an envelope that Tomi had used previously to connect with Ete. While this wasn't ideal, they decided that if they didn't tell Tomi which session it was from, it would be less likely that she would rely on her memories, rather than her current perceptions.

"Now, I'm going to give you a set of coordinates, and I want you to open your mind to that location," Ray said. "Using the instructions from the envelope, I want you to navigate to these coordinates: 63.6200 degrees north, 146.7161 degrees west. I'm going to give you a few moments. Let the shapes, colours, and patterns flow into your mind, and when you are ready, please report back what you are perceiving."

Tomi was quiet for a few moments, every once in a while scrunching up her face in confusion or frustration, at times moving her head slightly as though she were looking around with her eyes closed.

"It's…confusing," said Tomi finally.

"You don't have to understand it," reminded Ray, "just look for the raw data."

"Okay…I'm seeing a room. Yellow. Yellow walls, but a pale yellow. It's a bit hard as there isn't much to look at. Four yellow walls. No windows. The carpet is grey, industrial carpet. Like an office."

"Okay, is there anything of interest in this room?" asked Russel.

After a moment, Tomi said: "There's a door to my right."

"Great," said Ray. "Can you travel through that door?"

"Yes, I can," said Tomi. After a few moments, she continued. "It's another room. It's longer, like a shoebox shape. It's like another office. Again, it's empty. It's pink, kind of a worn down, dull pink. Same carpet. And there's another door."

"Okay, can you sense any other beings, any other intelligence, either in this room or the adjoining rooms?"

Tomi waited for a feeling. "No. I don't sense anyone. Anything. It feels lifeless."

"How do you feel in this place," asked Ray. "Do you get a sense of what the purpose of it is?"

"I don't...I don't feel good. It feels stressful here. Almost like I'm trapped. It's...I don't know what the purpose is, exactly. It feels purposeless. Like it's meant to have no purpose. I don't understand, that's just the feeling I get."

"I understand," said Ray. "Why don't you try the next door."

"Yes...it's beige," Tomi said, with a touch of distaste in her voice. "This one has a green carpet, it's worn down. This room is L shaped. Wait, there's a flashing. Something..."

"Can you find the source of the flashing," asked Ray, his voice a little more upbeat that they may have found something.

"It's...like a fluorescent light. You know how they go off and on when it's burning out? It's like that."

"Hmm, okay," said Ray. "Does this room have another door?"

"It has two on the far wall," Tomi said.

"Okay, try to sense which one is drawing you in, and go through it," instructed Ray.

Cream. Another beige. Another that was a light blue with a grey hue.

"Okay, I'm starting to think this series of rooms goes on forever," said Ray after the seventh room. "Let's try something different. Let your mind ease back just slightly and leave this place. Clear your mind." Ray gave Tomi a few minutes to get recentred. "When you are ready, I want you to navigate to the time and place where you first met Ete."

"Okay, I'm getting a colour first. It's like a pale orange." Tomi sighed. "It's another room. This one has a window, there are those vinyl, plastic sort of Venetian blinds. They're closed. Let me see if I can pull them up. What the? There isn't actually a window behind them. Just a wall. This place is so weird."

"Okay, please leave this place and get centred again," said Ray. He took his glasses off and rubbed his eyes, then pulled out his phone and looked up coordinates. "I want you to clear your mind of the envelope. We aren't using it anymore. Instead, I want you to navigate to 43.078765 degrees north, 79.078456 degrees west."

"It's…okay, it's loud. That's my first sense, it's a roar. A steady roar. I'm outside. It's, kind of hard to see. It's smoky. No, it's misty. There's a lot of water in the air, splashing. I'm moving to get a different perspective. Okay, I can see it now, it's a waterfall! Multiple waterfalls. A bridge. The sounds are just overwhelming."

"That's excellent, Tomi," said Ray. "You can leave that place, and get yourself centred again. This time instead of coordinates, I want you to try to find a person. I want you to try to find Dr. Ib Johansen. Can you navigate to his location?"

Tomi was silent for a few moments. "Okay, I can see him. At least I think it's him."

"Focus on the raw perceptions, what are you experiencing?"

"Okay, I see hair," said Tomi. "It looks like the back of a head. A man. He's sitting at…a desk. At PSI? No, it's not PSI. He's at a desk, but it's his home, I think."

"Okay," said Ray, "what is this person doing at the desk?"

"Writing," said Tomi. "No, drawing. Writing and drawing. On a piece of paper. I can't make out what it is exactly. Now he has his phone in his hand, and he is taking a picture of it. Now he put the paper in a box below the desk. The shredder. He shredded the paper."

"Great," said Ray. "Now I want you to leave this place. Get yourself recentred, and we will try one more."

Ray stayed silent for a few minutes, giving Tomi time to clear her mind of the scene.

"Just like you did with Dr. Johansen," said Ray, "I want you to try to navigate to Ete. Wherever Ete is, here on Earth or somewhere else, I want you to try to locate Ete and navigate there."

After a few moments, Tomi said, "It's white. It's…not a light. It's not white. Off white. Oh my god, it's another room. It's another one of those rooms."

"Okay, can you perceive Ete, or any other being in this or any nearby rooms?" asked Ray.

"No," said Tomi after a pause, "no, it's lifeless."

"Okay, I want you to leave this scene, and let your mind clear. When you're ready, I want you to become more aware of your physical body, of your toes and fingers, your limbs. Become aware of your surroundings. And when you're ready, you can open your eyes again and rejoin us," said Ray.

While Tomi started to move a little and ease back into being present in the attic, Barry slid his chair closer to Tomi and Ray. When Tomi opened her eyes, she looked over at Ray with bleary eyes, and said, "What the hell was that? What was in the envelope? What was that place?"

Ray sighed. "I have no idea. Purgatory."

"The envelope," said Barry, "was from the last time you connected to Ete. Ib gave it to me to bring along in case it could be useful. But obviously, it was not the same result." He turned to look at Ray. "Do you think the problem was that we were reusing the same instructions?"

Ray considered this. "No," he said. "No, I don't think so. First, we tried to navigate to where Tomi last met Ete. And she was stuck in limbo, that endless, boring maze of rooms. So then I had her navigate to Niagara Falls."

"That's what it was!" said Tomi. "I thought it might be, but I didn't want to guess. I've never been there, so I wasn't totally sure."

"Yes," said Ray. "And I would say you were bang on in that one. Then I wanted to test finding an individual. Perhaps Barry could check with Dr. Johansen to find out how accurate you were."

"No need," said Barry, pulling out his phone. "I got an encrypted message just a few minutes ago. It was a picture from Ib. Take a look."

He held out his phone to show the image. Tomi saw that it was a picture of a hand-drawn map. It had some features on it such as a bridge, mountains, and a little house. There were also written directions on one side of the page.

"You said he was writing and drawing," said Barry. "And here it is. And by the way, these are our directions. Ib has a safehouse ready for you when we leave here."

"Safehouse," repeated Tomi. She wasn't sure if she should be reassured that she had somewhere to go, or terrified that she *needed* a safehouse.

"So," continued Ray, "accurate on Niagara, accurate on Dr. Johansen, and then we tried to navigate to Ete. And you were back in that purgatory. It seems to me that there's some block. It's almost like you're being blocked from connecting with Ete specifically."

"A psychic block," said Barry. "What is that? I mean, how can that be?"

Ray sat back in his chair, his forehead furrowed. "I don't know. I mean there are stories of this kind of thing, sort of using a remote viewer to kind of protect something, or yes, try to block another remote viewer. Even violence. But the who, the why, the how. I just don't know."

Tomi had a chill run down her spine, giving her body a little shake. "So, what do we do, then? How do we get through the block?"

Ray stood up. "We wait. And we try again tomorrow. For now, let's make some dinner and tell some stories."

Tomi went back to her room for a rest, eventually following the smell of cooking garlic and onions down to the kitchen. She found Barry seated at the counter enjoying a glass of wine, while Ray had multiple pans going, a tea towel thrown over his left shoulder.

"Smells amazing," said Tomi.

"Don't bother asking if you can help," said Barry, "he won't let you."

"That's right," said Ray, placing a wine glass in front of Tomi. "You are guests in my home, let me be the great host I strive to be."

"Well, you certainly are that," said Barry. "Tomi, I was just telling Ray that, though we could get used to his hospitality, we shouldn't overstay our welcome. So, we will leave tomorrow, now that Ib has arranged a place for you to stay."

"Okay, sure," said Tomi, a little sad to leave this beautiful and welcoming home and host.

"But," said Ray, "before you leave, we'll try again to connect with Ete."

Tomi smiled, appreciating that Ray was invested in this. Her face then turned serious, remembering the chill she had up in the attic. "Ray, earlier you mentioned stories about psychic blocks, and you mentioned assassinations. In your time doing this, have you seen this studied? Or used?"

"No," Ray said, pouring steaming pasta into a colander. "It's certainly something that was talked about. We never tried these things at SRI. We never would have. But while we were contracted to do this work, the Army also set up their unit. And it's possible there have been other efforts that remain classified."

Ray finished plating the food, and brought it over to his guests, taking a seat.

"There was talk or maybe fear," he continued, "that especially strong remote viewers might be able to interfere with a person's physiology. That a strong enough psychic might be able to actually manipulate matter and stop someone's heart. Now, in the Cold War, you can imagine how from a military or intelligence perspective this would be of profound interest, both from an offensive and a defensive perspective. A completely untraceable assassination."

"Give humans a gift, and they'll find a way to turn it into a weapon," Barry said with a shake of his head.

"Ain't it always the way?" agreed Ray. "So, you can also imagine how an exceptionally gifted remote viewer could be seen as an asset to be used. Or, seen as a very real threat."

"Another reason why we want you in a safe location," said Barry, looking at Tomi.

Ray nodded. "Listen to your friend."

Tomi gave a nod, feeling both vulnerable and powerful simultaneously. *What is this bizarre world I've stepped into*, she thought.

"It's...well it's still hard to wrap my mind around the fact that my consciousness can travel. But to think about actually impacting something, the material world, in this state. Well, even after all I've experienced, it's still hard to accept," said Tomi. "I mean, really, how does this all work?"

Ray smiled. "God, I'd love to know. All I'm sure of is that our consciousness isn't attached to the body. Or if it is, it isn't stuck. Have passport, will travel."

Tomi smiled, imagining her astral body flying around with a passport.

"In one of your letters to my grandma, you said that the reality we know doesn't make sense," Tomi said. "Do you understand it more now?"

Ray laughed. "I think I understand it less."

Tomi and Barry both smiled at his honesty. "No really," Ray said, "I mean of course I understand more. Or at least have more informed hunches. But I think what has made me feel less certain of how remote viewing actually works is realizing how intertwined it is with various phenomena."

Ray took a sip of his wine, Tomi and Barry awaiting his next word, wanting to glean everything they could from his decades of research.

"You see, it's impossible - well, not impossible - it requires willful ignorance to entertain remote viewing as a legitimate phenomenon without also becoming aware of the evidence for near death and out of body experiences, channelling, or for UFOs and non-human intelligence in our midst. You can't. They all intertwine somehow. And the evidence for one inevitably becomes evidence for another."

"Elves," added Tomi. She expected Ray to laugh when she brought up elves. Instead, he nodded, wiping his mouth with a red cloth napkin. He cleared his throat and used his fingers to count his words. "Dreams, drugs, meditation, and death. What do they all have in common?"

Both Tomi and Barry inhaled deeply as they considered the question.

"Our consciousness exists in each of those states?" suggested Tomi. Ray nodded, and looked at Barry.

"Hmm. They're all altered states of continued consciousness. You know, our consciousness is continuous, and exists in each state, though each of those states alters our perceptions," Barry suggested.

Tomi nodded. "Each state lets us perceive reality differently. Each gives us an alternative view on reality. Or maybe a different reality, altogether. But our consciousness is continuous."

Ray nodded silently, using some bread to sop up the remaining pasta sauce.

Barry tilted his head back slightly. "Dreams, drugs, meditation, death. What about faith?"

"Faith? Say more," said Ray.

"Well, in each of those states we can reach out of our reality and into another, right? Or maybe another reality reaches into ours. Well, that happens with faith, too. You know, the burning bush. Miracles.

Levitating monks. The shepherd girls in Fatima. Is it possible that through faith these other realities can intersect, or we can perceive a different reality?"

Ray nodded slowly, considering this. "Interesting. Yes, interesting. Now, think about who connects in this way. What people are more likely to have these experiences, to have access to these other realities."

"Children," said Tomi, thinking about a documentary she had watched about children remembering their past lives, and even visiting and reuniting with their past life families. "Young children are the best at remembering past lives."

"Yes," agreed Barry. "And children are often the family member that first talks about abduction experiences. And ghosts. Because they don't know yet that these things aren't supposed to exist, so maybe they haven't learned to tune it out yet."

"Mmhmm," agreed Ray. "There's some research happening now around neurodivergent people having more of these experiences. Perhaps because they often have different levels of sensitivity, they are able to perceive different realities a little better? I mean, these other realities may be just under our noses."

"Or right there in the periphery," said Tomi. "Ray, Ete communicated to me, more than once, that something is coming. Like something big for humanity. For the Earth. Is this a message you've heard before, in your work with remote viewing?"

Ray nodded while collecting his thoughts. "In remote viewing, yes and no. We've talked about the Moon bases and potential hostility. But not an urgent message like that, no."

"You know, in the literature of UFO experiencers - and yes," said Barry with a laugh, "I am a nerd about this stuff - repeated over and over are people who receive messages, warnings about how humans are treating the Earth. Many have seen images of mass destruction, nuclear war, and disasters. It can be really traumatizing for some."

"Cataclysms," said Ray, nodding.

"Yes. And you know, in my research, I came across several documents that seemed to show a level of knowledge, or level of interest, in the CIA and the intelligence community generally, about global cataclysms. So," Barry said, wine glass in hand, starting to smirk, "here's a conspiracy theory to enjoy: our governments know that a global cataclysm is pending, and that's why they don't really try to stop major pollution and climate change."

"Hey, that is a fun conspiracy theory," said Ray. "If they know that some big thing is coming, say in 2027, and perfecting carbon capture or radically changing our economic system isn't going to make a lick of difference, then why bother? Then again, that might give our leaders too much credit, my money is on gross incompetence."

While Barry shared a laugh with Ray, Tomi felt another chill run down her spine just when Ray had said *2027*. She wasn't sure if it was the close proximity in time that caused her reaction, or if it was a date she had heard, or felt, before.

Maybe it's a sense of loss, she thought. The beginning of this journey had seemed magical, as she grew by leaps in her spiritual development. *Now it just feels like the future is so uncertain.*

Sensing Tomi's change in energy, Ray finished the wine in his glass, and said, "Well, we have work to do tomorrow, and you will have a long drive ahead of you. Probably time to call it a night. But Tomi, before you leave tomorrow, I just want to say that I know this journey is hard. You're probably questioning all kinds of things. Maybe even your sanity at times. But I hope you keep going with it. Just follow your intuition because more often than not, it will be right."

Tomi smiled at this kind and honest advice. "Thank you, Ray. It really is helpful to hear you say that."

"And your grandma. Esther. She would be so proud of you, I'm sure of that."

After breakfast, Tomi and Barry packed up their bags, and placed them by the front door. Ray was at the kitchen table, making some notes.

"Are you ready to give this one more try?" asked Ray. "I sure would like to meet this Ete."

They climbed the stairs up to the attic. Barry sat quietly by the window, while Tomi sprawled out on the couch and began breathing exercises.

"Take your time and get yourself centred. Clear your mind and relax your body. And let me know when you are ready to begin," said Ray.

After a few more minutes, Tomi said: "Ready."

"Okay, now Tomi I am placing a sealed envelope here on the table beside you," said Ray, shuffling an envelope out of the notes in his hand. "I want you to focus on the envelope and the instructions inside. This time I'm not going to give you coordinates. Everything you need is in the envelope."

Tomi continued to breathe slowly and waited for the eyes-closed darkness to give way to lines, shapes, and colours.

"I see a rectangle," she said. "A rectangle forming. Within a larger rectangle. It's becoming clearer now. It's a wall. And a door. Green. Like the green of those old appliances from the seventies. Yeah…I'm in the rooms again."

"Hmm, okay," said Ray, disappointed. "Why don't you proceed through the door."

"Okay, yeah. This is a big room. Like a big old office room. It's light brown. There are a few doors along the far wall. These rooms are empty, but they're so…eerie, I guess."

"Okay, hmm," said Ray, looking at his notes and deciding how to proceed. "I want you to raise your awareness from this place. Try to get a feel for what it is that is bringing you to this place."

After a few moments, Tomi said, "I'm floating. I'm actually rising up. I'm coming to the ceiling. I'm going through it. Darkness."

Tomi's face scrunched, as though she was trying to squint her way through the dark. "No. It's another floor. Another floor of these rooms. This one is light purple. Worn down grey carpet. There's nothing here."

"Do you think you can continue climbing? Is there a top floor?" asked Ray.

Tomi's head slowly shifted back and forth on the pillow, her body answering with a no. "It feels impossible. Like…something isn't going to let me out of here."

"Can you get a sense of who is creating this place, or creating this block?" asked Ray.

Tomi waited for the information to come to her. "No. It feels like it was an order. Someone made the order, and whoever it is, they're carrying it out. I mean, I don't feel hostility."

"Okay," said Ray. "I don't think we will be connecting to Ete today. I want you to leave that place and come back to a blank, relaxed mind. When you are ready, I want to try something else. I am going to have you travel to the street outside my house. At my front door is a doorbell. Let's do an experiment, and see if you can ring the doorbell."

"Okay. Yes, I'm seeing a streetscape. It's coming together slowly," said Tomi. "There are cars parked on the street. One just drove by. So many beautiful trees."

"Can you make out some buildings?" asked Ray.

"Yes. I'm in front of a set of brown townhouses. They are old, and so pretty. Let me look around. I see the number one-hundred and eight."

"Yes, that's my house number," said Ray.

"Okay, so I'm across the street and down a little. Let me head towards your house. Wait. I just noticed something," said Tomi.

"What did you notice?"

"I…I don't know exactly. Something is pulling my attention." Tomi paused to gather information. "One of the cars parked on the street. I don't know, it's pulling my attention."

"Can you approach it?" asked Ray. "What do you see?"

"Yes, it's dark. A dark sedan. The windows are tinted," said Tomi. "I'm getting closer. I'm looking in. There's a man in a dark suit sitting in the car. He's just leaning back in the driver's seat. He's watching."

"What is he watching, Tomi?"

The answer appeared in her mind. "He's watching me."

"Are you saying he's watching you right now?" asked Ray. "Watching you physically?"

"Yes. Well no," said Tomi, "he's watching this house. He is waiting for me to leave the house."

"I see," said Ray, attempting to sound unconcerned. "Tomi, there is a back door at my house. Can you travel around the side of my house and look around there?"

"Yes," she said, then went quiet as she began shifting her focus to the rear of the home. "Yeah, I see a little fenced in backyard. I see the back door. I'm looking out from the door, and I can see the street behind the house. Yes, there's something pulling me here."

"Okay, follow that pull," said Ray.

"There's another car," she said. "Another agent. It's narrow but where she is parked, there's a clear view of your back door."

"Hmm, okay," Ray said, suddenly wondering how he was going to get these people out of his house unmonitored. Barry shuffled over to Ray, trying not to make any noise that might disrupt Tomi's viewing. He took the pen and papers from Ray's hand, placed them on the table, and began writing. He handed it back to Ray. The note read: *My car is parked on Eugenie Street, just west of N Park Ave.*

"Okay, Tomi, I want you to navigate back to the front of my house. And I want you to continue travelling down the street perpendicular to the front of my house. Are you able to find that?"

"Yes," said Tomi. "It's all so very clear, I can see each of the leaves on the trees along the street. Okay, so I'm moving down this small street. It's a bit narrow, lots of parked cars. The buildings are long, like one continuous wall. On both sides."

"Yes, that's correct," said Ray. Barry, looked out the window beside him, and saw that the window looked out the front of Ray's home. From up in the attic, he looked out over the street she was describing. He saw the way the buildings on each side were indeed continuous, and there were cars parked along both curbs, leaving just enough space for a car to travel between them.

In that centre lane, for just a moment he saw a dark figure, like a shadow, walking in the opposite direction.

"When you get to the end of that street, you are going to go right. And continue for one block. Let me know when you are there," said Ray.

After a few moments, Tomi said, "Yes, I'm there. And I see Barry's car! It's a bit…unique looking, it's easy to recognize."

"Okay, great," said Ray. "Now just like with the front and the back of the house, can you look around, or sense if the car is being monitored as well?"

"Yeah. I'm looking. I feel that it is, but…I'm not feeling pulled to any of these cars. Like I don't feel like there's an agent in a car. Okay I'm beside Barry's car now, and I don't see…wait, a man is sitting on a bench just across the street. He's got a newspaper in his hands, but, I don't know. He looks out of place somehow."

"What is he wearing?" asked Ray.

"Sunglasses. He's wearing a dark suit. But no tie. He's…he's got the newspaper up, but he's sort of looking over it, at the car. Yes, I think he's here to monitor the car."

"Okay," said Ray, "can you-"

"Oh, umm…" Tomi interrupted.

"Tomi? What is it?"

"He's not looking at the car. He's looking at me. He sees me," she said.

"Tomi, are you sure?" asked Ray.

"Yes, I can feel it," Tomi said. "He's doing something. He's got his hand up to his face. He's talking into it. He's getting up. He put his newspaper in the garbage beside the bench. He's not looking at me now, but he's moving this way."

"Okay, Tomi, I want you to move. Go in the same direction you were going in. See if he follows you," Ray said.

Barry heard a car engine turning over, and looked out the window in time to see a parked car pull out and speed off.

"Yes, he's following me," said Tomi, her voice sounding anxious. "He's got a bit of distance, like he's not trying to stop me. Just watch me."

Barry again came over to Ray and wrote on his papers. He handed it back, and Ray read it: *The car out front just drove away.*

"Okay, keep going. What do you see coming up?" asked Ray.

"I'm coming up to an intersection. There's a bus stopped here, letting off passengers," she said.

"Tomi, hurry," said Ray, "get on the bus."

"Okay. Okay, I just squeezed in the back door. The doors are still open. The bus isn't moving."

"Can you see the man who was following you?" asked Ray.

"Yes, yes, he's running now!" said Tomi. "He's running towards the bus. He's almost here."

Barry wrote again on the paper. *We need to go <u>now</u>.*

"The door closed! He didn't get on! The bus is moving away," said Tomi.

"Okay, Tomi," said Ray, his voice conveying urgency, "I'm afraid there's no time for a slow return to your body. I need you to leave that scene and return now. Feel your digits, feel your limbs, and when you're ready, open your eyes."

Tomi opened her eyes, tried to sit up and had to pause, shaking her head like she was shaking off cobwebs.

"Tomi, we need to go now," said Barry. "The car out front has left. It's probably chasing that bus, but it won't be long before they realize you're not on it."

Barry came over to Tomi and helped her up. They headed towards the stairs, and he held onto her as they descended. Tomi relied on Barry to get down the stairs, but as they got to the ground floor, adrenaline was pumping and making her more aware of the present moment. They grabbed their bags.

"Ray, I'm so sorry we are leaving like this," said Barry, Ray still coming down the stairs.

"Don't be, go, get her somewhere safe," said Ray. "And you, Tomi, you stay safe. And get some answers. I mean it Tomi, Esther really would be proud."

"Thank you Ray, for everything," said Tomi.

"Go," said Ray, and they headed out the front door and down the street in the direction of the Saab.

"That was wild. That was wild!" Tomi said, laughing, breaking the long silence.

They had made it to the car, and threw their bags in the back seat. Barry had immediately started the car, put it in gear, and started navigating out of Chicago. They got on the I90, and soon the city turned into suburbs. They drove in silence, each taking turns to look around at the cars beside and behind them.

Tomi kept laughing, cathartically breaking the tension of their escape. Barry looked in his mirror, and quickly at Tomi. Finally, he cracked and laughed with her.

"That was really fucking wild," laughed Barry. "I feel like we're in a car chase scene from a movie. When did we become action heroes?"

They both fed off each other's laughter, eventually settling into the drive. After a few hours, they stopped for gas and a bathroom, and picked up some lunch.

Tomi eventually fell asleep in the passenger seat, her body crashing from the wild morning. When she finally awoke, she saw the sun had moved lower in the sky. She looked around to see that they were now driving through a forest.

She realized her mouth and throat were dry, and took a swig of the cold coffee from the gas station that she hadn't finished earlier.

"Sorry I fell asleep there, I'm sure you're tired too. Thanks for doing all of this driving. I'd offer to switch but I can't drive a manual," said Tomi.

Barry shook his head and smiled. "I wouldn't let you drive this car even if you could, after you called it *unique*," he said with a laugh.

"Hey, I haven't even asked, where are we going?" Tomi asked, looking around at her surroundings. "And where are we now?"

"Well, Ib has got things all set up. We are in West Virginia, and we aren't far from where you're going," he said, pulling out his phone to consult the map Ib had sent him. "Some professor that Ib knows has this cabin here. Ib has rented it in the past I guess, but this person is on sabbatical somewhere, gave Ib the keys and told him to enjoy it while he's away. Anyways, based on this map, it's pretty secluded, and so hopefully you'll be well off the radar there."

"Wow, sounds almost like a vacation," said Tomi. "What happens then?"

"Well, I am going to be dropping you off," said Barry. "I will head back to PSI to keep up appearances, while I reach out to some contacts I have in the IC. And hopefully, I will get some answers about what kind of trouble you're in, or what's going on. Ib and I will come back to the cabin on the weekend. Hopefully with a plan based on what I learn. And in the meantime, you can get some rest, and see if you can get through this block and communicate with Ete again."

Tomi, still a little groggy, considered the plan. It was a good plan, considering where they were at. And she was appreciative of all their efforts. While she had always been a person who enjoyed alone time, she worried about being alone in a cabin in the woods. And trying to remote view on her own. She already felt so detached from reality. *That kind of isolation is not going to be good for my sanity*, she thought.

As though she shared her fears out loud, Barry continued. "Ib gave the keys to Kirsten, so she's already there. She's got groceries and everything, so you should be safe there, and she can take care of you."

Tomi smiled, thankful for these friends, and happy to know where she would be sleeping, at least for a week.

During the conversation, Barry had steered off the paved road, and down a narrower gravel road. The road weaved left and right as it climbed in elevation. He consulted the map a few times as he turned again down a smaller road, and finally, turning down a narrow, overgrown driveway. They drove, covered in the shadows of the trees overhead, until the driveway curved up to a log cabin with a green metal roof.

Another car was already there, and Kirsten was at the trunk of it pulling out her luggage. Kirsten turned and clapped her hands in excitement. "We're on vacation!" she said, as Tomi opened her car door.

Chapter 12

Carl Jung

While Barry followed Ib's instructions for getting the power and water turned on in the cabin, Tomi and Kirsten were in the kitchen putting away the groceries Kirsten had brought. The cabin was rustic, made of wood inside and out, with a small kitchen with white cabinets and a blue ceramic tile countertop. Kirsten handed Tomi a bag of vegetables and fruit to put away.

"So how great is this," said Kirsten, "mini vacay for us!"

"I'm so glad to see you here," said Tomi, "but you know I'm here because I might be in danger. I have no idea what might happen. Kirsten, I'm worried you are putting yourself at risk by staying here with me. I will be fine here on my own if you wanted to go back with Barry."

Kirsten laughed. "Yeah right, I'm not leaving you here on your own. Don't worry about it."

"Aren't you worried?" asked Tomi.

"Please, I've got you to protect me. I mean come on, you're like this big bad witch bitch, I'm safe with you," Kirsten laughed.

Tomi smiled. "I thought psychic spy sounded pretty cool, but I like big bad witch bitch even better! Okay. I just want to make sure you know what you're getting yourself into.

"I do," Kirsten said. "And I'm here to help in any way you need."

Tomi paused to put her hand on Kirsten's. "Thank you. For being here. We didn't really find answers about my grandmother with Ray. And every time we tried to remote view and connect with Ete, I was blocked somehow. So while we're here, I need to find a way to make a connection."

"Sure, I'm here for whatever you need," said Kirsten, lifting a box onto the counter. She opened the folded cardboard top and started to pull out bottles of wine. "But how about tonight you forget about all that and we drink wine?"

Tomi smiled. "That actually sounds perfect."

Barry came around the front of the cabin to find Tomi and Kirsten pulling Adirondack chairs out from a wooden shed beside the cabin. The cabin had a small grass lawn around it, and beyond that the ground was covered in pine needles and shade from the abundant trees.

They placed the chairs at the front of the cabin beside a wine bottle and two glasses.

"Now that looks like a good idea," said Barry, rounding the corner and seeing their setup.

"Can we get you a glass?" asked Kirsten.

"No, but thanks, I need to hit the road," he said. "So, the power is on. It's off-grid, there's a battery system but you'll want to avoid using much electricity. There's a diesel generator that will kick in, but again that's only temporary. Ib and I will be up here on the weekend. We will try to keep communication light, but let us know if there are any issues and we can be here sooner."

Barry paused, searching for words. "Just…I don't know how to say this. I'm sure everything will be fine. But if there is an emergency, just…remember that calling 911, well, they may not be your friends. I would only do that if you absolutely have to."

"Don't worry Barry, I've got this," said Kirsten. "We've got books, we've got wine, we'll be fine."

"There's firewood over by the shed. It's fall, the nights will be cool, and the wood stove is the only heat in the cabin. No phones other than encrypted messages. And last thing, these woods are beautiful, but I don't recommend venturing too far," he said. "There are bears, coyotes, and well -"

"Okay dad," Kirsten laughed. "Ten years in Girl Scouts, Barry, it's not my first forest."

"Okay, sorry for being patronizing, I just want to make sure you're safe before I leave," he said.

"It's sweet, thanks Barry," said Tomi, hugging him. "Thanks for everything and for getting me here. Drive safe, okay?"

They saw him off in his car, and headed to the chairs they had placed in the light of the descending sun. From the front of the cabin, the land sloped down, leaving the treetops lower and revealing an expansive view of the forest sprawling out before them.

Tomi felt her body start to relax as she took a deep breath, pulling the clean mountain air into her body. As her muscles relaxed, she realized how tensely she had been holding them. This moment of peace was a reminder of how destabilizing the past few days - few months - had been.

"Tomi," Kirsten whispered. Tomi looked to Kirsten, who pointed into the woods, off to their left. A few trees in, she saw a white-tailed doe moving through the woods.

"Oh, it's so beautiful," said Tomi.

The deer suddenly stopped, as though it heard a noise or sensed danger.

"Do you hear that?" whispered Kirsten.

Tomi listened, and realized that the subtle sounds of the forest had stopped. *Silence.* Then the snapping of a branch as the doe raced off through the forest, and a flash in her peripheral vision.

"Did you see that?" asked Tomi.

"Yes," said Kirsten tensely.

"I saw…I don't know. Like a flash of darkness, over there." Tomi pointed towards nine on a clock, deeper in the woods than the doe had been.

"Yes," said Kirsten. She looked at Tomi, her eyes exaggeratedly wide. "Baaaaaaarry, come back!"

They both laughed, and Tomi realized she could hear birds singing again.

"Okay," said Tomi, drawing in a deep breath and holding out her glass, "it will be fine with me if that doesn't happen again. More wine, please."

Kirsten smiled and grabbed the wine bottle. "Good attitude," she said. As she finished filling Tomi's glass, they could hear movement in the woods off to their right. Then a male voice.

"Ib? Is that Ib Johansen back again?"

Tomi and Kirsten turned towards the voice to see a middle-aged man with dark hair propped up at the front by a blue bandana tied around his head. He wore a dark fleece, dark pants, and old brown leather boots, with a backpack strapped over his shoulders. In his hand was a simple metal mug.

"Oh," he said, as he stepped into the clearing around the cabin, "you are not Ib Johansen!"

"Neither of us," laughed Kirsten.

"But we are friends of Ib's," added Tomi.

"Oh, well any friend of Ib's," the man said, walking towards them. "The last time Ib was here we had a truly profound conversation about consciousness. Over a few of those," he said, pointing at Tomi's glass of wine.

Kirsten smiled and paused for a moment, unsure of what to make of this visitor emerging from the woods. Finally, she said, "would you like some wine? I can get you a glass."

"Oh, I couldn't say no," he said, pouring what looked like coffee out of his mug and onto the grass. "No need for a glass, I'm prepared."

Kirsten shrugged and filled his mug.

"Tak! That's thanks in Danish. Ib taught me. I'm sorry, drinks before an introduction, that was rude of me. I'm Sixto, and I live about a half mile in that direction," he said, pointing in the direction he had emerged from. He spotted a large log a few feet away, pulled it over to Tomi and Kirsten, and used it as a stool.

"I'm Kirsten," she said, as Sixto reached out to shake her hand. "And this is Tomi."

Tomi looked at his hand as she reached out to shake it, and saw a face tattooed on the webbing of skin between his thumb and index finger. It was much like the face her grandmother had drawn on the napkin, that upside down, egg-shaped alien face.

Kirsten noticed Tomi staring at his hand. "Who's your friend there?" Kirsten asked, pointing at his tattoo.

"Oh, this," he said, stretching out his hand. "I got this many years ago when I was a much younger man. I had read the book

Communion around the time a friend and I were getting tattoos, and I thought this would be cool. Many years later you could say my relationship with this guy," he said, pointing at the face, "is a little more complicated."

"How so?" asked Kirsten. Tomi's mind was spinning slightly at the strangeness of a man with an alien tattoo showing up in the remote woods, while Kirsten, with her free-spirited demeanor, seemed unphased.

"Well," he said, "to start with I'm an experiencer, or what we used to call *abductee*. I know most people roll their eyes at that, but I've had experiences going back to when I was a child. And with the magic of satellite internet, I actually host an online experiencer group."

"Well isn't this a small world," Kirsten said.

"Wait, are you an experiencer too?" he asked incredulously.

"Mmhmm," Kirsten said, mid-swallow of wine, pointing to herself, then Tomi, "we both are."

"Well, that's one hell of a coincidence to meet you both all the way out here," he said, shaking his head at the remote odds.

"You shouldn't confuse coincidence for synchronicity," Kirsten said, raising her glass.

"Isn't that the truth," he said, with a look of wonder.

Tomi sat quietly and listened to Sixto and Kirsten chatting. Not only was she unsettled by the sudden change of subject - as though the universe couldn't allow her one evening off - she also found herself surprised by Kirsten's admission on behalf of both of them.

"Really, it's ridiculous that in twenty-twenty-three we usually have to start conversations without a universal understanding that there's an alien presence here on Earth," Sixto said. "Although I don't like the word alien, it assumes they're extraterrestrials from some far-off galaxy, and I'm not sure that's the case, so I prefer NHI, or non-human intelligence."

These experiences were all so new to Tomi, she had never stopped to label it, or come to embrace a term like *experiencer*. Of course, she thought of Kirsten as an experiencer, as she had had a longer time to make peace with her abduction experiences.

It's like the label just made these experiences more real, Tomi thought.

"But, I have to also remind myself," he continued, "that everyone is at a different place in a journey of discovery. And also that, while I'm perfectly comfortable talking about it, for a lot of people there's something very unsettling, very disquieting about the phenomenon. Some people are deep down terrified of what it all might mean."

At that, Tomi's mind stopped spinning and she felt calmer and more present. *Maybe it is okay if some of us are terrified,* she thought.

"Let me ask you," he said, leaning in, "something we've been talking about in my experiencer group is this feeling, as though we are being prepared for something. Like things are really heating up. Have either of you felt that?"

Kirsten looked at Tomi, stifled a laugh, and said, "yes, things are definitely heating up."

"Yes, interesting," he said, straightening his back again. "It's like something is coming."

"Something *is* coming," said Tomi, nodding. Sixto looked at her as she stared at the ground, looking somber.

"Well," he said, finishing his mug of wine and standing, "I should get back home while there's still some daylight. But I would really love to hear more about your experiences. Can I invite you to dinner at my cabin tomorrow?"

"Oh," said Kirsten, looking at Tomi for an answer but not finding one. "Sure, that would be lovely. But how do we get there?"

"Well," he said, "you'll find over there, where I exited the woods, there's a little path. I painted blue circles on the trees to mark the way. Follow the blue circles and you'll find my cabin."

"Okay, we'll find our way there," said Kirsten. "And hopefully we won't find anything weird in the woods on the way! We just saw…something, moving over that way." Kirsten pointed in the direction of where the deer had been.

"Yes, I saw it," said Sixto calmly. "There's a rather large owl that lives nearby. Nothing to worry about."

Sixto took a few steps, then stopped and turned. "You know, meeting you both here, well, I just can't get over how synchronistically arranged the universe seems to be lately. It really is something. I'll see you tomorrow!"

After Sixto left, Kirsten lightened the conversation again, and had Tomi laughing as she recounted her worst online dating experiences. Eventually they went inside where Kirsten fried some vegetables and tofu for Buddha bowls. They ate at the small table in the cabin, then cleaned up and made a fire in the wood stove.

Kirsten poured the last of the bottle of wine into their glasses, and said, "Let's go check out the stars!"

They stepped out of the cabin, and Tomi immediately felt a chill, surprised at how much the early fall temperature had dropped. They walked a few feet into the middle of the clearing and looked up. The night was perfectly clear and moonless, letting the stars light up the night sky.

Kirsten flopped down on the cold grass and tugged at Tomi to do the same. She lay down beside her, less comfortable letting her hair lay in the grass and dirt, but she forgot about it as she focused on the tapestry of stars filling her view. The Milky Way streaked across the sky, brighter than she had ever seen.

"It's so beautiful," said Kirsten.

"Seeing stars like this makes me think of my grandmother. She always used to tell me I was made of stardust."

"I love that," said Kirsten. "I want to be made of stardust!"

"You are!" said Tomi. "Years later I found a Carl Sagan quote where he said we are all made of star-stuff. And he was being literal. Our bodies really are made of materials created in far off, long-dead stars. The universe is so majestic."

"It sure is. Oh, look, see that? That one that's moving?" Kirsten said, pointing into the sky.

"Oh yeah, what is that?"

"That's the International Space Station. Just spinning around the Earth. There are people up there looking back at us," she said. "Isn't that wild?"

Tomi imagined herself looking down on the Earth from space, and thought about Ete saying she will learn to fly their craft.

"And that," Kirsten said, pointing again, "that is Polaris."

"The North Star, right?" said Tomi.

"Right! Well, for now," she said.

"For now?"

"It changes. A lot of people don't realize that, but it shifts," Kirsten said. "The Earth moves in a cycle, and so the North Star changes. Like if you went back to Ancient Egypt, it was a different star that marked north. And in like ten thousand years, it'll be a different star again," Kirsten said.

"I had no idea, where did you learn that?" asked Tomi.

"Ten years of Scouting," Kirsten said, with a laugh. As she laughed, a sound of movement came from the forest. Tomi couldn't make out the direction it came from.

"Did you hear that?" asked Tomi, sitting up.

"Yeah," said Kirsten, quietly. "I just saw some red eyes from over there. Let's just assume it's Sixto's owl. And maybe it's time to go inside."

They went back inside, brushed their teeth, and got ready for bed. Kirsten put another log in the wood stove.

"Okay, so I'm pretending I'm not freaked out," said Tomi, "but I'm a little freaked out. Can I sleep with you tonight?"

"Uh, no, I want to be alone in the middle of these creepy woods," she said sarcastically, smiling.

The bedroom was colder, separated from the wood stove by a wall. They climbed under a quilt and a few layers of blankets and waited for warmth, facing each other.

"I really respect how comfortable you are talking about being an experiencer," Tomi said. "You're comfortable and confident wearing that badge. I'm still getting there."

"You will," said Kirsten. "Believe me, I wasn't always so comfortable in my own skin. It's taken work."

"You know, when I was a kid and my grandmother taught me stuff, I was comfortable because she was. But after she was gone, I was never comfortable with this side of me. Like Sixto said, some people are afraid of what it means. That was me," said Tomi. "Is me."

"Maybe the experiences you've had," Kirsten said, "the remote viewing, all those experiences, do you think maybe it all came along to knock you off your path? Or maybe you were off the path you were meant for, and it's knocking you onto the right path?"

Tomi considered this and thought about what it means to be comfortable in your own skin. "Yeah, I think so. I feel more, I don't know, more me. Like this was always a part of me, and I just buried it, and now I'm more me."

"Good, I like you," Kirsten said, smiling. "I know that it's not easy. But think of all the amazing things you've seen, learned, and experienced."

"It is amazing," said Tomi. "I don't know, I kind of feel like I've been running from this side of me, but it's been like trying to outrun your shadow. It's just…I guess I just like reality. Or what we think of as reality. I can understand it. I can hold it. It's safe. And now it's like that safe feeling is disappearing."

"I understand that," said Kirsten. "But what if there's so much more beyond that reality? Doesn't it excite you to find out more about what the universe is all about?"

"It does," said Tomi. "I think I'm like a person at a pool putting their toes in the water, then their leg, to get used to the temperature. I think you would just jump in!"

"Hah, I'd be the one jumping in fully clothed," laughed Kirsten. "And a pool is a good analogy. Once you're in, you can let go in the water. Just let your body go. Float, move with the current. I don't know Tomi, the universe is just so beautiful. And magical. I don't understand it at all, but I feel like being around you, I understand a bit more."

Tomi smiled. Kirsten flipped around to turn off the lamp beside the bed.

In the darkness, Tomi could hear Kirsten yawn.

"You know, for as long as I can remember, I've had this recurring dream," Kirsten said, in a drowsy voice. "I'm on this giant hill, I mean giant, it's an island with ocean all around it, but it's like a different planet. Gravity is different, you can let go the way you can in water. You can almost float. Anyways, that pool analogy made me think of it."

Despite the darkness, in Tomi's mind she could see the bright green grass sloping up the hill, and the waves lapping against rocks at the bottom.

Chapter 13

"If quantum mechanics hasn't profoundly shocked you, you haven't understood it yet."

Niels Bohr

Tomi woke up, not suddenly, but that restful wake up when the sunlight gets brighter and brighter and eventually convinces your body that it's time to rise. The curtains were a light cotton, and even with them closed the sunlight filled the room. She looked over to see Kirsten still sleeping, her long blond hair covering her face.

I'm so glad she's here, thought Tomi. As much as she was concerned about putting her at risk, she was so grateful to not be alone.

Tomi entered the kitchen, put the kettle on, found a French press in a cupboard, and made coffee. She poured herself a mug and stepped outside. Usually, Tomi was selective about her coffee, grinding her own beans and choosing the darkest roasts she could find, but in this case the store brand, pre-ground coffee tasted great when paired with the fresh air and the view of the expansive forest.

"Hey, what's this?" said a voice behind Tomi. She turned to see Kirsten emerging from the cabin, mug of coffee in one hand, and a piece of paper in the other. She came and sat down in the chair beside Tomi.

"Wow, look at that view in front of us," said Kirsten, breathing in the mountain air.

"What is that?" asked Tomi, reaching for the paper. There was a yellow sticky note on it.

"I'm not sure, I saw it sticking out of the little mailbox there by the door," Kirsten said, motioning to the door behind her.

"*It's always nice to meet fellow travelers,*" Tomi read from the sticky note. "*Don't forget dinner tonight, just follow the blue marked trees. A member of my group passed this on to me, and I thought you might find it interesting. It's a slide from an actual slide deck internal to the Department of Defence, about the UAP phenomenon (or what us old guys call UFOs). Sixto.*"

Tomi peeled off the sticky note, and tried to make sense of the various acronyms.

"What does it say?" Kirsten asked. She shuffled her chair closer, and Tomi held it out so they could both read it. "*DoD Threat Scenario, AATIP Sub-Focus Areas,*" she read out loud.

"*DoD* is Department of Defence," said Tomi, "but I don't know *AATIP.*"

"*The science exists for an enemy of the United States to manipulate both physical and cognitive environments in order to penetrate U.S.*

facilities, influence decision makers, and compromise national security," Kirsten read from the printed slide.

"Psychotronic weapons," read Tomi, *"Cognitive Human Interface, Penetration of solid surfaces, -"*

"That's true," said Kirsten. Tomi looked at her to explain more. *"Penetration of solid surfaces.* In the abductions, they went right through the walls. And so could I. Through the walls and out into the craft."

"Right. Wow, Kirsten. That's wild," Tomi said. She looked back to the slide, and continued reading: *"Instantaneous sensor disassembly, Alteration/Manipulation of biological organisms, anomalies in the space/time construct, unique cognitive human interface experiences."*

"Well a lot of that sounds terrifying," laughed Kirsten. "What does that last one mean, do you think? *Cognitive human interface experiences?"*

Tomi read the line a few times and considered it. "Could it be about how they communicate? I'm just thinking of when I've connected with Ete, it's not like we are talking. Not physically. It's all in my mind, I can hear the words, or see them. Or see colours or images, or even just know something."

"Telepathic," said Kirsten. "That's true, too."

Kirsten took back the paper, and read out the last line on the slide: *"What was considered "phenomena" is now quantum physics.* Okay, now I'm regretting not paying attention in physics class," Kirsten said, with a laugh.

They sipped their coffee and listened to the sounds of the forest. Tomi looked back at the printed slide again, and considered the word *threat*. She wondered if people like the General, people in the military, if they actually knew Ete, would still see them as a threat. *Or could they know more, something I don't?* She wondered.

They went inside, made more coffee and oatmeal, and had breakfast. Afterwards, Tomi told Kirsten that she should try to remote view and see if she can connect with Ete.

"Okay, so I have no idea how to be your guide or whatever," said Kirsten, "so just let me know how I can help."

"Just sit beside me and hold my hand again, and I'll let you know what's happening."

Tomi laid down on the couch in the small living room, the woodstove beside her still warm from the night's fire. For a long time, Tomi laid there, silent but for her breathing. Eventually, she said: "Okay, I am ready. I'm going to try to focus on finding Ete."

After a few more minutes, she spoke again. "I'm in a room again. It's grey. Empty, an old empty office it feels like."

"Can you see anything interesting?" Kirsten asked, unsure if she should be coaching or not.

"Yes. Well, no," Tomi said. "It's…darker, this room, darker than the last. There are more fluorescent lights burnt out. There's one flashing. I don't like the feeling here."

"Can you leave this room?" asked Kirsten.

"There's a door. I'm…hesitating. I sense a presence…"

"In the next room? Could it be Ete?" asked Kirsten.

"No," said Tomi, "it feels…darker. Okay, I'm going through."

Kirsten felt worried and realized she was starting to squeeze Tomi's hand.

"No," said Tomi, "there's nothing here either. It just feels…like there's someone here, with bad energy. But there's not. I'm done with this."

Tomi allowed herself time to come out of her deep state, eventually wiggling parts of her body, and opening her eyes. When she did, Kirsten was smiling at her.

"Well, that sucked," Kirsten said. Tomi laughed and nodded. "Come on, let's go be with the trees instead."

They each filled a metal bottle with water, and headed into the woods behind the cabin, moving up in elevation. With the cool nights, the bugs were light, though parts of the forest were so thick, they had to navigate around to keep moving forward. Eventually, Kirsten pointed towards a clearer direction, and said, "That's a game trail. That will be easier to walk."

While Tomi loved nature, she hadn't spent a lot of time deep in the woods, and let Kirsten be her guide, following along behind her as they ducked under some branches or climbed up a rock. Eventually they emerged into a small clearing, where they were able to look out and see the landscape below them, the cabin's roof hidden by the trees.

"What the?" said Kirsten. Tomi saw Kirsten taking a few steps towards the edge of the clearing, where there was a large tree stump. On top of the stump was a fresh, red apple.

Tomi followed Kirsten to get a closer look. "How weird. It's like it's set there as a gift."

"A gift from the forest?" laughed Kirsten. "Although, that sort of makes sense, since the whole forest knows we're here."

"How do you mean?" asked Tomi.

"The mycelium network," she said. "Have you heard of it? Mycelium is this long fungus that wraps around tree roots. And it's basically the internet, but for the forest!"

"What?" said Tomi, unsure if Kirsten was being serious.

"Yes! And it shares water and nutrients with plants that need it. And it lets the plants talk to each other," Kirsten said. "So when you're moving around the forest, the whole forest knows. No secrets here."

"That's...so beautiful," said Tomi, looking around at the trees, suddenly wondering if they have souls. too.

"Isn't it?" Kirsten reached out and held the end of a pine branch in her hand, tickling the needles. "We look at them and see individual trees. But there is no individual tree. It's part of this much bigger whole. The forest."

"Just like people," Tomi said.

A feeling of safety came over Tomi, as she visualized each of these trees, the whole forest, holding her close. She felt the urge to drop to the ground and touch the earth. She leaned her back against the tree stump, and sat cross-legged, the palms of both hands touching the ground. Kirsten saw what she was doing, and sat cross-legged on the other side of the stump in silence.

Tomi focused on her hands and the feeling of the cold ground. The more she focused, the more she could feel that what Kirsten said was true. She imagined her spine growing down, sprouting roots that dug deep into the Earth, weaving around the roots below her.

Can you help me speak to Ete? she asked.

She focused and waited. She felt the ground under her buzzing, a whole world of life and activity that had always been there, though she never thought much of its existence, just below her feet.

An image of a network, a wild and winding network of tunnels, with flashes of energy travelling, zipping here, then a ninety degree turn and zipping there. The image started to give way to simple, straight lines. A room was forming in her mind again.

No, you don't want that. She wasn't sure if she saw the words or felt them, first.

Tomi felt the image in her mind shifting again, from darkness to something subtle, then back to darkness, like making a phone call, getting a busy signal, and trying again.

Atlah-Toa. The letters formed in her mind. *What is that?* she tried to ask. The picture went back to darkness. She tried to refocus, ask again, but could feel that intense connection fading away.

Though she was disappointed the connection faded, she felt a wave of gratitude for the brief feeling of connection and receiving information, even if it might be nothing more than gibberish. But more than that, she felt intense gratitude to the ground below her. It felt like she had made a new friend.

She tapped the ground a few times as thanks and stood up. Kirsten heard her moving, and stood up to face Tomi, the stump between them.

"So, what happened?" Kirsten asked.

"Well, I had a…an intense moment there. I didn't quite connect, but I got a word. Or two, I don't know. *Atlah-Toa.* I have no idea what it means. Or if it is anything at all," she said.

"Atlah-Toa? Huh," Kirsten said.

Tomi looked around. "But you are right about this forest. It really is amazing, it…what is it? What's wrong?"

Kirsten was looking down with a puzzled expression. "Tomi, did you take the apple?"

"Yes, I know about the apple," said Sixto. He was standing outside of his cabin where he had greeted his guests, who shortly after exchanging hellos asked about an apple on a tree stump in the woods. "I put it there. It's a gift for sasquatch."

Sixto's cabin was more rustic and clearly a home rather than a weekend retreat. Tibetan prayer flags were strung between trees in the small yard, with a string hammock hanging between two other trees.

"A gift for…sasquatch?" asked Tomi.

"What, you don't believe in bigfoot?" he asked with a smile.

"I…guess I haven't really thought about it," Tomi said.

"Hey, believing in sasquatch isn't any crazier than believing we've been abducted by another species, is it?" Sixto said with a chuckle.

"Have you seen sasquatch here?" asked Kirsten.

"No, unfortunately I haven't, or fortunately, depending on your perspective. But I leave the apples out for them anyways to show that I'm friendly, and I respect their place in the forest. Look at this," he said, taking a few steps closer to his cabin, and pointing at a small pile of stones placed on an upright log. "Feel them, they're so smooth. Sometimes the apple will be gone, and often there's a stone left for me. They are river rocks; the water has eroded them to be smooth. What are they doing on a stump up the mountain?"

Tomi and Kirsten held them in their hands, rubbing them and feeling the smoothness. "When we were there," Kirsten said, "we both sat down, leaned up against the stump in meditation. When we got up, the apple was gone."

"Far out!" said Sixto, dragging out each word. "And you didn't hear anything approach, or a bird flying over you? Wow. How cool. There are many stories, and indigenous beliefs, of sasquatch being a type of shadow creature. Physical sometimes, a shadow other times. Almost like they can move between states, or dimensions. That's very cool!"

While Sixto's eyes were lit up with excitement, Tomi felt more creeped out than fascinated. She wasn't buying Sixto's explanation, though she thought it may be because she didn't want to imagine a creature of that size reaching for an apple sitting just above her head.

"Come on in," said Sixto, motioning for them to follow him inside. "I'm just working on dinner."

They stepped in and found that the inside was also far more rustic, with old, basic furniture, and a small rustic wood kitchen. In one corner of the cabin, there was a large desk with two monitors, the only overtly modern part of his home. His living room had an old brown couch, a couple of chairs, and the rest of the space was taken up by cluttered bookshelves.

"I'm just making some veggie and haloumi skewers that we will grill. Let me just finish my chopping here. Hey, why don't you pull a card?"

He pointed towards a small table between the living room and kitchen. It had about a dozen small statues - Tomi recognized Buddha and Ganesh, but was unsure of the rest. There was a singing bowl, incense, and a stack of cards spread out messily in the centre of the table.

Tomi stepped towards the table, reached for a card, then hesitated. "What do we do? Just pick one?"

"Yeah," he said, looking down and chopping a zucchini. "Have an intention first. A question, something you want advice on. Say it to yourself, and pick the card that draws you to it. Then you can check that book there," he motioned towards a stack of books beside the table, "look up your card, and see if it tells you anything. And if you don't like what it says, just pick another card! That's what I do," he said, looking up now and smiling.

I almost can't tell if he believes in the things he speaks of or not, thought Tomi. He was earnest yet lighthearted at the same time, not what you expect of an eccentric hermit, or conspiracy theorist, as many would label and dismiss him.

Tomi thought about what she should ask, and didn't know where to start. She thought about John. Her grandmother. Ete. Eventually she settled on a generic question. *Is this path I'm on the right path?* she asked in her mind.

She slid a few cards around and pulled one that caught her eye. She flipped it over to see an old man in a long cloak holding a staff and a lantern. "Nine. The hermit."

"Interesting," said Sixto, now piercing vegetables with metal skewers, "what does the book have to say?"

Tomi bent down to grab the book. She saw the top four books in the stack were all books on tarot. She picked up the top book and looked at the cover: *The Symbolism of the Tarot* by P D. Ouspensky. She flipped to the index, found The Hermit, and turned to the right page.

Tomi had expected something that would explain the meaning of the card, or give some clear guidance. Instead, she read through several paragraphs that painted a scene. At first, she read silently.

After long wanderings over a sandy, waterless desert where only serpents lived, I met the Hermit.

He was wrapped in a long cloak, a hood thrown over his head. He held a long staff in one hand and in the other a lighted lantern, though it was broad daylight and the sun was shining.

"The lantern of Hermes Trismegistus", said the voice, "this is higher knowledge, that inner knowledge which illuminates in a new way even what appears to be already clearly known. This lantern lights up the past, the present and the future for the Hermit, and opens the souls of people and the most intimate recesses of their hearts."

Tomi paused, thinking about all the higher knowledge that has been passed on to her these past few weeks and months. If her journey was to light up the past, present, and future, she thought she was indeed on the right path.

After a few minutes of silence, Kirsten said: "So, anything interesting?"

Tomi scanned it again and began to read what spoke to her most:

"The lantern, the cloak and the staff are the three symbols of initiation. They are needed to guide souls past the temptation of illusory fires by the roadside, so that they may go straight to the higher goal. He who receives these three symbols or aspires to obtain them, "strives to enrich himself with all he can acquire, not for himself, but, like God, to delight in the joy of giving".

"Initiation unites the human mind with the higher mind by a chain of analogies. This chain is the ladder leading to heaven, dreamed of by the patriarch"."

Sixto nodded. "Interesting," he said. "And did that answer your question?"

"I'm…not sure," said Tomi. "I think it did, indirectly. Profoundly."

"Well, the lantern on the card is the lantern of Hermes Trismegistus," he said." Now Hermes Trismegistus – which means *'Hermes Thrice Great!'* Don't you love that name? - anyways, Hermes is a remarkable figure. Maybe there's more you can get from him. Take a look at that," he said, pointing to a framed poster. Tomi stepped towards it to get a closer look. It was made to look old, and looked to be a mountain with lines of small text written on it.

"That is the Emerald Tablet," Sixto continued. "Well, a seventeenth century drawing of it. It's a Hermetic text, perhaps written by Hermes himself! It's where the saying, *as above, so below* comes from."

Tomi looked at the little tower, houses, trees, sky, and sun, such a beautiful scene surrounding the writing. *As above, so below,* she repeated to herself, thinking about the communion she had with the forest and the earth beneath her feet earlier in the day.

"Your turn," said Sixto, nodding to Kirsten.

Kirsten stepped towards the table, paused, closed her eyes, and reached down to pull a card. "Ooh la la, The Lovers," she said. She picked up the book and read silently.

While Kirsten read, Sixto was finishing his preparations, and Tomi shifted her focus to a painting she hadn't immediately noticed, as it was partly hidden, hung between two bookcases. The painting was dark, a grey-black with darker shadow figures. At the bottom of the painting were yellow-orange sections, jutting into the darkness. *Tongues*, thought Tomi. *Tongues of fire.*

"So, anything interesting?" Sixto asked Kirsten. Kirsten had gone from joking about her card to having a look of depth and concentration. She had a delayed response, looked up to acknowledge what Sixto had asked, and said, "Yeah. It's a bit long, but this part was interesting. It talks about the *everlasting mistake with men,"* Kirsten said, looking up from the book and laughing. "Though I don't need a *book* to tell me about the everlasting mistake with men!"

Tomi and Sixto laughed.

"It might be hard to limit it to just one," joked Sixto.

"Okay, where was I?" Kirsten read aloud:

"The everlasting mistake with men, is that they see the fall in love. But Love is not a fall, it is a soaring above an abyss. And the higher the flight, the more beautiful and alluring appears the earth. But that wisdom, which crawls on earth, advises belief in the earth and in the present. This is the Temptation. And the man and woman yielded to it. They dropped from the eternal realms and submitted to time and death. The balance was disturbed. The fairyland was closed upon them. The elves, undines, sylphs, and gnomes became invisible.

She looked up and smiled at Sixto. "I thought you would like that part, what with your bartering with sasquatch." Sixto laughed and nodded. Kirsten continued:

"This Fall, this first 'sin of man', repeats itself perpetually, because man continues to believe in his separateness and in the Present. And only

by means of great suffering can he liberate himself from the control of time and return to Eternity--leave darkness and return to Light."

"Love is a *soaring above an abyss*. That's, well that's beautiful," said Tomi, thinking of Ete. "A…friend, said something similar to me recently. Did it answer your question?"

Kirsten let out a big laugh and said, "Well, I expected something a bit juicier from The Lovers. It is beautiful though."

Sixto laughed, "Like I said, I just ignore the ones that I don't like. Speaking of leaving the dark for the light, let's go outside and build a fire so we can cook like cavepeople."

"Science has taught us so much, but in some ways, we are no different today than we were in Galileo's day," said Sixto, using tongs to flip the skewers on a grill propped up over his fire pit.

"How so?" asked Kirsten. At this point Tomi was a little lost, unsure how the conversation even got here. While Sixto was interesting to listen to, she was grateful to have Kirsten's extroversion to hold up their end of the conversation.

There was so much about this day, this present moment that reminded Tomi of all she had been through these past few months. She was having trouble engaging while her mind was working overtime, processing.

"Well, we don't sentence people to death if they disagree anymore, sure," he continued. "But we definitely ridicule and marginalize ideas that don't conform to the mainstream. Don't conform to accepted science. Which is such a shame, because if we were allowed to really ask questions - and I mean academics and non-academics - if we were really allowed to ask questions, it would just make our science better. If it was okay to dream a little, and not be afraid of being wrong."

Sixto started to pull the skewers off the grill and onto plates.

"Right, I see what you mean," said Kirsten. "I remember I had a science teacher who was like that, like when you asked a question that wasn't part of the textbook, he would act like it was ridiculous. Or if you questioned something, it was like you were questioning science itself. One time I asked what happened before the Big Bang. Like, what was going on then? Okay, so everything was super dense and suddenly exploded, but how did it *get there* in the first place? And what is *there*, for that matter? He didn't like that one."

"Oh, you are so right to ask that! I love that one," he said, handing Tomi and Kirsten their plates. "You see, in their minds nothing can exist unless it's material. Unless you can observe or measure it, it doesn't exist. That's the accepted, materialist view. And so, nothing existed before that you could measure, so it doesn't matter. As though a universe suddenly exploding from a kernel of popcorn with no intervention, no outside spark to light that fuse, makes sense."

"Oh, this tastes amazing," said Kirsten, popping a blackened cherry tomato into her mouth.

"You know," Sixto continued, "Terence McKenna once said, 'Modern science is based on the principle: 'Give us one free miracle and we'll explain the rest.' And that's just it. Everything must be purely scientific, oh except that one miracle where the whole universe emerged from nothing, just don't ask about that one."

"I think that's one reason - *hoo, hoo.*" Kirsten started talking, then put a piece of hot halloumi in her mouth and started blowing air out of her mouth to cool it down. "Sorry, I think that's one reason why an alien – or nonhuman intelligence, as you said - presence here on earth is so threatening, because it makes us rethink…well, everything we know."

"Totally," he said. "The implications are so enormous. I mean what if we find out that something else was involved in our evolution? Or even that we were seeded. Pohhh!" he said, making a brain-exploding motion with his hands. "But really, that's why I had to leave the academy. I couldn't do the research I wanted to do. On my own, I can."

Tomi was quietly enjoying the dinner and felt nourished from it already. She looked around at the surrounding trees, and seeing that the forest was dark, realized that dusk had fallen. As she looked at the dark line of trees, she noticed tongues of flames flickering up from the fire, and thought about the painting inside.

"That painting was interesting," Tomi said, "the one that's sort of dark, with shadows, and fire at the bottom. What is that?"

"Oh, that," he said, "that was from my latest attempt to become an artist. It's my depiction of the Cave."

"Which cave?" asked Kirsten.

"Plato's Cave, from The Republic," Sixto said. "Have you read it?"

Kirsten shook her head as she finished her last skewer.

"I've heard of it, but I'm not sure what it is," said Tomi.

"Well," started Sixto, "I think it might make sense in the context of this very conversation. And I think it's so important for us experiencers. Because we know what most people don't. Okay, quick recap: There are prisoners in a cave, and they're chained up and can only look at the cave wall. And they've never been out of the cave, so it's all they know. Behind them is a fire, and their captors make shadows on the cave wall. And to the prisoners, *those shadows* are reality."

"Oh, I think I've heard of this," said Kirsten.

"Well one day, one of the prisoners escapes," he continued. "They see what is making the shadows, then leave the cave, and see the land, the water, and finally the sun. So now they know, they experience the true nature of reality. So, should they go back for the others?"

Tomi thought he was asking rhetorically, but after a few moments, she answered: "Yes?"

"Well, Plato would agree with you," he said. "He said it's our responsibility to go back and let everyone know that the reality they believe in is an illusion. Now, how do you think they welcomed this news?"

"They didn't believe him," guessed Tomi, feeling amused at the way Sixto slipped right into professor mode.

"Worse. They killed him," he said.

"Talk about shooting the messenger," said Kirsten.

"Exactly," said Sixto. "But Plato believes we still need to do it."

"So, we are the prisoners who escaped," said Tomi flatly, not liking the implications.

"Exactly," he said. "And if today you say that science hasn't fully explained our reality, that there are phenomena humans experience that can't be rationalized, and ask people to step out of their cave, well, you may not be killed but you will surely be called a crank, or conspiracy theorist, or looney."

Kirsten laughed. "I've been called worse."

Sixto laughed along, then continued. "And here, we three, we know there is a nonhuman intelligence here on earth."

"Multiple," said Tomi.

"Multiple," Sixto repeated while nodding, as though Tomi the student gave the right answer. "But if we go out and tell people that, talk openly about it, talk to someone about it on the street corner, we would be called crazy. And reminded that the shadows on the cave wall are all that really exist."

"So why do it?" asked Kirsten.

"Well," he laughed, "you may have noticed I live like a hermit in the woods, so you won't see me preaching on the street corner! Anyways, there isn't much light left. Let me walk you back through the woods."

Tomi and Kirsten had thought ahead and brought flashlights from the cabin, which proved necessary on their hike back. Sixto led the way with a miner's flashlight strapped to his forehead.

Other than walking into some spider webs, and a scratch on Tomi's hand from a stray broken branch, they made it back without event. As they emerged from the woods to the clearing around the cabin, Sixto gave a bow in jest and said: "And you are returned safely to your castle. Thank you for the company and conversation. It's always a treat to share an evening with fellow travellers."

"It was so lovely, thank you," Kirsten said, giving him a friendly hug.

"Sixto, before you go," said Tomi, "I want to ask you something. Is there a way to, I don't know, get in touch with the aliens? Invite them to connect?"

"Oh sure," he said with a shrug, as though it was a simple, everyday question. "Human-initiated contact. I mean, not everyone agrees that it works, but I've had some results."

Tomi was encouraged. Perhaps she could find another way to connect with Ete since remote viewing hadn't been successful. "How does it work?" she asked. "How do we do it?"

"Well, there are protocols out there which you can research," he said, "but basically, I just meditate and invite contact. I put that invitation out to the universe. Because it's all about consciousness, right? So, you get into a deep meditation, and invite the phenomenon to make contact. You can do it outside, at night. One of you could meditate, the other could be on the lookout for visitors in the sky!"

"Oh, so you might see like a UFO?" Kirsten asked.

"Your mileage may vary," he said with a laugh.

"What about…inviting communication. Or real contact?" asked Tomi.

"You mean inviting abduction? I mean, you could try to put that invitation out," Sixto said, looking concerned. "But, well, my advice is to be *very* careful. You know, when you open the door to the other side, you can't be sure what might step out of it. And even if you can communicate with something benevolent, well if that door is open, other things can come through. Even attach to you and follow you. Like a hitchhiker."

"I see," Tomi said, already certain she will ignore those warnings and attempt it. "I will be careful. Thank you for sharing that. And for dinner, and helping us get back."

As they walked into the cabin, Kirsten said, "You're going to want to do that, aren't you?"

Tomi scrunched her face. "Yes? But I won't if you don't feel comfortable."

"Please, I'm on this rollercoaster with you," Kirsten said. "But how about not tonight? I'm ready for bed."

Although she was also tired, Tomi had a rough night of sleep. She would fall asleep, wake up to the bright moonlight coming through the drapes, then fall asleep again.

When she did sleep, her dreams were intense, vivid, like the type of dream a fever brings on - sweaty and disorienting.

The dream was a memory. Tomi was a child, awake, lying in her childhood bed. She was under the covers. It was dark, but with a little bit of light coming from the window, she could see she was in the room she grew up in.

And she was scared, frozen in fear. She was being watched. Her bedroom had a wide window, covered by white plastic blinds. The blinds were just a smidge too short, and the glow of the streetlight snuck through at the bottom.

But so too did their watching eyes. There were a few of them. *Three? Four?* She could feel their stare deep in her bones. She couldn't move. She was frozen in her bed with fear.

It was the kids from school. She knew it. They were outside her window, the cool kids. She barely interacted with them at school. They intimidated her. They ignored her. And now here they were outside her bedroom, watching her. Waiting for her to do something weird or awkward. Waiting to judge her and laugh.

Although none of it made sense - *why would kids be out this late? why would they gather to watch me sleep? Why does it make me so scared?* – in Tomi's mind, she knew it was them.

She looked at her hand, gripping the top of the covers. She saw a fresh scratch on her hand, but couldn't remember cutting herself. She touched it.

Tomi awoke, saw Kirsten beside her, and breathed deeply. *This dream was a memory,* she thought. *I remember these nights, paralyzed in my bed.* She looked at her hand, gripping the top of the covers, and saw the scratch she got on her hand in the woods.

She fell asleep again. Again, she dreamed she was a child, in bed. *They* were watching her again. *The kids* were watching her, and she was frozen in fear.

The dream repeated throughout the night.

Chapter 14

"If human reactions to the vision of a UFO are varied, the opposite holds true for animals: their reaction is unmistakably one of terror."

Jacques Vallée

*T*omi *awoke. She opened her eyes. The room was bright. Brighter than it should be. She was sleeping on her stomach, and flipped over to look at the window. Light was streaming in through the thin drapes. It was too bright to be coming from the moon.*

She turned halfway over to face Kirsten. She saw Kirsten laying on her back, her pillow on the floor. Her body was straight as an arrow. Like a mummy, Tomi thought.

Tomi put her hand on Kirsten's arm, lying flat beside her body. Her arm felt cold. She squeezed it. Kirsten didn't react.

"Hey, Kirsten. Wake up," she said, in a loud whisper. She put her hand on Kirsten's shoulder and gave her a shake. Kirsten didn't respond.

She turned back over to look at the window. It was like there was a spotlight on the cabin. She wanted to turn back to her left, to try waking Kirsten again, but her body didn't move. A wave of fear ran up her body, starting with her toes, hanging in the air just off the bed.

She felt her skin break out into goosebumps. She had the unmistakable feeling that she was being watched from the window.

"Okay, so we will meditate together at first," said Tomi. "Then when I give you a signal, I want you to scan the skies. See if you can see an orb, or UFO, or whatever. And if you do, let me know. Does that sound okay?"

"Yeah, sure," said Kirsten, sounding hesitant. "I'm just…what are we hoping for exactly? That Ete shows up in a UFO? Takes us for a little spin. Like, is that actually the goal?"

Tomi shrugged. "I'm not sure what will happen. Maybe some kind of sign or something? I mean if Ete showed up and could explain what happened to my grandmother, sure, that would be the ultimate goal."

Kirsten laughed. "Invite Ete in for some wine? Okay, I'll scan the skies and try to wave Ete down. I just - I don't know, Sixto freaked me out a little bit. Careful, okay?"

"Okay."

They stepped out into the middle of the clearing in front of the cabin. Tomi dropped to the ground, sat cross-legged, took Kirsten's hand, and guided her to also sit cross-legged, facing her.

"Okay, let's start with meditating," Tomi said. She felt anxious for this to work, and knew she would need to spend a good deal of time breathing and relaxing her body to get into a deep meditation.

They had made sure to have an easy, no stress day, to save energy for this, tonight.

After some time, Tomi had cleared her mind and was at peace. She sat with this for some time, then felt that she was ready to hold this state of peace while also taking action. Tomi squeezed Kirsten's hands, and could sense her getting up to watch the skies.

In this deep, peaceful state, Tomi tried to open herself to the wider consciousness, to communicate, make a broadcast she hoped would travel along some super spectrum and magically arrive in Ete's consciousness.

Ete, I need to communicate with you. Please, make contact. She would say this in her mind, feeling it leave her individual consciousness, and watching with her mind's eye as it floated off to wherever it needed to go.

Then she would wait, and after some time, would repeat it again. She was in this state for what felt like hours, until she felt a physical presence beside her.

"Tomi, I think it's time to call it a night. It's late. I've been looking all over. Beautiful stars. But no UFO. I'm sorry," Kirsten said softly, knowing Tomi would be disappointed.

Tomi became more aware of her body and opened her eyes. "Yeah, let's go to bed. Thanks for trying this with me."

Even though the window had been closed in the bedroom, the drapes, hanging from a rod fastened just above the window, blew open, stretched

out horizontally, lifting from the bottom up; but instead of drifting back down after being blown open, the drapes held their rigid, horizontal position in the air. Light streamed into the room, casting tall shadows onto the ceiling.

Tomi's body was frozen. She could sense people in the room. She could smell them. A deep sulfur smell entered her nose, familiar and repulsive. Then the smell was gone.

It was replaced by a flash of light, somehow brighter than the light that had already flooded the room. Her eyes were frozen, open. The ceiling got closer.

I'm floating, *she realized.*

Her body rotated and she could see that the blankets were undisturbed, like she'd floated right through them. Beside her empty side of the bed was Kirsten, still asleep. Tomi tried to scream, to call to her. It was as though all her energy travelled up her body to her throat, where it hit a block, a terrified scream just lodged there. She didn't make a sound. Her throat burned.

Her body rotated again, and she saw she was approaching the wall beside the window, headfirst. She tried to brace her body as her head approached the wall, but instead of impact, there was a moment of darkness, and she emerged outside.

She saw the source of the light, but it was so bright she could hardly make out what object was creating it. She floated towards it. Though she was terrified, she had always dreamed of floating, free of gravity and a heavy body.

From the light, she could start to make out silhouettes. Four of them, standing in a row. Four silhouettes of children. But not children, *thought Tomi.* No. They were never children.

"I'm sorry that didn't work out tonight," said Kirsten, sleepily. They were lying in bed facing each other, Tomi on the left side and Kirsten on the right. Tomi could only see half of Kirsten's face, the other half buried in the thick feather pillow.

"It's okay," said Tomi, though she was feeling frustrated that she couldn't connect with Ete again. She was starting to wonder if she ever will. Or ever had. "We tried. We could try again."

"I believe in you," said Kirsten. Tomi smiled. She thought it sounded silly, and yet it filled her with confidence.

"Do you believe that souls live multiple lives together? Like a family or cluster of souls?" asked Kirsten, changing the subject after a pause.

"Or a classroom of souls? Yeah, I do," said Tomi, thinking about the soul cluster vision Ete had shown her the last time they connected.

Kirsten held eye contact for a moment before continuing. "This one time, years ago, I was driving in this residential area, not far from home. I was turning left, and on the corner there were two women walking a dog. As I was turning, I made eye contact with the one, and we both just held it, and it was the most intense feeling. I just felt that I knew her. But I didn't. I mean I could feel it deep in my soul that I recognized her."

"I know that feeling," said Tomi.

"I didn't realize it at first, like I eventually broke eye contact and kept driving, but I couldn't get it out of my mind. It was like I saw someone from my soul family or something. I went by that spot a bunch of times, but never saw her again. Not that I'd know what to say."

"Hello soul sister," said Tomi, both laughing.

"Anyways. That's how I felt when I first met you," Kirsten said. "Soul sister." Tomi smiled. She thought about Kirsten dreaming about the hilly island. She hadn't told her the details of her past life regression, had never told her about her special place. She thought about telling her now. But she didn't. In a moment, she fell asleep.

She was inside a craft. Or is it a building? *Tomi thought, looking around. It couldn't be a craft, it's too big, like a giant empty warehouse, or airplane hangar. She could see the walls off in the distance, but they seemed distorted, making it hard to identify her surroundings. Everything was bright.*

And all around her were people. She looked around, seeing all kinds of people standing in long lines. She realized she too was in a line. In front of her was a little boy in pyjamas, his mother beside him, but not holding his hand. They faced straight forward, taking slow, shuffling steps. She realized she was moving forward, too, keeping pace.

Where am I going? *she wondered. She looked to her right. There was a woman wearing a hijab and a beautiful evening gown, like she just walked out of a five-star restaurant. Beside her was a man in plaid pants and a white undershirt, walking barefoot. She looked down and realized she was barefoot and in her pyjamas, too.*

Tomi looked to her left and saw a young man in a suit, his tie loosened, stepping straight forward. It was like being at an international airport, with people of all complexions, and all sorts of different clothes. Then she saw Sixto.

"Sixto. Sixto!" she said. He was in the next line beside her, no more than three feet away. He stared straight forward, unphased by someone beside him calling his name.

"Sixto?"

He stepped forward, his line moving faster. She watched as he stepped behind a large privacy barrier.

Move forward. *She heard the words in her mind, rather than through her ears. She turned to her right and they were there; their faces just like her grandmother's drawing or Sixto's tattoo.* Small greys, *she thought.*

They were short. Tomi guessed four feet. Though they were small, when Tomi looked into their large, dark eyes, she felt her body flush in fear. She couldn't move. These beings were not like Ete.

You don't need to fear. Move forward.

She stepped around one of the privacy barriers, which were assembled to create semi-private rooms within this huge structure. Tomi blinked her eyes. Everything was bright.

She was put on a table. The two greys were standing beside her. She couldn't look at them. She looked to her right, and saw a human, a woman, with long straight gray hair, wearing a long white lab coat. She was touching some machine.

"Hey! Ma'am. Ma'am! Help me!" Tomi yelled. The woman slowly turned to look at her, emotionless, then looked back at the machine.

Tomi looked towards her feet, and saw two more humans, a man, and a woman. The man was also working on a machine, and the woman touching a screen. It's like they work here, she thought.

She looked back to her left. The two greys were gone, and in their place was a taller grey. Tomi looked into its eyes and this time didn't feel terrified. She's female, thought Tomi, unsure how she knew this. The being placed her hand on Tomi's forearm. Tomi felt calm in her presence. She had seen this being before.

I know you, Tomi thought.

You know why we have to do this, Tomi heard in her mind. We won't hurt you. You know it's for the best.

The being turned and walked away. The two smaller greys came back. Tomi looked away from them. She saw another bed near hers. There was a little girl on this bed. The taller, female being was now over with the child, reassuring the little girl. Tomi stared at her and suddenly lost her breath. That little girl is Kirsten, she thought. She was sure of it.

The little girl made eye contact with her. Tomi watched a small grey lift a device, and place it behind the child's ear. There was a puff. What did they do to her? Tomi thought, her stomach on fire with anger at them harming a child. Harming Kirsten.

Then darkness.

Tomi woke up to the sound of birds. The thin cotton drapes blew open with the gentle breeze coming through the open window. The sun softly lit the pine wood floor. She turned her head over to see Kirsten, head on her pillow, her eyes open.

"Good morning," said Kirsten. "Good sleep?"

"Yeah," Tomi said, yawning. "I guess so. I think I slept right through. I'm kind of still tired though."

"Then don't get up!" said Kirsten. "We're on vacation, remember? Besides we were up late trying to call ET."

Tomi smiled, remembering their uneventful attempt at human-initiated contact.

"Well somehow in the night, we switched sides," said Kirsten. "Have some crazy dreams and roll over me or something?"

"What?" Tomi lifted her head and looked around the room, and realized Kirsten was right. She had been on the side of the bed closest to the window, but now was on the other side, as though they'd gotten up and switched in the night.

"Well that's super weird," Tomi said, laughing. "I'm not responsible for what I do when I'm unconscious. And no, I don't remember any dreams actually."

"I had a dream last night," said Kirsten. "I had a dream that I saw you somewhere, but you were just a kid. We both were. It felt super real."

"Ha," Tomi laughed, "and did I have my cool braces?"

"I don't know, I only remember that I saw you," Kirsten said, fluffing her pillow and settling her head in again. "Where did you grow up again? San Fran?"

"Close, Oakland. You are from Durham, right?"

"Yeah, well I was born in Alaska actually! My dad was there for work. But then we moved to Durham when I was around two." Kirsten was silent for a moment. "I wish I knew you as a kid."

"Me too," Tomi said.

Kirsten turned her head on the pillow, and Tomi looked at Kirsten's ear, unsure why it drew her attention.

After laying in for a while, they got up, made a French press of coffee, sat outside, and enjoyed the peace of the nature around them.

Chapter 15

"The more you fly in space the more you see an incredible amount of things out there and that sort of brings to you, really a certainty, that other living creatures are out there.

Some incredibly primitive, more primitive, some just ah proteins coming together, amino acids and some just single-cell organisms and other civilisations that have been around for a million years that are doing unimaginable kinds of things."

Franklin Story Musgrave, NASA Astronaut

Ib stared at the drawer full of neatly folded tops and leggings, clueless about how to pack for a woman. When he was asked to pack a bag so that Tomi had more clothes, Ib thought that would be a simple task. Instead, he found that his bachelor lifestyle had left him with a few knowledge gaps.

It's been a long time since I've lived with a woman, Ib thought. *Not that I was ever attentive enough then to know what she would have packed.*

He started grabbing stacks of folded clothes, placing them in the luggage he had pulled out of her closet. Ib decided his strategy would be to jam as much as he could into the bag. He opened the next drawer to find socks, bras, and underwear. *Oh boy*, he thought.

It took using his body weight, but he got the clamshell luggage closed enough to get the zipper all the way around. He then followed instructions to open John's closet, move a box out of the way, and enter a four-digit code into a small safe.

Ib entered the code: *2-0-2-7-*.

Ib opened the safe door and found Tomi's passport. They had no plan for the next steps yet, but they thought it best to keep options open. He closed the safe, replaced the box in front of it, and left the bedroom. *So cold and empty*, Ib thought.

As he carefully descended the stairs outside the bedroom, Ib thought about being in his own bedroom, years ago, packing his own bags, his wife Dagmar already long gone. *So cold and empty.*

Ib put the luggage at the front door. He figured if the house is being monitored, they're going to know he visited anyways, so why not go in the front door.

So far in Barry's conversations with intelligence contacts, it seems that Tomi is in no immediate danger. But she is a person of interest. Barry had been told that all could be forgiven. But she would need to meet. To come in. They wanted her for something.

Ib reached to open the door, then paused. He thought for a moment, then turned and headed towards John's office. He scanned the wall and found the picture that intrigued him so. He looked closely. A young John with another serviceman, John's arm around the man, both smiling. *I know this man*, thought Ib.

He looked around, looked back at the picture, and pulled it off the wall. Ib went back to the front door, and opened the zipper on the luggage just enough to slip the picture in between some clothes.

He opened the door, stepped out, and put the luggage in the back of his car. He looked up and down the street, but didn't see anything suspicious.

Ib got in his car and headed home. He pulled out his phone, and recorded an encrypted voice message: "Tomi, got your clothes and passport and - and yes, well, there is much to discuss. We will see you in two days. Stay safe. Ib Johansen."

Tomi was on her knees on the floor of the kitchen in her home. The sun shone brightly through the kitchen window, covering her in light.

Crunch. Crunch.

She turned to find the source of the sound. A man was beside her, a spade in his hand. There were stakes driven into the floor and a line was tied between the stakes to mark off a square, as though it were an archeological dig. The man was digging into the tile floor, but instead of resistance, the floor lifted onto the shovel as though it were made of dirt. With each shovel full, he dumped the debris into a box with four wooden walls, and a grating at the bottom for sifting.

Crunch. Crunch.

He put down his spade, picked up the box, and looked at the contents. Tomi looked at his face. Wrinkled, perhaps too much sun in his life. He had a curious, determined look.

The man started shaking the box back and forth. Tomi watched sand start to drift to the floor, falling slowly as if it were snow.

"Just imagine what might exist just below us, and we don't even know," the man said. "What we can't even imagine."

The sand stopped falling and was followed by full pieces of tile and wooden subfloor, flowing illogically from the tiny holes. Like the sand, they also fell gently to the floor until the sifter was empty.

The man picked up the spade again and dug it deep into the floor.

"If you dig like that, won't you damage whatever might be under there, whatever it is you're trying to find?" Tomi asked.

"That's precisely the point," the man said, digging deeper into the floor.

Slop.

"There," the man said, holding up his shovelful of wet debris, dripping water. "Tomi, why are so many ancient holy sites built above sources of water? And how much of our history lies below the seas, waiting for us to discover it?"

Tomi peered into the hole and saw water flowing under her floor. *This isn't right,* she thought. Where's John? *Wait 'til he sees the floor.*

"I'm dreaming," she said.

"That you are," the man said, looking intensely into her eyes. "Atlah-Toa, Tomi. That's how you get my attention. Tell me you know about Atlah-Toa."

"Who are you?" Tomi asked, but the man was fading. She woke with a start.

"Hey, are you okay?" Kirsten said. "You were having a bit of a rough dream. You're sweating."

Tomi felt her forehead, wet but cold. She looked around to see that she was in the living area of the cabin. Her head on a pillow in the middle of the couch, curled up like a bean. Kirsten was sitting upright on the couch, just beside Tomi's head.

Tomi looked up to see that Kirsten was deep into a book, having been reading while Tomi napped. Tomi read the title on the spine, *Evidence From the Ancients*. Then she was drawn to the small black and white picture of the author on the back cover of the book. *It's him. The man from the dream,* Tomi thought. *Tell me you know about Atlah-Toa.*

"Um, who wrote that book?" Tomi asked with an urgent tone.

"Arthur Minear," she said. "Why?"

"So why do you need to contact him?" asked Kirsten, walking behind Tomi through the narrow path heading to Sixto's cabin.

"I...I don't know," said Tomi. "He told me to. In my dream on the couch."

"Okay, stop for a second?" Kirsten asked. Tomi stopped to face her, though she looked impatient. Her phone had been switched off in case it was being tracked. She knew Sixto had the internet, and had mentioned that he used a VPN to ensure his location wasn't traceable. She figured his paranoia - or reasonable caution? - could come in handy.

"Do you think maybe you saw the picture on the book, and that's why you dreamed about him?" Kirsten asked. "I'm not saying it wasn't something…profound, I guess. I just know we're trying to keep a low profile, and I'm worried."

"That could be it, I accept that," said Tomi. "Just like all of my remote viewing, like all of this, it all could be just something my mind is making up. But I guess I just *know*. I've been able to feel what's real, so far. And I feel it now. I don't know why but I think I'm supposed to talk to him."

Kirsten took a breath. "I'm ride or die, so if you say you need to contact him, let's do it."

"Thanks." Tomi smiled, turned, and started walking again. "So, what's the book about, anyways?" she asked, turning her head to try to look at Kirsten when she spoke.

"It's umm, it's pretty interesting, actually," Kirsten said, pausing between words as she navigated through branches. "Basically, he makes the case that human civilization is actually way older than we think. That there were advanced civilizations before, and they got wiped out in the Great Flood."

Tomi slowed to look back at Kirsten. "The Great Flood. You mean like, Noah's Ark?"

"Yeah! He talks about it. But the Bible isn't the only place that talks about this flood. Minear goes through all these cultures that have the same flood myth. In the Middle East, the Americas, Africa, and Europe. All over. He believes that there was mass destruction that wiped this earlier civilization out, and so *our* civilization as we know it wasn't the first for humanity, but was actually a rebuilding, or relearning of civilization after this global cataclysm."

"Global cataclysm," Tomi repeated. She thought about the vision Ete had shared with her, that huge, beautiful city being erased by a wall of water. She picked up her pace, more certain now that she was right about contacting Minear.

They emerged from the woods into the clearing around Sixto's cabin. They looked around but didn't see him at first, until Kirsten touched Tomi's elbow, and pointed to the treeline behind the cabin. There was a large stone coming out of the hill, and perched atop it was Sixto, bandana around his head, cross-legged in meditation.

"I guess we just wait," said Kirsten in a whisper. She took out her phone, connected to Sixto's network, and found a message from Ib.

"Ib picked up the stuff you asked for," Kirsten said. "They'll be here in two days."

Tomi half listened to Kirsten's update, scraping her foot back and forth on the grass impatiently. She thought if she stared at Sixto he might sense her gaze and realize they were here. After a minute or so with no change in his posture, Tomi gave up.

Tomi forced two loud coughs. Sixto started to move.

"Tomi, that wasn't cool," said Kirsten, a cheeky grin on her face.

"Oh, hi there!" said Sixto from his perch, stretching out his limbs and climbing off the rock.

"Oh, I'm sorry we disturbed you," said Tomi. "I was hoping you might let me use your computer to send an email. And maybe show me how I can send it so it can't be traced?"

Sixto looked at her seriously, then smiled, pointing a finger at Tomi. "You don't want the *man* to track you. Smart. I like it. Sure, I can help."

Sixto helped Tomi create an encrypted email account. "And with my VPN, your location should be untraceable," he said. "I'll give you some privacy and wait outside."

Tomi searched for Arthur Minear's email address, and though she went through pages of searches, couldn't find anything better than the general email address on his website.

He probably gets so many emails. She thought about how to get his attention. *Tell me you know about Atlah-Toa,* he had said.

She moved the cursor to the subject line, and typed, *I know about Atlah-Toa.* She wrote a short email about her need to talk to him and clicked send.

She was about to close the browser, having accomplished her goal and hesitated. She had been disconnected from the world for a week now, and her curiosity got to her. She logged into her personal email account. *I'm covered by the VPN,* she thought, *and I'm not sending anything.*

She opened her inbox to see the typical spam messages, along with several from John. They had subject lines from *Tomi, please answer your phone,* to *Where are you?* to *Help me fix this.* She opened the most recent message.

Tomi,

I need you to call me or message me. I've learned some troubling things about your new friends. They don't have your best interests in mind.

I'm worried about you. Even if we are done, I still want to help you. I know you are in some trouble, but if you will come in with me, I know we can fix it. I can protect you.

Call me.

John

"Tomi, everything work okay on there?" asked Sixto through the door.

"Yes, thanks," said Tomi. "Just finishing up."

She logged out, deleted the browser history, and came outside to join Sixto and Kirsten.

"Thank you so much for letting me do that," said Tomi. "Thing is, now I'm hoping to get an answer. I may need to pop by a few times to check for a reply."

"You're welcome to any of my stuff anytime you need. And hey, if consciousness really is primary, as I was just saying to Kirsten, none of this stuff materially exists anyways. Now, what would such knowledge, if deeply understood and shared by everyone, do to the Nasdaq, I wonder," Sixto said with a laugh, though he wasn't joking.

Arthur Minear sipped his tea as he opened his email inbox - 324 new emails. He did strive to at least scan all emails his fans - and detractors - sent to him, but after a time away, that goal felt like climbing a mountain.

And climbing a mountain he had just done. In the corner of the room was his luggage, still unpacked, his least favourite chore after returning from the field.

What do you think about this theory? the subject of one email read. He continued to scroll. He would come back to these, but for now he was scanning to see if there was anything urgent.

His wife Peggy would be home in an hour, to find that he had returned early. He planned to surprise her with dinner on the stove when she got home, but gave in to this distraction. After four weeks away in the desert, it felt good to be connected to the world again, although he wouldn't have given up a second of this trip.

Usually, he would find out about archeological discoveries after they had been announced or published. He wasn't an archeologist by training. Instead, he believed his role was to make sense of discoveries from an alternative perspective, one where what we know of our past is an incomplete picture, only small pieces of a much larger human tapestry.

In Arthur's tapestry of humanity, the ancients didn't create remarkable things with limited technology. The ancients were people with technology and an understanding of our place in the world that was truly advanced. Perhaps more advanced.

But on this trip, he got to be part of the discovery. He'd been tipped off to it, and on this expedition, he had found something truly ground shaking, if incomplete. Something that again affirmed Arthur's belief that what we call myths are often based on truth. *And what a truth I've found*, he thought.

What you fail to understand, another email subject line that caught his eye. Sometimes even better than a supportive email is one where the detractor twists themselves in knots to explain away Minear's theories, like setting up bowling pins for him to knock down with his extensive knowledge.

He kept scrolling, and as he got to the top of his inbox, his stomach sank to the floor. *I know about Atlah-Toa*, the subject line read.

How could this be? He had made this discovery with an archeologist he partnered with. Then there was their guide and a translator. Four people. But everyone was sworn to secrecy. Of course, his wife Peggy knew, but she would never spill the beans, not until he was ready to share it with the world.

He clicked the email.

Hello Mr. Minear,

I need to talk to you urgently.

Thomasina

He shook his head in wonder. *Well, well*, he thought. *Who is this Thomasina, and what secrets might she share?*

Barry sipped his martini, looking around at the few patrons at Rory's Tavern and decided none of them were here to slip him classified information. Whoever he was waiting for was already twenty minutes late, unless they were perfectly disguised as a sleepy regular.

While Barry had had many covert, off-the-record meetings with intelligence officials over the years researching his books, none felt quite as mysterious - or important - as this one. Barry couldn't help but feel a bit like he was waiting for his own Deepthroat, like he was a character in some sort of paranormal-mystery-thriller.

Of course, everything had felt a bit like a mystery-thriller since Tomi had come to PSI, and into Barry's life. And while it had been destabilizing, it was also the most alive Barry had ever felt. Instead of writing fringe history, he was helping to make it.

A woman entered the Tavern, looked around, and took a seat at a table with a few other regulars. *Not Deepthroat*, he thought. The fact was he had no idea who he was waiting for. He had been making subtle inquiries with some contacts he had in Intelligence. Mostly, they hadn't learned much, but after a short, in-person meeting with Summit, he had learned that Tomi wasn't in immediate danger.

And that if she would consider coming in for a meeting to develop an understanding, this all could be resolved.

And then things got weirder, first with the photograph, then the note.

Last night, Ib had come to Barry's home to avoid speaking on the phone. He pulled a framed picture from his bag and showed it to Barry. "Recognize anyone?"

Barry stared at the photo. "I give up, who are these men?" he asked.

"This one is John, Tomi's husband," Ib said, putting his finger on the man on the left. "I took this from his office. I know, I know, what's happened to the respectable Ib Johansen, stealing from a client's homes? Anyways, this man. Look closely."

Ib pointed his finger at the man on the right in the photograph. Barry squinted.

"The General," he said, with an edge of sadness in his voice, thinking first of what this might mean for Tomi. He looked again, hoping it was just a fleeting similarity. The man in the picture was fifteen, maybe twenty years younger, but if it wasn't the General, the resemblance would be uncanny.

"It's him," Barry said with a sigh.

"It's just…" Ib started, then paused, his whole face furrowed as he tried to make some sense of the photograph. "We were with the General when we picked Tomi up, remember? John answered the door. It sure didn't seem like two people who were old military buddies."

"Yeah," said Barry slowly, thinking back to that day, the day of the unforgettable investigation of Mars. "Or was it two people pretending they didn't know each other?"

They continued discussing the photograph and what it might mean, but came to no conclusions. They agreed they would tell Tomi only when they saw her in person.

Then there was the mysterious note. A small piece of paper, ripped roughly from a notepad, was waiting for him this morning, secured under his windshield wiper.

I have important information that you are seeking. Rory's Tavern 8:30 pm tonight. Alone. I will find you.

Barry looked at his watch and found Mickey had one arm pointing to nine, and the other to twelve. He sipped the last of his martini and was about to stand up to leave, when another person came in the door. They had a dark jacket on, and a dark baseball cap pulled low. He couldn't make out a face.

They approached the bar and ordered a drink. While they waited, the person scanned the bar, stopping just before looking at Barry in the back corner. They paid for their drink and took a sip. Then another. *Not Deepthroat*, thought Barry.

Just then, he watched them scan the bar again, once again avoiding looking directly at Barry. After another sip, the person turned and walked quickly over to Barry's table, and sat down. They took their sunglasses off, pulled off the hat, and looked Barry in the eye.

"Meena?" he said, clearly surprised. He remembered Meena, Summit's wife, who had been at PSI for Tomi's first remote viewing. Normally he wasn't great at remembering faces, but Barry remembered every detail of being in the large room at PSI, looking at that rough sketch of his watch projected on the screen.

"I have information that you need," she said quietly, looking over each shoulder and leaning in. "About Tomi."

Barry could see that she was extremely nervous. "Please, tell me, don't worry, we are alone back here."

She opened her mouth to speak, then took a drink, her nervousness making her mouth dry.

"I know that Summit told you to encourage Tomi to come in," she said. "You cannot do this. I don't believe it will be safe for her."

"What makes you believe that?" asked Barry.

"It's…it's all lies," she said, struggling to get the words out. Barry could see she had tears welling in her eyes. He realized whatever she had to share was so important that it pushed her to betray someone she loved.

"It's okay," he said, encouraging her to continue. "Whatever you have to say, just know I think you're incredibly brave, and I truly honour that. This is between us."

Meena wiped her tears, drew in a deep breath, and closed her eyes for a moment. When she opened them, her voice had regained its strength.

"Tomi is not a person to them," she said. "She's an asset. The time we all went to PSI for the test, that wasn't what it seemed. It was presented as though Summit's work was going to find out about your work and research, reviewing it in case they wanted to contract with you. That's not true. It was a setup. And that wasn't Tomi's first time remote viewing."

Barry was stunned. "Tomi lied?"

"No," she said. "From her perspective, it was true. To her it really was her first time. I don't know how, but they've blocked her memories. They've been training her from a young age, using her without her knowing. From what I gather, they determined, or hoped, that she could be more powerful, a better asset, if she used her gifts while not under their control. So, this was all their plan, to wind her up and let her go."

Barry's mouth was wide open, struggling to take this in. It was big, and most people would hear something like this and think such a big deception, some mind control conspiracy, would be impossible. From all his research on covert and special access programs, none of this sounded impossible. He'd heard crazier.

But this wasn't some program he was researching for a book. This was Tomi. His friend.

He sighed deeply. "And she never knew."

"She never knew. And John discouraged her from getting her own job, her own life," Meena continued.

"So John was in on it," Barry said, thinking about the photograph.

Meena nodded, as a tear dripped down her face. Barry could see this information was weighing on her.

"So John was her handler. How far back did this go?" Barry asked.

"Them taking her in, training her, wiping the memory of it, that started when she was a teenager," Meena said, shaking her head.

Barry leaned back, trying to take it all in. "How did you come to know this?"

Meena breathed, then exhaled deeply. "My husband, well, I believe he's a good man. And that he works for some very bad men. He works so hard to provide for us. And he really believes that his work is keeping the country safe. I just, I needed to say that."

"I understand," said Barry, nodding.

"But he's not always the most diligent with secrecy at home," she continued. "Usually he locks any documents up, but every once in a while, he leaves things out on his desk. Yesterday, I could hear him in his office speaking to you. I heard what he told you about Tomi. Frankly, our walls are thin, and when I heard him say her name, it caught my attention and I, well, I listened."

She took another sip of her drink, her throat bone dry from anxiety.

"After her talked to you, he had a phone call. It was quick. He came out of his home office, then said he had to go out for work. After he left, I found that he had a file open on his desk. The label on it said *Starlight 9*. When I started to flip through, I realized Starlight 9 was Tomi. I started to go through it, and I read about what they did to her."

"And you had to come forward," said Barry. "That's really, really brave of you, Meena."

Meena wiped tears from her face. "It's just wrong what they did to her, Barry. She's not a human being to them, throughout the folder they just call her *the asset*. It's just wrong. I love my husband and support him in every way, but when I saw this, I just…couldn't let this be."

"I understand. It's between us, Meena. Nobody will know that we met today," said Barry.

Meena nodded. "Keep her safe," she said. She put on her hat and sunglasses, got up, and left the Tavern.

Tomi took a deep breath. She put her hand on the mouse and clicked the link. A new window opened on the monitor, launching a video call. First she saw her own video appear. She realized she hadn't looked much at herself lately in the mirror, but she thought she looked different somehow. *Or maybe I'm just seeing myself differently*, she thought.

The second video was loading. She looked out the window to see Sixto and Kirsten outside the cabin, his arms waving dramatically as he talked to Kirsten. They had been chatting with Sixto often these past two days, visiting a few times a day to see if Minear had responded.

Finally this morning, she got his reply. It was cold and to the point: *8:30 pm GMT. Click this link for a video call. Arthur.*

She looked at the time on the computer monitor: 3:30 pm. She hoped she got the time difference right.

Finally, the loading stopped, and a video appeared of an older man, grey, neatly cut hair, wearing a white collared shirt. Tomi smiled when she saw him. His face expressed a serious, suspicious demeanor.

"Mr. Minear, thank you for speaking with me," said Tomi.

His expression didn't change. "Atlah-Toa," he said flatly, in his Cornish accent. "There are four people in the world other than me who know about it. And now apparently there's a fifth. So why don't you start by telling me how you came to know about it?"

Tomi's stomach turned. She hoped this conversation would start easier. How can she explain what she knows?

"Mr. Minear," Tomi said, "do you believe in the mystical?"

Chapter 16

"This is the way the world ends

This is the way the world ends

This is the way the world ends

Not with a bang but a whimper."

T.S. Elliot

Tomi told Arthur about her experiences, and was relieved when he already knew about remote viewing and wasn't immediately skeptical. She told him about her search for her missing grandmother, about the being she had been communicating with, and about her psychic block.

Then she told him about the dream. About Arthur being in her kitchen, digging up the floor and finding water. And telling her to say she knew about Atlah-Toa.

"That was two days ago, and I emailed you immediately after," she said, "though I'm not sure why I've been…I don't know, directed, to contact you."

Arthur had been sitting forward, as though being closer to the screen would help all of this make sense. He leaned back, exhaled, and considered. She could see that his demeanor had changed as she talked, looking less suspicious and more curious.

"Well, that's quite a story,' he said. "And normally I might be inclined to write you off but for two things: first, I can see that you're earnest in what you're saying, and second, well, you said the magic words. Atlah-Toa."

They looked at each other for a moment through the screen, both knowing they have much to discuss, but unsure where to begin. Arthur broke the silence.

"The dream is interesting. I'm not sure the symbolism of digging up your kitchen, that I don't know, I suggest a therapist would be better prepared for that one," he said with a small laugh. "But finding water is interesting. And it's true that many ancient holy sites are in fact built over underground water sources. And it's also true that I often talk about the many cities that may have existed along coastlines in the antediluvian age, that are now underwater. I'm certain there are critical and history-changing discoveries at the bottom of our seas and oceans that are being ignored by mainstream archeology."

"Antediluvian?" Tomi asked.

"Antediluvian means *before the flood*," Arthur said, his eyes starting to light up. "You see, we are a species that forgets. And the ancients told us this. There are five rivers in Hades, the Greek underworld. One was the River of Unmindfulness, called the Lethe. It was said all who drank from it experienced complete forgetfulness. I think as a species we've drank from it, and we've forgotten our true history."

"So…what is the truth, then?" she asked.

"Well, much of my life's work has been searching for evidence that there was an advanced, global civilization that once existed, a civilization that was completely wiped out at the end of the last ice age – and largely forgotten. And mainstream academia refuses to study it, refuses to even entertain the possibility."

Arthur paused to adjust his camera, then sat back in his chair, now in his element sharing the theory he'd been working to prove for decades.

"You see," he continued, "as a species, we like the narrative that we started from zero, from scratch. The story we tell ourselves is that we started with early cities and agriculture in the fertile crescent six or seven thousand years ago, and it was nothing but a linear progression towards our technological peak today," he said, inverting his arm to show the ascent of civilization. "And yet if we look at the incredible megalithic structures from all over the world, we can see that the ancients had deep knowledge of writing, astronomy, spirituality, and the most incredible construction methods. Often with precision we couldn't match with today's modern tools and technology."

"Why do you think this idea, that humans have had civilization before, is so challenging for people to consider?" Tomi asked. She wasn't sure what it was she needed to learn from Arthur, what knowledge he had that spurred the universe, or whoever was behind that dream, to contact him.

"Oh, I've been asking that for thirty plus years," he said with a shake of his head. "I think as a species we like to be special. The first, the smartest, the best. And yet when you look at megalithic construction, it's clear that our ancestors had technology and techniques we simply don't understand today. I think the other reason people don't like it, is the way that forgotten civilization ended. If it ended in total annihilation, which is what all the evidence points to, well, if it happened to them, it could happen to us. I don't think we like to entertain that possibility."

She thought back to Ray and Barry talking about all the warnings of cataclysm UFO experiencers have received. *Something is coming*, Ete had said.

"So, what if we didn't start from zero?" he continued. "What if we were actually at a civilizational peak? Then after the cataclysm, the survivors of this lost civilization tried to preserve as much knowledge as they could, record it in stone and in myths passed down to us today. Isn't that what we would do today if nearly all traces of our current civilization were erased? Save what we can and try to pass it on?"

She thought about Ete talking about the coming of a new age, but warning that it would be painful and destructive.

"Now, what makes more sense," Arthur continued, "that homo sapiens have been around for three-hundred, maybe three-hundred and fifty thousand years, and for three-hundred and forty-four thousand of those years we plugged along with slow technological developments as hunter-gatherers, then suddenly, *wham*, in just six or seven thousand years, we invent agriculture, build pyramids and megaliths all over the world, invent cities, writing, religion, construction, science, split the atom, walk on the moon, and network the world. All of that in the most recent two percent of human history."

Minear leaned back in his chair, confident in his argument, ready to bring it to a conclusion. "Or, Tomi, does it make more sense that human nature is to learn, grow, develop, and share knowledge? And who knows how advanced human civilization might be if it weren't for a comet or volcano or massive flood coming along like a giant eraser, and periodically forcing humanity to start all over again."

"A cycle," Tomi said. She thought back to asking Ete about Atlantis. *That's not what it was called,* Ete had said. You will know, one day.

"Yes, a cycle," Arthur said. "And our ancestors told us this, if we would only listen. Whether it's Plato telling us about Atlantis, the ancient Hindus and Mayans telling us of majestic former ages of humanity, or the flood myths that exist all around the world, our ancestors were clearly trying to communicate something important to us."

She thought again of the vision of the massive, circular city being engulfed in a wall of water, that feeling of terror returning. *Can't you do something? Help them?* Tomi had asked. *We did,* Ete had replied. She wondered what Ete had meant. *Where did they go?*

"This all…I mean I don't know the evidence, but I feel that it's right," said Tomi. "Like I can feel it in my bones. In my DNA."

"And there is so much evidence, Tomi," he said, his enthusiasm for his theory animating his voice, nothing like the stoic, suspicious figure from the beginning of this call. "From ancient maps that point to knowledge of places like Antarctica that shouldn't have been known at the time, to archeological sites like Gobekli Tepe that are older than our established timeline for civilization, to myths that stretch across oceans, yet tell the same story. And this story is so often one of cataclysm. Like a warning from the ancients."

"A warning that it could happen to us?" Tomi suggested.

"I think so," he said. "That's why we really need to listen to what our ancestors were trying to tell us."

Arthur let out a deep breath, his excitement for the topic waning, replaced with the look of fatigue that being a lone voice from the wilderness will bring.

"Everywhere, Tomi, all over these flowers are poking up through the cracks in the concrete. These flowers are breaking through the establishment story of planet Earth, the story of humanity," Arthur said. "These flowers are our ancestors, trying to tell us their story."

Tomi felt her eyes close. An image of her grandmother came into her mind, then her grandmother's mother, who she'd once seen a picture of. Then her great-great-grandmother, and on, and on, linked by ancestry, passed through generations of women. She imagined all their stories, their incredible knowledge, woven into and passed on through their shared lineage.

She opened her eyes. "I've been learning a lot lately that what we think of as reality, of our history, it's…an illusion," Tomi said deeply.

"Yes, an illusion," Arthur said, nodding. "Humans, we just inherently need to feel like we've got it all figured out. What if we walked through life knowing, embracing that we in fact know almost nothing?"

Tomi leaned back in her chair, wondering why it felt like everyone was out to destroy her safe worldview.

"But many don't agree with you," Tomi said, a statement as a question.

"That's an understatement," Arthur said with a laugh. "Some people are critical not just of the evidence I present or my conclusions, but feel as though questioning the dating of ancient sites questions, or takes something away from other ancient cultures. I would never. Ancient Egypt, for example, was the most spiritually developed civilization we know about. We are still unravelling their truths."

Arthur leaned forward, his voice energized again, as though his detractors might be listening.

"So, what if we prove conclusively, for example, that the Great Sphinx really is much older, and was created by a much older culture, as some geologists have argued. Does that take anything away from the Ancient Egyptian construction, writing, art, astronomy, alchemy? Of course not. We are the benefactors of the Ancient Egyptians. So much of their accomplishments have been handed down to us, just as they were the benefactors of generations and civilizations that came before them."

"Right," she said. "An unbroken chain of humanity."

"That's right. Do you know about the Lascaux caves? They hold some of the most remarkable cave art, created some forty-thousand years ago. Well, Picasso visited the cave, and afterwards, he said: 'Since Lascaux, we have invented nothing.'

"Wow," said Tomi, her mind forming a picture of a pre-historic savant, creating and experimenting in a dimly lit cave. She looked over to Sixto's painting of Plato's Cave, the shadows dancing with the fire.

"Picasso said this about forty-thousand-year-old cave art. I'm saying the same, that we need to give more credit not only to our recent ancestors and their accomplishments and knowledge, but also to the truly ancients, those ice age and older humans who, as we can see from the cave paintings at Lascaux, were remarkably intelligent, creative, and in touch with not only the world around them, but the sky, too. And they sure had warnings for us," he said, tilting his head for emphasis.

"What sort of warnings?" Tomi asked, leaning in, starting to sense that this might be the information she was sent to Minear to glean.

"You know, if you study the ancient wisdom, the mythologies - which I tend to see more as histories - if you look at these stories from all around the world, all different times, you might say that ancient humanity was obsessed with cataclysm. Absolutely obsessed," he said, shaking his head.

Tomi felt a chill. Ever since she started down this path, this rabbit hole she'd tumbled down, this word, *cataclysm*, kept circling around her.

"A civilization destroying flood, talked about all around the world," Arthur continued. "Sky serpents depicted around the world, as a warning of comet strikes. Perhaps these aren't just myths, or stories, as most people think, but are actual records of past cataclysms. When you look at some of these stories you see clear warnings, some with references to sky positions. Maybe they were saying, 'Hey, future humans, this is what happens on earth, a big eraser comes and almost scratches us out, and we have to start again. And that eraser will come for you too, so be prepared.'"

"Maybe they weren't really obsessed with the apocalypse," Tomi said," but they were actually obsessed with warning their descendants about it. To save us."

Arthur sat back in his chair. "What a beautiful thought," he said.

Tomi breathed deeply. Some force directed her to have this conversation, to get this history, or this warning that things may be destroyed, may fall apart, but she didn't know why. She thought about her grandmother saying that to her when she was little, *things fall apart*. She said it often, and once showed her the poem it was from.

"I'm just...I don't know, this poem is in my head. *Things fall apart*," she said, shaking her head, trying to remember the rest.

"*Turning and turning in the widening gyre*," Arthur said. "Yeats."

"Right. *Things fall apart; the centre cannot hold*," Tomi said, the words coming back to her.

"*Mere anarchy is loosed upon the world*," Arthur said grimly.

Tomi nodded, remembering being chilled by those words. But her grandmother had wanted her to know it. *Why?*

Tomi felt frustrated. While this was an engaging conversation, she was no closer to figuring out her next steps. Nothing Arthur said pointed her in any direction that got her closer to Ete or her grandmother. She decided before ending the call, she would ask directly.

"Mr. Minear -"

"Arthur, please," he said warmly.

"Arthur, I've told you the situation with being blocked from contacting…a being. And needing to, so I can find out what happened to my grandmother. Maybe this isn't your area of expertise - psychic communication," she said with a bit of a grin, still hearing how strange such a question might sound, "but is there any chance you have some advice for me?"

Arthur sat back in his chair, looking like he was deciding whether he wanted to answer the question. Finally, he said, "Actually, I do."

"I'll start off by saying I'm not a UFO person," Arthur said. "I know about Ancient Aliens and all the books, and there might be some compelling evidence there, but it's never been my interest. Wherever the technology and knowledge came from, my point is that the ancients had it, and had a remarkable understanding of their world."

"Yes, I understand that," Tomi said.

"But what I do know something about is ancient wisdom. Now, you've connected with this being through some sort of transfer, or connecting of consciousness. And now the path to that connection is blocked. So, what if there's another route to making that connection? A bypass?"

"Well, I tried Human-Initiated Contact, but that didn't work," said Tomi.

"Well, what I'm going to say, I don't want you to interpret as me encouraging or promoting drug use."

"Okay…," Tomi said, a bit taken aback that this older, articulate man brought up drugs.

"Ancient people understood the spiritual world and had a closer connection to it than we can imagine in our modern, distracted age. When the ancients needed to communicate with the spirit world, well, all around the globe cultures found natural psychedelics to help aid in that process," he said.

"You mean like what, magic mushrooms?" Tomi asked.

"Sure," Arthur said. "Go around the world, whether it's mushrooms or cacti or vines or flowers, natural psychedelics were used to gain wisdom and knowledge, and receive guidance from the spiritual world. There are Egyptian hieroglyphs that show priests bringing lotus flowers to the Pharaohs. Well, the lotus flower was used as a psychedelic. In Siberia, shamans would ingest the Amanita

Muscaria mushroom and filter out the poison through their urine, then share that urine with the people, so they could safely experience the drug. I shouldn't say drug. Medicine."

Tomi was stunned. Sure, she'd have a few drinks now and then, and had smoked pot here and there, but a hallucinogenic was not something she had ever tried. Even considered trying. "I…don't know what to say. I suppose this makes sense. I just have no idea how to…I mean, what do I do?"

"Well, if you really want to go for it, perhaps consider DMT - dimethyltryptamine. In South America, Indigenous people have used it for thousands of years, through a medicine they brew called ayahuasca. But you can also create it fairly simply in its basic molecular form," he said.

"DMT," she said, writing it down on a notepad on Sixto's desk.

"The spirit molecule, they call it, and for good reason," said Arthur. "Many people report encountering beings, and many believe that those beings are not just a hallucination. They believe they encounter actual beings. As though it's a shadow dimension, and the DMT allows them enter it, perceive it, and interact with it."

Tomi took a deep breath. Ete had talked about this shadow reality.

"Now, like I said, I'm not encouraging you to do this," Arthur said. "And it would be a very intense experience, and there's no guarantee it's a pleasant one. I'm just saying that if I were in your situation, I would ask myself, what would the ancients do?"

"I can't thank you enough for responding to me, and sharing this all with me," Tomi said, as they prepared to wrap up their conversation. "I'm going to look into your suggestion. And this conversation on ancient history, and the cycle of cataclysms. I don't know the reason, but I think this is what I needed to get from you."

"Well, I hope this information serves you well," said Arthur. "It sounds like quite a journey you have been on. I can only imagine the epics the ancients would have written about it."

Tomi smiled. "I wish you -", Tomi started, then paused. "Wait, so what is Atlah-Toa?"

Arthur blushed. "I thought I may get away without saying," he said with a laugh. "Well, I told you four people plus me know about this, and now you. I ask that we keep it that way. You've been incredibly open with me, and for some reason, I have a feeling this information may be useful to you, so I will share."

Tomi leaned forward as his voice grew quieter.

"For the past four weeks, I've been in southern Turkey. I won't say where exactly, but myself and an archeologist I've been working with, made a discovery. A big one. Have you heard of the Emerald Tablet? Hermes Trismegistus?"

The Emerald Tablet. She looked across the room to the picture Sixto had pointed out just days before. "*As above, so below.* As a coincidence - or I should say, synchronicity, I'm looking at a picture of it, now."

"Remarkable," he said, shaking his head. "Then you know that the texts we have are later recreations, translations. But no actual tablet of emerald, of course, has been found."

Tomi nodded. She looked down at her hand and imagined holding a piece of the tablet. She thought she could feel the cold of the stone, the weight of it in her palm.

"These words, these translations, were passed down, and had significance to alchemists, who linked it to the Philosopher's Stone. So of course, finding the original, finding there really *was* an Emerald Tablet, would be an awfully big deal."

Tomi saw him pause, taking a breath to contain his excitement, a smile coming to his face.

"We found it, Tomi," he said. "Well, a part of it. It is broken. We estimate we have a third of it. And it's just small, I mean, this third can fit in the palm of your hand, with small and precise characters chiseled into the stone."

He held up his hand to demonstrate, as though he were holding the stone in his hand, rubbing the text with his thumb.

"Now, as if this discovery wasn't remarkable enough," he continued, "the Tablet had another surprise for us: there is text on each side. On the back of the tablet, there is text that we believe was not handed down like the text of the Emerald Tablet was. No, this text is new. Unknown. There is still work being done on the translation, but it talks about the destruction of a great city."

"Atlah-Toa," she said.

"Atlah-Toa," he nodded. "I believe, and if we can find the lost pieces, I hope to prove it, that this text is a history of Atlantis. And that this ancient text might be giving us the real name of Atlantis, or at least something closer to it."

That's not what it was called, Ete had said. *You will know, one day.*

"Arthur, something tells me you're right," she said solemnly.

Tomi stood up from the computer and felt momentarily dizzy, realizing she had been sitting at that chair, and occupying Sixto's home, for some time. She breathed and tried to gather herself, her mind swimming. Tomi felt like she was being handed a picture, but only one puzzle piece at a time. And with each piece she's handed, she must start rearranging the others to make the puzzle fit together.

I'd do anything for some stable ground right now, she thought.

Taking the note from the desk, she stepped outside, thinking she would find two people annoyed at being locked out for the past two hours, and instead found Sixto and Kirsten laughing, as she tried to teach him to do a headstand.

"How did it go?" Sixto asked from the ground, where he'd just tumbled.

"It ah, it was interesting. And heavy," she said, looking towards the sun, making its descent towards the treetops. "And well, he did have an idea for how to make contact. I, well I need to figure out how to make," she looked at the note and stumbled through pronouncing it, "dimethyltryptamine."

"Oh, I can help you with that," said Sixto casually, brushing dirt from his hands as he stood up.

Tomi tilted her head back. "Of course you can," she said, incredulous. *Just another coincidence*, she thought.

Sixto described - or rather, acted out - the process of extraction. Kirsten took notes, which Tomi appreciated, feeling overwhelmed and unable to take in more information today.

After Kirsten repeated things back and confirmed she understood, she sent an encrypted message to Barry and Ib.

We need you to pick up a few things.

First is, uh, root bark...

Chapter 17

"Do you not know, Asclepius, that Egypt is an image of heaven, or, to speak more exactly, in Egypt all the operations of the powers which rule and work in heaven are present in the earth below?

In fact, it should be said that the whole Cosmos dwells in this our land as in its sanctuary. And yet, since it is fitting that wise men should have knowledge of all events before they come to pass, you must not be left in ignorance of what I will now tell you: there will come a time when it will have been in vain that Egyptians have honoured the God head with heartfelt piety and service; and all our holy worship will be fruitless and ineffectual. The gods will return from earth to heaven.

Egypt will be forsaken, and the land which was once the home of religion will be left desolate, bereft of the presence of its deities…"

"**W**ell, it's a good thing I have a contact in the gardening world," Barry said with a laugh, handing the bag of root bark to Kirsten, who was already set up in the kitchen, ready to get to work.

Barry and Ib got themselves settled in the second bedroom, while Tomi checked out the packing Ib had done for her.

The luggage almost exploded when she opened it, with stacks of folded clothes expanding and tumbling out onto the bed. *He must think I'm never going home again,* she thought.

While Kirsten was hard at work in the kitchen, following Sixto's directions, Ib, Barry, and Tomi sat chatting in the living area, as rain poured down outside.

"We need to update you on what we've learned this week and talk about our next steps," said Ib. "I'm afraid some of it may be difficult to hear," he said, thinking about the framed photograph in his bag.

"Okay," said Tomi, "I'm not sure how much more destabilizing things can get, so hit me."

Barry and Ib looked at each other, and through that look, decided Ib would start. "Well to begin with, the word that we got was that you're not in immediate danger. And that if you come in to see them - see the General - that something can be worked out."

Tomi nodded. "I know."

Barry and Ib gave her a curious look.

"When I contacted Arthur Minear, I may have also looked at an email from John," she said. "He warned me about the people I'm with, that you all don't have my best interests in mind. And that I should come in with him."

Barry looked at Ib and nodded. Ib started rustling through his bag, pulled out the framed photograph, and handed it to Tomi.

"This is John's picture," she said, giving Ib a concerned look. "Did you take this off his wall?"

"I did," he said, "which I know is technically wrong. But I did it for a good reason. I want you to look closely at the man beside John."

She analyzed the photo. "He's familiar but I'm not sure."

"Tomi," said Barry, "it's the General. With John."

"I…I don't understand," said Tomi, staring at the photograph. "Why wouldn't John tell me that he knew him?"

She looked to Ib and Barry for an explanation.

"Tomi," said Barry as gently as he could, "your first session at PSI was no coincidence. I don't know how it was done, but they have been training you, using you covertly for years."

"I…don't understand. I only met the general the day you all picked me up and took me to PSI," she said, her face scrunched up in confusion.

"I know it doesn't make sense, but I don't think that's true," said Barry, trying to be gentle in his voice. He wondered what would be more destabilizing for Tomi: these past few months where she pushed through the boundaries of reality, or finding out that the core relationships, the story of her life, has been an illusion.

"Somehow," he continued, "they've been able to suppress the memory of this in you. When John's company came to PSI, it wasn't what it was presented as. They wanted you to go down the road you've gone. This was by design."

Tomi's face had been stonelike, as though it would be her defence against painful information. Her stony face started to crack. She looked towards the kitchen where Kirsten was continuing to work away, oblivious to the gravity of the conversation happening in the next room.

"I…" Tears were welling up in her eyes. "I don't understand. Why?"

"I guess," Ib said, "their theory is that you would be better able to do - whatever it was they wanted you to do - if it were your idea. If you were consciously choosing this path, rather than being directed."

"So…John knew?" she said, looking at the floor. "I just, don't see how that's possible. He didn't even want me to do this work."

Barry and Ib nodded. "Tomi, I'm so sorry," Ib said. "It appears that John was aware. And likely helped to facilitate the mission."

"It wouldn't be the first time that an intelligence operation used romantic relationships, even marriage, as part of an operation or investigation, I'm afraid," said Barry, pulling on his years of research.

Tomi shook her head, tears streaming down her face.

"So, you're saying my marriage was a sham? An intelligence operation. I just…so I just can't trust anyone in this world," she said sadly. She closed her eyes and imagined herself back in her own world, her peaceful, perfect hilly island.

"Tomi, I'm so sorry. I can't imagine…I just hope you know, feel that you can trust us," said Barry.

She didn't respond. Tomi sat hunched over, her eyes still closed. A full, passionate person, now physically deflated.

"Tomi," said Ib, "based on what we've learned, obviously we don't want you to go in and meet with them. You are their asset — their words, their perspective - and they want to maintain control of you."

"So, we need to come up with a plan for what comes next," said Barry. "Where we go next, how we can keep you safe."

Tomi opened her eyes and stared at the floor. She felt the room spinning. Tunnel vision was setting in, and she lost her peripheral view. Her world was closing in.

"I need to go lay down," she said.

"Of course," Ib said, standing as she got up. He watched her head into the bedroom, and close the door firmly, wishing there was something he could say that could heal her.

Tomi buried her head in the pillow, wishing she were home in her own bed. She felt claustrophobic in the cabin, wishing she could be alone and push the world away. She planted her face into the pillow to dampen the sound of her screams and cries.

Eventually she cried out, feeling like her body was emptied of emotion. Instead, she just felt hollow. She fell asleep, sleeping through the afternoon and into the evening.

Sometime later, she awoke to the mattress shifting as someone laid down beside her. She opened her eyes to see Kirsten's face on the pillow beside her.

"Hey," she said.

"Hey," replied Tomi, her voice broken and raspy.

"Barry and Ib got me up to date. Tomi, I'm so sorry, I can't imagine what you are feeling right now," Kirsten said.

"The nap helped," Tomi said. "So did screaming into the pillow." Kirsten smiled. "I just…I've always felt kind of alone in this world. I just had no idea how alone I am."

Kirsten put her arm around her. "Ride or die Tomi, you've always got me, okay? You can bank on that."

Tomi tried to smile, and nodded her head, laying on the pillow.

"You can cry if you want, I'm here for that," Kirsten said with a smile. "And I brought you some dinner, it's over there on the dresser. Or if you want to get up you can. And I can sleep out on the couch if you want space to yourself."

"Thanks," Tomi said. "You can stay. Amazingly, I feel like I can go right back to sleep for the night."

Tomi sat up in the bed and faced Kirsten. "When I was having my cry, I kept hearing my grandmother's voice. She used to say, 'They thought they buried us, but they didn't know we were seeds.'"

"That's perfect," Kirsten said.

"I'm not going to let him win," Tomi said, the sadness on her face slowly shifting to determination. "Them win."

"Yes!" said Kirsten, sitting up and trying to encourage Tomi's resilience. "And if we ever see John again, you leave him for me," she said, punching her right fist into her pillow.

Tomi smiled. "When I was sleeping, I kept having this feeling that this was it. That this was the last bit of the old me that needed to die. Weirdly, it feels cathartic. Like there's nothing left back there now. Now it's just forward."

"That's such a great way to look at it, Tomi," said Kirsten. "You've found your gifts, you've found your purpose, and you've found your people. It's been so swift and chaotic, and yet this amazingly resilient person has emerged. I'm proud of you."

"Thanks. I'm kind of proud of me, too," Tomi said. "And you're right, I've found my people. I'm just going to put my trust in you. And Ib, and Barry."

"And Ete?" asked Kirsten.

"And Ete. Come on," she said, getting out of the bed. "Let's go look at the stars a bit before bed."

They left the bedroom to find Barry and Ib talking quietly. They stopped talking and looked at her. Tomi tipped her head towards the door, indicating they should follow.

"You heard her," Kirsten said, following Tomi out the door, "we're going to look at stars."

Tomi stepped out onto the cold grass with her bare feet, the grass wet with the day's rain. Someone turned off the light in the cabin, and she was surrounded by darkness. She didn't turn when she heard her friends approaching behind her. Instead, she looked up to a clear, starry sky, the day's rain clouds having retreated. She remembered Kirsten telling her about the stars changing their position, the great precession, and felt that she had become a small part of a long, long story.

"I've decided," Tomi said, still staring up at the stars "that I'll try the DMT and see if I can break through. And we will see what happens. Now, the last time I connected with Ete, the time was present day, and the location was underground in Alaska. So if we don't get the answers we need tomorrow, that's where I will go."

"We will go," said Kirsten, putting her hand on Tomi's shoulder. "You're not going alone."

She could sense Barry and Ib nodding behind her. Tomi opened her mouth to argue, but held back, deciding to let go and trust in her friends.

As they continued looking at the night sky, Kirsten pointed out Mars, glowing a bright, faint red. Tomi imagined the dot of light growing, becoming a glowing craft, first just a light in the sky, eventually blocking out stars as it moved closer. She imagined the craft, a real, physical craft, approaching silently, hovering in front of her. She imagined Ete, a real, physical being, in front of her, coming to pull her out of this situation.

"I'm heading to bed," Tomi said eventually. "Big day tomorrow."

"O Egypt, Egypt, of thy religion nothing will remain but an empty tale, which thine own children in time to come will not believe; nothing will be left but graven words, and only the stones will tell of thy piety. And in that day men will be weary of life, and they will cease to think the universe worthy of reverent wonder and of worship. They will no longer love this world around us, this incomparable work of God, this glorious structure which he has built, this sum of good made up of many diverse forms, this instrument whereby the will of God operates in that which he has made, ungrudgingly favouring man's welfare, this combination and accumulation of all the manifold things that call forth the veneration, praise, and love of the beholder.

"Well Tomi, earlier this year, before you met me, did you ever imagine you'd be making crystallized dimethyltryptamine hoping to launch yourself into another dimension so that you can talk to an ancient being from Mars?" Ib said, laughing hard at the situation.

"I mean, when you say it that way, I suppose a few things have changed," Tomi said with a laugh.

Tomi made herself comfortable on the bed, working to relax her body and mind and clear out all the negative emotions of the past twenty-four hours, hoping they wouldn't manifest in this experience.

Kirsten had borrowed a bong for the experiment, along with some herb from Sixto. She weighed out the small white crystals and sprinkled them in the bowl.

"Okay Tomi," said Kirsten. "So first, we're going to light this, and you inhale. Sixto said it would be harsh, but try to hold it as long as you can. And we're going to do that three times. He said the first time, it will change your vision. Second, you will be in a full psychedelic experience. The third, well I guess that's when you'll hopefully go out of body and find Ete."

"Okay," said Tomi. "You will help me?"

"Yes," said Kirsten. "I will need to! You'll be off in your own world, so I'll have to help you to keep going. And then I'll be here holding your hand. He said it will only last for ten or fifteen minutes, but for you, it will feel much, much longer."

"We will give you some space," said Ib, touching Barry's elbow to move them out of the bedroom. "Good luck, Tomi."

Tomi sat cross-legged on the bed and breathed deeply a few times. "Okay, I'm ready." She looked at the bong. "I'm embarrassed to say I don't know how to use it," she said.

"Oh sweet, innocent Tomi," Kirsten said with a playful smile. She gave Tomi a quick lesson in using the bong and lit the bowl. Tomi sucked in thick smoke. *Harsh is right!* she thought, as she tried to hold in a hacking cough.

"Very good!" said Kirsten. "Keep holding it!"

Tomi held the smoke in as long as she could, then finally exhaled with a series of deep, cutting coughs.

"Oh my God," she said when she stopped coughing. Kirsten tried to put the bong in front of her again, but Tomi was looking around at the walls.

"It's pixelated," she said. "It's like the wall is made up of tiny pixels, tiny little boxes."

These little pixels started to move around, exchanging position. In her peripheral, they started to swirl.

"Tomi, next one," said Kirsten, lighting the bowl again and holding the bong to Tomi's mouth. Tomi breathed in, only half paying attention to the smoke entering her body, watching as Kirsten's face became pixelated.

"Great, now hold it," said Kirsten.

Tomi stopped feeling her body. For a moment, she felt immediate terror at losing feeling in her physical body, but that terror was quickly replaced by a feeling of pleasant vibration, as though every particle in her body was in a state of vibration and weightlessness.

The walls, the room, and Kirsten were gone. Tomi found herself on a path made up of bright stones. *The yellow brick road!* Tomi thought. The path wound through a field of blue grass. Bright flowers sprung up along the path, and swirling colours entered her view.

"Tomi, one more," said Kirsten.

Tomi saw small beings popping up from the ground along the path, small elves, but instead of being made up of solid colours, their skin and clothes were like a bright, intricate mandala pattern of colours, slowly moving and shifting.

"Hello," Tomi said.

The first elf that popped up turned to call to the others. "It's Tomi! Tomi is here!"

"Hello Tomi," they all said at once, with high-pitched voices.

"Do I know you?" asked Tomi kindly. The room and the cabin were gone now as she became immersed in this world of colour. She felt so light and free.

"We've been expecting you," that first elf said. *Papa Elf*, Tomi thought. The other elves muttered in agreement, their voices high-pitched and so friendly. She wondered if Sixto had ever met these elves.

"You know Sixto?" one of them said in an excited voice. "We love that guy!" said several of them at once. Tomi smiled at them.

Papa Elf caught her attention, and she followed his eyes as he turned to look down the path. She looked deep down the path and saw two reddish pyramids. *The pyramids on Mars*, she thought. She recognized them from remote viewing, from her investigation of Mars. But when she first saw them, they were barren, and here they were, pristine, surrounded by lush blue grass. She looked up to see the two Martian moons hovering in the sky.

"Tomi," said Kirsten, pressing the bong to her mouth. "You need to do one more."

"Sorry," said Tomi to the elves, "I think I need to go."

"Come back soon! Come back soon!" they said enthusiastically, waving their colour-changing arms.

Tomi inhaled, this time unaware of the harshness of the smoke.

"Great Tomi, keep holding it," said Kirsten.

Cough! Tomi finally hacked out the last of the smoke, fell back into the bed with her eyes closed, looking like she had fallen asleep.

Kirsten placed the bong on the side table, and held Tomi's hand, wondering where she was.

The scene around her started to swirl, and soon Tomi felt a whoosh of energy pushing her forward. The swirling slowed, and there she was, standing at the top of her hilly island, looking down at the water crashing on the rocks at the bottom of the hill. Like before, the grass was a deep, bright green, and colourful, exotic flowers grew throughout the grass. She looked closely at a beautiful violet flower, and realized it was sentient. It looked back at her. She didn't speak, but instead felt energy exchange between them. *You are so beautiful*, she thought. *So are you*, she received back.

She looked up to see a night sky with an impossible number of stars. She could see the stars drifting into galaxies, colourful swirls in the sky with billions of tiny points of light. Though the sky was dark, there was light all around her, the light thick like smoke.

She felt a presence and turned to her left to see a figure approaching. It was a man, tall and lanky, with a black vest and black cowboy hat on, a grey handlebar moustache framing his face. The energy felt familiar.

"Ete?" Tomi asked, confused.

"Hey there, Tomi. I see you've made it through the block," Ete said in a deep male voice with a Western accent.

"Why do you look like…like Sam Elliot? The actor?" Tomi asked.

Ete's thin face and moustache curled up into a smile. "Heck Tomi, it's your trip," Ete/Sam said with a chuckle.

Tomi looked around at the magical scene around her. It felt like a hologram, and at the same time, more real than anything she had experienced before. The scene was so beautiful, she found herself distracted, forgetting the purpose of reaching Ete.

"I didn't find my grandmother," she said finally, staring at the flowers blowing in the gentle breeze.

"I know," said Ete.

"You told me to find her," Tomi said. "I failed."

"You're on exactly the right path to find her," said Ete. "There is no destination without a journey."

Tomi nodded. She looked at Ete/Sam Elliot, a bright sparkle in his eyes. She followed his gaze, and realized his eyes were reflecting the swirling galaxies in the night's sky.

"It's…so impossibly beautiful. Is this real? Are we really here?" she asked.

"Can we have an experience that isn't real?" Ete replied. "And how can we even start to understand the beauty of the universe?"

Tomi searched her mind for a quote, something she remembered from high school English. She remembered reading it over and over in class, dreaming of understanding the mysteries of the world around her.

"*There are more things in Heaven and Earth, Horatio, than are dreamt of in your philosophy,*" said Ete.

Tomi looked at Ete/Sam, and said, "that's it. Shakespeare. Do you read our writing?" asked Tomi.

"It came from you," Ete said.

Tomi paused again, filling herself up with the movement of colours all around her, the swirling beauty, the feeling of lightness. She focused again on the vibration of her body, feeling each electron matching the vibration of the hilly island and the sky and stars around her. She had never felt more in harmony, more at peace.

"Did you send me to Arthur Minear?" she asked.

"Yes," said Ete.

"Why?"

"He got you here, didn't he?" Ete/Sam's mouth curled into a half grin. "And because you needed to know."

"About cataclysms? The cycle? Why do I need to know this?" she asked.

"As I've shared, our solar system is moving into a new age. A time where the connection to - well, to the source - is closest. This could be a time of major spiritual evolution for humans, a time when you learn to finally transcend your material reality. And you can feel it coming, can't you Tomi?"

Tomi felt a sense of deep emotion, a sense of loss that comes before a major change, an end of an era. "Yes, I do," she said.

Ete/Sam took off his hat, and looked up at the endless expanse of stars. Tomi stared up at the sky, then closed her eyes, as if to take a picture. When she opened her eyes, she was no longer on the hilly island. She was back in the glowing room, Ete's home deep under the surface of the Earth. She could see the light emanating from the walls, this time swirling through the air. Ete was transformed to her normal form, and was seated in meditation with several other beings.

"So why are you telling me? Why do I need to know?" asked Tomi. She realized Ete wanted her to sit on the meditation stool, and communicate telepathically. She took a seat, and saw the six beings seated on their floating stools, slowly gliding around the room, never bumping into each other, as though the stools were performing a well-choreographed dance.

"It's time. It's time for you to know." Ete's words echoed in her mind. "We're all going to have to start working together soon."

And she knew we did.

Tomi looked at the beings, so few of them, and thought of their species dying, like a star blinking out of the universal sky.

"Is there anything I can do to help your species?" she asked sadly.

"When we agree to live, we agree to die," said Ete. "Remember, there are no opposites. Death is part of life, every step of the way. Even though our species is dying, our future is clear. It's humanity's future that's not. You humans have so many of your nuclear weapons, just ready to fire, always an instant away from destroying your entire species. At any second, you can be erased by your own hand. You humans are Schrodinger's Cat. You're both alive and dead in the same instant."

"You're right, but I can't do anything about nuclear weapons," Tomi said. "Shouldn't you be telling this to our governments, to the President?"

"There are some in your governments who know that this is the nature of the earth," said Ete. "They even know that it is impending. Yes, past cataclysms have started with floods, asteroids, volcanoes, but the real eraser of civilization is the sudden change in climate following these events. People don't maintain civilization and record essential knowledge when they are starving. And if this time it's nuclear weapons, that will be your fate, too. The question is whether humanity will choose cataclysm, or work together to prevent it."

She nodded at this and looked down solemnly.

"*Things fall apart,*" Ete said. "*The centre cannot hold.*"

"Yeats," said Tomi. "Did that come from me, also?"

"What, you think we've never been to a library?" Ete said. She felt Ete's humour, as though a message of emotion.

"You humans are at your most beautiful when you are sharing truths," Ete said.

Darkness will be preferred to light, and death will be thought more profitable than life; no one will raise his eyes to heaven; the pious will be deemed insane, and the impious wise; the madman will be thought a brave man, and the wicked will be esteemed as good. As for the soul, and the belief that it is immortal by nature, or may hope to attain to immortality, as I have taught you, all this they will mock and will even persuade themselves that it is false. No word of reverence or piety, no utterance worthy of heaven will be heard or believed…"

Tomi found it difficult to keep focused. She had a momentary realization that she was experiencing a psychedelic trip, that she was bilocated, here underground with Ete, and in bed at the cabin, Kirsten by her side. She then felt herself sucked back into the experience.

"When will this happen? The cataclysm?" she asked.

"It doesn't matter when it happens. Just that it will," Ete said, with such certainty it troubled Tomi. "That's the path of the Earth. It's like a giant blackboard that periodically gets wiped clean. A planet with a reset button. Whether it's an asteroid strike, solar flares, systems breaking down from sudden climate change, or perhaps in your case, self-inflicted nuclear destruction. The point is, something will come along and wipe it clean. Just as your ancestors warned you."

Tomi thought she could hear, could feel, millions of screams at once. She shook her head and focused. "Will humans survive?"

"Maybe," said Ete. "Some. They did last time, but it was like starting again. Remember, Earth is a great classroom for souls. And this is part of what it is to live here."

"But, I mean, will it happen soon?" asked Tomi, feeling herself distracted by the swirls of light, twirling between the moving, seated bodies.

"What is soon?" asked Ete, Tomi again sensing amusement. "Take heart, death is never the end of life. And it won't be the end of the Earth. The earth will need to heal. But some ready humans may take the next step."

"How do we do that?" asked Tomi, feeling a sense of desperation, confusion.

"Transcending," said Ete. "By entering what you might call another dimension. A differentiated reality. Everything vibrates at a different frequency, these different realities. It will be a time when some will raise their vibration and access that other reality."

"How do we do it?" Tomi asked.

"You will help them," said Ete softly. "We will help them. There are others who will help. But it will be up to humanity, ultimately. You will either be reset, to try again, or you will be ready to step forward to a higher reality. If it's not too late."

"Humanity is in the last stages of incubation before you can move to the next dimension," said Ete. "But can you do it before the next great reset?"

"If you know that something bad is coming," said Tomi, "can't you stop it? Like if it's an asteroid, blow it off course or something?"

"This is Earth," Ete said. "If it isn't one way, it's another."

Tomi was transfixed, watching the figures slowly floating around the room, the swirling light bending around their bodies. She looked at Ete, whose eyes suddenly popped open, large and dark. It gave Tomi a sudden fright, then a feeling of calm.

"Come," said Ete, waving a long, thin arm, and the scene suddenly swirled and transformed. Tomi and Ete were standing in the giant cave as before, the rugged walls and impossibly large cavern protecting the giant, dark-stoned pyramid.

As before, the light shone off the walls of the cavern, twirling and swirling as it filled the room, thick and white. It reached the exterior of the pyramid and seemed to seep into the giant dark stones. *Like the stones are eating the light,* Tomi thought.

"Look at it," said Ete, her words appearing in Tomi's mind. "Look at it singing."

This time, they were much closer to the pyramid, the solid wall of blocks cut so perfectly you couldn't fit a piece of paper between the seams. The pyramid stretched so high Tomi needed to tilt her head up to see it all. From the top, she could see that it was moving, vibrating, could see the surrounding light being energized by the vibration. *It's dancing,* she thought.

"That's right," said Ete. "It's singing, it's dancing. It's emitting a frequency. You remember I talked about frequencies? This is different from the pyramids you know. This pyramid emits a low frequency, designed to interfere with humanity, to put up a wall between the human soul and the rest of the universe. It makes you feel alone, solitary, it makes it harder to access your soul lives, and the wisdom of your ancestors. There's a bigger human past that you could know if not for this."

"Well, who made it?" asked Tomi. "Can it be turned off?"

"When it is time, Tomi, *you* will turn it off. You will destroy it. And when you do, it will be like pulling a lid off a boiling pot. And we have to hope that humanity is ready. When a species prepares to move on to the next dimension, it's painful, it's chaotic. It's a raging fire. And that's when humans can transcend."

"But when all this has befallen, Asclepius, then God the creator of all things, will look on that which has come to pass, and will stop the disorder by the counter force of his will, which is the good. He will call back to the right path those who have gone astray; he will cleanse the world of evil, washing it away with floods, burning it out with fiercest fire, and expelling it by war and pestilence. And thus he will bring back his world to its former aspect, so that the Cosmos will once more be deemed worthy of worship and wondering reverence, and God, the maker and maintainer of the mighty fabric, will be adored by the men of that day with continuous songs of praise and blessing.

Such is the new birth of the Cosmos; it is a making again of all things good, a holy and awe-inspiring restoration of all nature; and it is wrought inside the process of time by the eternal will of the creator."

Hermes Trismegistus, Asclepius III

"I...I don't know how. I don't know if I can. When?" stammered Tomi, struggling to imagine how she could accomplish such a thing, destroying this massive, magnificent structure.

"When the time is right," said Ete. She turned to face Tomi, and though her mouth didn't move, the words and the meaning behind them seemed to flow into Tomi's mind. "There will come a day when humans must make a choice, to embrace their consciousness, to evolve into a being that has a deeper spiritual responsibility for the universe. For each other. That's how you transcend."

Though the word that Ete used was *responsibility*, Tomi knew that what she truly meant was *love*.

"And I will play a role," said Tomi, though she already knew the answer.

"Tomi," Ete said, her presence moving closer to Tomi, "you must never forget the true nature of humanity, of your souls. When our bodies die, our souls go to the absolute, infinity, to consciousness at rest. We merge into the absolute, but we retain our individual experience of consciousness. If humans can see through this hologram, see that you are actually all the same, always a part of the absolute, you may then see that the true nature of the universe is unity, not conflict."

As Ete spoke, a vision of a bodhi tree entered Tomi's mind, an image she knew was being shared, uploaded to her by Ete. The tree had deep roots, the root system spreading deep and wide, mirroring the branches and leaves that reached for the sky. She focused on the leaves, and watched as each one turned a different colour, each unique, each leaf inextricably part of the whole of the tree, each having its own experience.

"The tree of the universe," Tomi said, the image now fading, but the feeling of having seen something beautiful lingered. "And when a leaf falls it breaks down, and returns to the tree."

"So what is a tree, and what is a leaf?" asked Ete. Tomi could feel Ete smiling, as though she shared a clever riddle.

"It's what we humans might call a classic chicken and the egg scenario," said Tomi.

She felt Ete smile at this, then felt her energy shift to become serious again. "Here," Ete said, reaching her long, thin hand into a pocket Tomi hadn't realized was part of the tight suit they wore.

Ete took Tomi's hand and held it, palm up, then took her own hand, and closed it over Tomi's, palm in palm. Tomi could feel something small and cold between their hands.

"You will need this," said Ete.

"Wait," said Tomi, feeling as if she was being pulled away, the light swirls slowing to a halt. "What about my grandmother?"

"All of your questions about your grandmother will be answered," Ete said. "In time."

Tomi could feel Ete getting farther away, getting smaller as she was being pulled back, back to the cabin, back into her body.

When Tomi thought Ete was gone, she heard her voice once more: "Tomi, wake up. They're coming now. It's time to run."

Chapter 18

"But presently, ... with no apparent change of weather, but all on a sudden, the sky burst asunder, and a huge, flame-like body was seen to fall between the two armies. In shape, it was most like a wine-jar (pithoi), and in color, like molten silver. Both sides were astonished at the sight, and separated. This marvel, as they say, occurred in Phrygia, at a place called Otryae."

Plutarch

Tomi opened her eyes. *Strips of wood,* she thought. *It's the ceiling. The cabin, I'm at the cabin. I was on DMT. I'm back now.*

She turned her head and saw Kirsten smiling at her. She blinked a few times to gain focus. *It just wears right off,* she thought. *Groggy, but the intense visions are just gone. Like nothing had happened.*

"Welcome back," said Kirsten. Ib and Barry had been listening, and popped into the room. "How was it?"

"It was, uh," she said, starting to wiggle her toes and feet and feel herself back in her body, "it was beautiful. And horrible. And scary. And Sam Elliot was there," she said, shaking her head.

She remembered the pyramid, seeing and feeling its vibration. She remembered Ete taking her by the hand, giving her something.

She wiggled her fingers, and could feel Kirsten's hand holding her own. She felt something cold between their hands.

Tomi looked at Kirsten, and could see she felt it, too. Kirsten's mouth opened as she lifted her hand from Tomi's. The four of them stared at Tomi's open palm, holding a rough, chipped triangle of green stone.

Tomi's thumb rubbed the stone, feeling tiny markings, writing, etched in the small stone. She knew immediately what it was.

"The Emerald Tablet," she said, as she sat up and looked at it more closely. It was small, no bigger than a package of Tic Tacs. Two sides were smooth, with the long edge rough, clearly broken from a larger whole.

She thought about Arthur Minear telling her he had found a piece of it. She had imagined it in her hand, and here it was. A chill ran down her spine, waking her sleeping muscles.

"Kirsten, can you explain this?" asked Ib, incredulous. Kirsten shook her head, looking at Tomi's hand in wonder.

Tomi suddenly sat up, remembering Ete's last words. "They're coming. Now."

"What do you mean they're coming?" asked Ib, as Tomi shot out of bed, adrenaline taking over.

"They. The General. I think, I don't know, but they're coming now," she said, pulling her suitcase from the closet. She stopped and held up the green stone. "Maybe they were waiting for this," she said.

The three stared at her without moving. "Get your passports, wallets, shoes. Let's go." They didn't move. "They're coming now!"

Everyone erupted in movement, running around the house to collect the bare essentials. They were about to burst through the door when Ib stumbled on his shoelaces. Tomi paused and breathed. *Slow down*, she thought.

She dropped to the ground and tied his shoes, knowing it would be faster than waiting for him to do it. She stood up, grabbed Ib and Kirsten by their elbows, and pulled the group together.

"Okay, we need to go," she said, trying to speak calmly. "But first, I want to say thank you, to all of you. Having you all in my life, here, now, I just can't -"

"It's synchronicity," said Barry. "It was meant to be. And we're not meant to be caught now. So let's go."

They exited the cabin and rushed towards the vehicles. As Barry fiddled with the lock on the Saab, Tomi heard the beat of a helicopter.

Whoosh, whoosh, whoosh, growing louder and faster. She ran to the edge of the front yard to look out over the bottom of the mountain. In the distance, she could see flashing lights, vehicles on the road below.

"No car!" she yelled. As they froze, partway into the vehicle, Tomi pointed at the sky. "Helicopter. They're going to cut off the road. They'll have us in no time. We have to go on foot. Come on!"

Tomi cut across the yard towards the small path heading to Sixto's cabin, and turned to see her friends running towards her,

Kirsten in front, then Barry, then Ib, struggling to keep up, older and in poorer shape.

Tomi led the way through the rough path, pushing branches out of her way as though she'd already memorized every inch of the trail. "Keep going!" she called out behind her.

She emerged from the woods to find Sixto standing in his small yard with binoculars, looking up at the sky.

"Sixto!" Tomi called.

"Three helicopters," he said, still looking through the binoculars. "Black helicopters, scanning the mountain."

"Sixto, we need your help," she said urgently, hearing Kirsten rush out of the woods behind her. "Those helicopters are looking for me. There's no time to explain, but I promise you," she said, taking his hand and looking him in the eyes, "we are the good guys."

"Oh, I know that," he said matter-of-factly. "Okay, you need to go on foot. Let me think." He stuck his tongue out the side of his mouth in concentration, and turned to walk towards the far edge of his clearing. "Yes, you take the yellow trail," he said, with a nod.

Barry had caught up, and Ib, breathing heavily, followed behind.

"We'll need a bit more information, please," said Kirsten.

"Right, well I've marked off trails all through these woods, like the blue one you just followed. And you will want to follow the yellow trail," Sixto said, pointing towards a tree with a faded yellow splotch of paint on the trunk.

"Okay, and where does it take us?" asked Tomi, already moving towards the start of the trail.

"Follow it, it cuts up and around the mountain. It's mostly tree covered, to hide you from the choppers. There is one clearing a ways up, maybe keep to the edge of that. At the end, it will come to a road. Go slow in the dark, and you should get there by morning. I'll be there to pick you up."

Tomi was about to start into the trail, but stopped, with a sudden feeling that she would not be seeing him in the morning. She turned and hugged him. "Thank you, Sixto."

"Anything for the good guys, right?" he said. Tomi looked at Barry's face, covered in sweat, and Ib, sweating and still catching his breath. Instead of launching herself into the forest, she put her arm around Ib, and helped him move through the rough brush.

They moved slowly as the sun descended and the forest grew darker. They had brought two flashlights, but tried not to use them, in case the light gave away their position. They found it was a trail in name only, the dark path full of obstacles. Each got scratches, and twice Ib got his feet caught on a fallen branch and stumbled.

"Tomi, you need to leave me," he said the second time, rubbing his hurt shin as he worked to stand up.

"Not a chance," said Tomi, pulling him up and leading him through the brush.

Several times they could hear the helicopters overhead, and stopped moving when they thought there was a chance they could be spotted. They continued their slow ascent, their mouths dry, bodies covered in sweat.

"Tomi," whispered Kirsten, who was leading the way. "We're at the clearing."

Tomi joined her at the edge of the forest. The sun was below the horizon, but cast just enough light for Tomi to see the large clearing, tree stumps where the forest had been, the area having been recently logged. Tomi looked around the sky and listened.

"I don't hear the helicopters," she whispered. "Let's walk the long way, but out in the clearing so we aren't struggling through the brush. We can jump back into the forest if the helicopters come back."

It was a new moon in the sky, with just the tiniest sliver of moonlight illuminating their way. They still moved slowly so that Ib could keep up, but were making much better progress through the clearing.

Suddenly Tomi felt chilled. She stopped moving, and the three behind her stopped as well. *What had she just heard?*

Click.

She felt eyes on her. Her sweat felt hot against her suddenly cold skin.

In a flash, the world lit up around them. Tomi spun around, disoriented, to see lights pointed at them from all directions. She closed her eyes, trying to help them adjust to the sudden, blinding flash.

She opened her eyes to see Ib and Barry with their hands in the air. She turned to look in the direction they were facing, putting her hand over her eyes to try to see through the intense light. She realized the lights were attached to guns, and that they were surrounded by some sort of SWAT team. Then *he* stepped in front of the light, where Tomi could finally see him.

"You think we don't have our own remote viewers? You can't hide from us, Tomi," said the General, stepping forward and smiling at her. "Now, you have done one hell of a job. We're proud of you, kid. Why don't you hand me that little rock, and then we can chat and get this all worked out?"

Tomi looked around again. She'd never had a gun pointed at her before, let alone being surrounded like this. She took a deep breath and closed her eyes. *What do we do next?* she thought.

"Come on Thomasina," said the General, in a tone that said he knew her well enough to know how to push her buttons. "Let's not get anyone hurt here. You've done your job, and done it well."

Tomi didn't open her eyes. She continued her rhythmic breathing.

"John, maybe you can talk some sense into your wife," the General said.

Tomi opened her eyes and saw John stepping out from behind the General, and into the light. He was uniformed with body armor, just like the others, except he didn't carry a rifle. He stepped towards Tomi.

Tomi shook her head and took a step back. She felt her body revolt, her skin crawled. *He doesn't know what I know,* she thought. *That I know he was my handler, not really my husband.*

"What the fuck are you doing here?" she said, her voice coarse with anger.

"I asked to be here," John said softly. "Tomi, I work with these guys. I couldn't tell you that before, but I'm telling you now. And I'm telling you, this isn't a joke. It's time to stop this game, and get you some help."

Tomi took another step back, wanting to run from him but knowing there were rifles pointed at her back.

"Look, they're trying to help you," he said, reaching for her hand.

She smacked his hand away. "No, I'm not going. Not with you, not with them."

"Goddamnit Tomi, let's go," John said, grabbing her firmly by her upper arm and pulling her towards him. Tomi tried to wrestle away and started to lose her balance.

"Don't you fucking touch her!" Kirsten yelled, lunging at John.

Gunshots.

"Hold fire! Hold fire!" yelled the general.

Tomi fell to the ground. She opened her eyes, and saw that John had fallen to the ground, also. He looked down, dusting his body, seeing he wasn't hit. He was fine.

Kirsten.

Tomi turned to see Kirsten on the ground beside her, blood staining her white shirt.

"No!" Tomi screamed, and scrambled to her, putting her hands on Kirsten's abdomen, trying to stop the bleeding. She looked at Kirsten's face, to see her eyes open, full of fear.

"Kirsten, no," she said, tears falling from her eyes.

Barry and Ib stepped towards them to help, but had guns pointed at them, and were told not to move.

Tomi looked at the General, then at John. "Help her you bastards!"

"You give me that rock, and we'll get your friend on a chopper and right to a hospital," said the General flatly.

"Fine," Tomi said, standing and reaching into her pocket to find the piece of the Emerald Tablet. *It means nothing if she dies,* she thought, as her bloodied hand gripped the stone.

Just as the General and the men around him stepped forward to retrieve the stone, the field lit up in thick, bright white light. Everybody stopped and looked up, frozen.

Tomi smiled as she looked at the bottom of a round craft, hovering silently, blocking out the stars behind it and filling the space around them with light. Suddenly that bright light got even brighter, like a flash that doesn't retreat. Tomi felt enveloped in the light, disoriented. She dropped to the ground to feel Kirsten's body, pressing her hands back onto her stomach.

Just as suddenly, the light was gone. The General looked up at the craft, and back to the ground. Their four targets had vanished.

A telepathic message, an announcement, entered his mind: *These four humans are now under our protection, with all the guarantees outlined in the IGF-EAR Shared Planetary Protocol Agreement of 1954.*

Fuck you, the General tried to send back. But he knew it was over. Tomi, his asset, his golden goose, had been claimed by the Others. She was theirs now.

Chapter 19

"Virtually every abductee receives information about the destruction of the earth's ecosystem and feels compelled to do something about it."

John E. Mack

Tomi felt disoriented in the bright light, and closed her eyes. When she opened them, the overwhelming light was gone, and was replaced with a light glow emanating from the walls around her.

She looked down at her hands, still putting pressure on Kirsten's stomach. Kirsten's shirt was covered in her dark red blood. *Too much blood*, thought Tomi.

Tomi looked at her face. Kirsten's eyes were open, and instead of fear, she saw life. Love. Kirsten was smiling. Tomi looked down again at her hands and lifted them off Kirsten's stomach. Blood didn't flow from her abdomen. Tomi pulled Kirsten's shirt up to find not an open wound, but instead two round scars, the skin already healing over.

She looked Kirsten in the eyes again, and wrapped her arms around her. "You're okay!" she said.

Tomi started to become aware of her surroundings. Ib and Barry stood beside them, their arms still raised, but they were no longer in the clearing, no longer outside. She had seen this place before. The inside of a UFO.

She turned slightly to see Ete, her big, dark eyes emanating kindness. Tomi stepped forward and took Ete's hand, so much larger than her own. Ete towered over her. She hadn't felt so small with Ete when remote viewing, but now could see clearly how tall and lanky Ete and her kind were.

"You saved her," said Tomi.

She felt Ete smile. *There's someone I think you'd like to see*, Tomi heard.

Tomi turned to see her, as radiant and full of life as the last time she saw her, long ago, when Tomi was a child. It was like she glowed, emanating light.

"Grandma," Tomi said, stepping towards her grandmother, hugging her tightly. Tomi breathed in, finding her grandmother's hair smelling just as it had when Tomi was a child. *She's really here, in the flesh*, thought Tomi, incredulous.

After an extended embrace, Esther let go and took a step back.

"Look at you, you are so beautiful and so special, as I always knew you were," Esther said.

"I don't," Tomi stammered, "I don't understand. How? I mean you look younger than I remember you. Where have you been?"

"Well, let's just say it all started with an investigation of Mars. Oh Tomi, there are so many stories to share. All in good time," she said. Esther brushed Tomi's hair with her hand and smiled at her. "I'm so sorry I haven't been around. Please know I've been with you. I've been in, well, in the other place. I've been preparing, Tomi," she said, taking her granddaughter's hand, "for our mission."

Tomi looked at Ete, and thought about the dark pyramid that she was to destroy, to pull the lid off the boiling pot, then thought about the napkin her grandmother had used to draw the vibrating pyramid. *Our mission.*

"Now, you and your friends have been through a lot," Esther said sweetly, stroking Tomi's hand. "What kind of grandmother would I be if I didn't have a treat for you?" she said with a smile, as she reached for a helmet that was secured on a panel in the centre of the craft. Tomi remembered Ete wearing this helmet when she had remote viewed being on the craft, the flying saucer.

She held the helmet, black and metallic, out to Tomi. "I believe someone promised you would learn to fly one of these," Esther said, nodding towards Ete. "It's pretty simple, really. Put this helmet on, and think about where you want to go. Let your consciousness travel there. And the craft will take us."

Tomi looked to the wall of the craft, and saw the walls of the craft disappear wherever she focused, giving her a view outside. She could see the dark landscape, the mountain still below them, the General and John somewhere down there.

"Anywhere…anywhere on Earth?" Tomi asked.

"Anywhere," said Esther.

Tomi closed her eyes and focused. *I want to go home*, she thought.

She slowly opened her eyes, and saw it approaching: her beautiful, hilly island, her refuge, somewhere in this vast universe. She could see the craft lowering gently, preparing to land towards the top of the hill. Tomi turned to look at her grandmother, and they joined hands. Kirsten stepped to the other side of Tomi, and took her other hand.

"It's…it's the place from my dreams," said Kirsten in wonder. Tomi gave her a knowing smile and squeezed her hand.

As the craft approached the island, Tomi suddenly felt scared, seeing the steep incline of the hill. *The craft will topple over if we try to land*, she thought.

As though the island heard her thoughts, the hill began to fold in on itself, bending inward, creating a giant flat shelf just where the craft would land. Tomi felt a gentle shake as the craft touched down. An area of the floor suddenly carved itself into a rectangle and opened, creating a ramp down to the surface.

Tomi led the way out, and everyone followed. She jumped from the ramp, feeling light as a feather, drifting down to the ground.

She turned to look at Ete. "The air is safe for us? We can breathe here?" she asked.

"You can, but you don't need to, here," Ete said telepathically.

Tomi closed her eyes, breathed deeply, and raised her hands to the sky. She let herself fall backwards, like a trust exercise with the ground, with the island, with reality itself. She flopped gently back onto the grass, almost fur-like in its softness, and looked up to the sky. It was a bright blue-sky day, and yet she could see the stars. So many stars it seemed impossible.

She felt a warmth, and sat up to see her grandmother seated beside her, also nestling into the grass. Tomi looked around and saw Ib sniffing a multicoloured flower, and Barry pointing out a star to Kirsten. And there was Ete, sitting down and yet as tall as a human, settling into a meditation.

Home.

Over her shoulder, Tomi heard a familiar voice call her name. She stood and turned, only to see a cliff and the seas below, stretching off into the horizon, towards the stars. Then she felt it, like the vibrational wave that hits you when a gong is struck. It was a pull, *a subatomic pull*, she thought. *I know this one. I've felt it before.*

She looked around and saw everyone else standing, looking towards the same horizon.

"Do you feel it too?" she asked.

"Yes," said Kirsten. "It called my name."

"Mine too," said Ib.

"Earth," said Ete.

"The fourth call," said Tomi, solemnly. "The fourth wave."

Tomi looked around at the landscape, so lush, soft, and perfect, a world like a hammock, cradling you in suspension. She didn't ever want to leave this place of pure beauty, peace, and harmony.

My home, she thought.

Tomi looked at her friends. Her people.

"Our mission. We need to go back," she said, turning to look again towards the horizon, towards the source of the call. "We have to go back to Earth."

About the Author

CJ Dearlove is a writer, artist, and community builder from Cambridge, Ontario, Canada.

www.ingramcontent.com/pod-product-compliance
Lightning Source LLC
Chambersburg PA
CBHW072045190726
48294CB00005B/1414